KT-131-058

FOOL'S GOLD

FOOL'S GOLD

A Liberty Lane Mystery

Caro Peacock

This first world edition published 2017
in Great Britain and the USA by
SEVERN HOUSE PUBLISHERS LTD of
19 Cedar Road, Sutton, Surrey, England, SM2 5DA.
Trade paperback edition first published
in Great Britain and the USA 2017 by
SEVERN HOUSE PUBLISHERS LTD

Copyright © 2017 by Caro Peacock.

All rights reserved including the right of
reproduction in whole or in part in any form.
The moral right of the author has been asserted.

British Library Cataloguing in Publication Data
A CIP catalogue record for this title is available from the British Library.

ISBN-13: 978-0-7278-8691-0 (cased)
ISBN-13: 978-1-84751-795-1 (trade paper)
ISBN-13: 978-1-78010-862-9 (e-book)

This is a work of fiction. Names, characters, places and incidents
are either the product of the author's imagination or are used fictitiously.
Except where actual historical events and characters are being described
for the storyline of this novel, all situations in this publication are
fictitious and any resemblance to actual persons, living or dead,
business establishments, events or locales is purely coincidental.

All Severn House titles are printed on acid-free paper.

Severn House Publishers support the Forest Stewardship Council™ [FSC™],
the leading international forest certification organisation.
All our titles that are printed on FSC certified paper carry the FSC logo.

Typeset by Palimpsest Book Production Limited,
Falkirk, Stirlingshire, Scotland.
Printed and bound in Great Britain by
TJ International, Padstow, Cornwall.

Northamptonshire Libraries & Information Services NC	
Askews & Holts	

ONE

Cephalonia. May, 1841

One moment there was just a pillar of white rock, twenty feet high or so, at the far side of the harbour, coming almost to a point at the top. Then a sculpture of a young Greek god was standing on it, arms extended, balanced as easily as a seabird, silhouetted against the white of the early morning sky. The area where he was balancing looked hardly wide enough for two human feet. If he wore clothes they weren't visible in silhouette. The outline of him looked as naked as a classical statue. Robert caught my surprise, looked where I was gazing and took my hand. The young man couldn't have walked there because the pillar stood on its own, some way out from the shore, and in the first surprise of seeing him you'd have guessed he'd flown. Logic said that he must have swum out and scrambled up, though that was surprising in itself given the steepness of the pillar. He seemed to stand there for a long time, then he was flying, rising up from the rock and curving down in a perfect swallow dive with his arms extended, sweeping them down at the last moment to enter the water so smoothly that just a small collar of white foam flashed round his vanishing feet. He must have gone deep because he surfaced at some distance from the rock with only a thin line of white spray showing where he was swimming towards the crescent of the beach. A tinkling sound like a small silver bell came from somewhere out of sight in the olive trees behind it. When he got to the beach he stood straight for a moment, flicking water droplets out of his hair, then vanished into the olive grove. The bell stopped. Above the olive grove was a long, rectangular house with a terracotta tiled roof, looking as if it dated from the time when the Venetians owned the island, and rather dilapidated, like many of the buildings round the harbour. Only the upper windows were visible above the trees and most of them were shuttered. The young man might have been heading there or into any of the fishermen's cottages near the beach.

'Or perhaps he really did come from Olympus,' I said.

I might have thought that I'd imagined him, under the influence of a place so magical, except that Robert had seen him too. We were sitting on the deck of our yacht where we'd come to enjoy the midsummer sunrise and the tiny cups of black coffee our steward had brought up from the galley. In reality, it wasn't our yacht at all, just a loan from a very generous friend who'd suggested we might borrow it for a honeymoon cruise rather than leave it tied up at Venice with the crew growing fat and lazy. The cruise was almost over and we were making our leisurely way back to Venice among the Ionian islands. For the past two days we'd been in the harbour at Agia Efimia on Cephalonia, just off the western edge of Greece, and in a few more days we'd be setting sail northwards, which was why we were determined not to waste the sunrise. We'd had weeks of happy wandering on the mainland and around the islands, had seen Delphi and travelled overland as far as Athens. We'd bathed in secluded coves, naked as Adam and Eve or the boy on the rock, lunched on white goat's cheese, sharp white wine and apricots warm from the tree, slept out on the deck under the stars – everything we'd wanted and more, but now we'd turned decisively northwards and home was calling. I was twenty-six years old, Robert was nearly ten years older, and we'd lived unusual lives. For five years I'd earned my living as a private investigator. As for Robert, if I mention that his own father had tried to kill him and very nearly succeeded, that's probably as much about his past as I should put down here. In worldly goods, I paid rent on a thin sliver of a house in a yard behind Park Lane in London and had forty pounds to my name. My dependents included a thoroughbred mare called Rancie and a housekeeper who mostly disapproved of me and my off and on apprentice, the street urchin Tabby. I wanted to see them again and, with them, my good friend, the groom Amos Legge. Even in paradise here I occasionally thought how good those spring mornings must be, cantering through the dew in Hyde Park. Robert had two half-brothers and was on good terms with them. He possessed, by inheritance, income enough for us to buy a small estate in the country and practise scientific agriculture and philanthropy, if that was what we wanted to do with our lives. Meanwhile, the world was large, and in our happiness we felt as young as the morning of it. When he'd brought the coffee, our steward had said there was a warning of rough weather on the way, but as the sun began to climb and the sky turned from white to blue it looked as clear as any other day. The harbour at Agia Efimia was small, mostly for fishing boats and, apart from our own vessel, the only one of any size was anchored not far out from the villa.

'Lord Byron came here to Agia Efimia,' I said. 'It was when he and Trelawny went across to Ithaca.'

Robert pretended to groan. We were still at the stage when finding differences between us was as absorbing as likenesses and he didn't share my enthusiasm for the man or his poetry. The late Lord Byron had been a hero of my girlhood because he'd died fighting for Greek independence. (Died, in fact, of a fever not far away on the Greek mainland before he'd had a chance to fight, but I'd put that to the back of my mind.) Byron had spent some months on Cephalonia while deciding what party to join of the several that were fighting each other as well as the Turks. My father had actually known him, and admired him, up to a point. I'd even met Byron's companion, the notorious pirate Trelawny, when I was twelve years old but had little chance to ask him about the poet because he'd tried to kiss me and my father had thrown him out of the house. Robert and I decided to take a walk in the hills for what would probably be our last full day on Cephalonia and were rowed to the shore. It was a perfect day for walking with the sun not yet scorchingly hot and a little breeze from the south. On our way we passed several of the features we called the 'mysterious pits' – rectangles several feet deep and about twice the width of an average grave that we'd noticed at various parts of the island in previous walks. Usually, but not always, they'd be close to some ruined shack or farmhouse. I guessed that they'd been made by local people digging for antiquities to sell. Some looked quite recent; others as if they'd been dug years ago. Occasionally we'd asked local people who spoke English what they were for but never got a clear answer. We came back to the yacht when

the sun was high and took our lunch on deck. I looked across
to the villa and saw that some of the window shutters had been
opened while we were away. Apart from that, there were no
signs of life. Then, just as we were thinking of going below
for a siesta, a small boat pulled away from the beach below the
villa where we'd seen the young man coming out of the water.
One man was rowing, another just sitting there, and it was
making straight for us. As they got closer the man just sitting
there called out in excellent English that he had a message for
us. I told our sailors to let a ladder down and he climbed neatly
on board. He was a cheerful-looking man of middle age, thin
and quite short, his round face browned by the sun, his teeth
white and his cap of hair so glossily black that I suspected he
might dye it. He bobbed a bow with just a touch of parody
about it, as if playing the part of a servant.

'Mr and Mrs Carmichael? Jolly, at your service.'

He handed me a piece of folded paper. It was addressed to
Mr and Mrs R. Carmichael, so I opened it and read. It was in
English, on plain paper, the handwriting black and decisive.

> *Villa Maria*
> *Wednesday*
> *I hope you will excuse an approach from a person who
> has not had the honour of being introduced to you. Please
> put it down to island manners. I should be delighted if
> you would come to dinner with us today. Yours with great
> respect, Matthew Vickery.*

'Villa Maria?' I said.

Jolly pointed across the harbour towards the rectangular house
with the terracotta roof. Robert was at my side, reading the
note. We looked at each other.

'Thank you. We accept,' he said.

Jolly bowed again and was turning to go but I was curious.

'Mr Vickery is English?'

A nod. 'Very much so, ma'am. In case you're wondering,
I'm his manservant-cum-butler and anything else needed. Also
English.' His speaking voice was surprisingly deep and sonor-
ous for a small man. He said Mr Vickery would send a boat

across for us at five o'clock and went as neatly as he'd arrived. Robert smiled, checked to see that nobody was watching and kissed me.

'I said yes on impulse. But you did want to accept, didn't you?'

'Yes. This Mr Vickery may know about the diving boy.'

So at five o'clock we were waiting on deck when the boat from the Villa Maria arrived.

TWO

The same man as before was rowing the boat, wearing an off-white shirt and looking like a local fisherman. He held it steady while I climbed down the rope ladder, keeping his eyes modestly fixed on the side of our yacht. With Robert settled in beside me, he rowed strongly for the shore. The boat was seaworthy but not smart, varnish bubbled and flaking, the plank seats we sat on with splinters enough to make me glad of petticoats. Somebody was waiting for us on the beach, a vivid patch of blue against the background of olive trees. As we came nearer we could make out details. He wore plain white trousers, like a sailor's, and over them a sort of tunic in dark blue embroidered with gold. His beard was brown and square cut, his hair long and swept back from a large head with a wide forehead, his nose a determined wedge, flaring out at the nostrils. He was tall and broad-shouldered, like a man who could do a spell of manual work if needed. As our boat grounded on the pebbles he waded out up to his knees to help pull it up on the beach.

'Good afternoon, Mrs Carmichael. Good afternoon, sir. Matthew Vickery at your service.'

His appearance was exotic but his voice entirely English. Close to, there were a few grey hairs in his beard. Mid to late forties, probably. He helped me out of the boat. His feet, planted firmly beside my white satin pumps on the pebbles, were as bare as Adam's and as brown as a peasant's. We shook hands. He was as easy and relaxed as if we were old friends who'd simply strolled across the park to meet him and suggested we should go up to the house. It was out of sight from the beach, hidden by the olives, and a line of steps went up towards it. They were old stone steps, perhaps made by the Venetians who'd built the villa. They must have been broad once but now the sides of them were crowded in with cistus and lavender so that we went in single file, Vickery leading the way. The olives fell away and the villa stood in front of us. From close to it looked large but less impressive than from across the water, cream-coloured paint flaking away in patches, a green trail from a broken gutter running down the wall. In front of it, facing the harbour, was a terrace with a line of terracotta pots containing jagged-leaved agave plants, some flourishing, some dead. Two men were standing on the edge of the terrace looking down at us. One of them was an Orthodox priest in a black cassock with a gold cross on his chest and stove pipe hat. He was a big man, even taller than Vickery and as broad-shouldered, his beard more grey than black, his eyes dark. The second man beside him looked small and ordinary by comparison with a round, pink face, sparse and straggly pale brown hair, and was probably in his thirties. Vickery introduced them as Father Demetrios and Geoffrey Panter. We exchanged civilities. Father Demetrios spoke excellent English and I guessed he was more than a local priest. Panter seemed ill at ease. There was no sign of the diving boy. Vickery led the way to an arbour shaded by a rampant and unpruned vine at the side of the villa where bottles of the local white wine waited in a terracotta cooler. He poured and did most of the talking, full of good humour. He'd heard that a new English couple had arrived on Cephalonia, learned our names from the list published from the governor's house and was delighted to find us in his harbour. He spoke as if all of the village belonged to him, though he cheerfully made it clear that the villa was rented for the summer like his yacht in the harbour. If he was curious about what we were doing he gave no sign of it. I asked him if he knew the island well. Quite well, he said. He'd been amusing himself cruising among the Ionian islands then decided to settle for a few months. One of the things that struck me was how few clues about himself Vickery gave. Usually when you meet fellow countrymen abroad you offer each other little bits of information about where you come from or what you do, perhaps search for acquaintances in common, but there was nothing of that from Vickery. He was a gentleman, clearly educated, but with something unconventional about him. One of the world's wanderers, perhaps. He was still as barefoot as he'd been on the beach and I found my eyes wandering to those brown feet with their strong, bent toes, feet you could imagine planted firmly on a ship's deck.

The sun began moving down the sky. They dined early, Vickery said. Perhaps it would suit us to go inside. We went by a side door into a large and unfurnished room with heavy curtains and a smell of damp plaster. After the sun outside it seemed more than half dark. Vickery advised that it would be best to keep near the walls because the floorboards in the middle weren't entirely trustworthy. We made our way through a door on the far side to what was clearly the more lived-in part of the villa, along a short corridor to the dining room. The long table of old pine was set with six places, glass and cutlery clean but in a variety of styles. A vase brimming with the pink and yellow flowers of lantana was in the centre. Altogether, there was a picnic air about it.

Vickery looked at Panter. 'Will Emilia join us?'

Panter shrugged. 'Her head was aching. I'll go and see.'

Vickery pulled out a chair for me on his right, next to Father Demetrios on the other side. The men had no sooner sat down than they were on their feet again because another woman had walked in. She looked as if she'd just got out of bed, her fair hair caught up in a casual knot with the ends sticking out, wearing something in gold silk that could just as easily have been a dressing gown as a dress, her full-bosomed figure clearly uncorseted. Her pale feet in gold Turkish slippers were bare and arched. She was small, probably not much over five foot, and at first glance looked to be in her early twenties, though a second look put her some five or more years older. Her face had high cheekbones, a good, straight nose and full lips, while her complexion was pale. A scent like tuberose wafted round her as she moved. Geoffrey Panter walked behind her like an animal keeper with a lioness. Emilia Panter. Vickery introduced us and her eyes met mine for no more than a second but long enough to show that they were brown and neither friendly nor unfriendly, giving nothing away. She looked longer at Robert and I guessed she didn't waste too much of her time on women. She said coolly that she was pleased to meet us in a voice that was deep and pleasant, though I detected a note of something in it. Well-buried cockney, perhaps. Panter pulled out a chair for her and sat down beside her but she took no notice of him at all. The food arrived, brought in by two male servants in white trousers and fishermen's tunics – lots of small dishes in the local style with Vickery urging us to try this and that dish, sometimes spooning things directly on to our plates. Emilia dissected a stuffed vine leaf, ate a few rice grains then abandoned her fork as if it were too heavy to hold. She played no part in what turned out to be pretty lively conversation and pointedly ignored her husband throughout the meal. Any fears that the presence of a holy man might make for a dull occasion were put at rest almost at once, with our host teasing Father Demetrios about some of the superstitions of his flock and the priest coming up with his own examples, laughing in great rolling gusts. He was clearly a sophisticated and well-travelled man.

'Yes, it's true. Some of them, they'll pray in church on Sunday morning and in the afternoon walk up to some supposed holy rock or well as their ancestors did two thousand years ago.'

'Very wise of them,' Matthew Vickery said. 'Why offend the old gods? I never go on a voyage without making an offering to Poseidon.' It sounded as if he meant it. Geoffrey Panter joined in the conversation with apparent reluctance, usually in response to a question from Vickery. I felt he resented our presence there and that we might have interrupted a quarrel between him and his wife. When he was speaking her attitude seemed to change from boredom to downright scorn. His accent was clearly public school English but he gave as few clues as Vickery about his connections. Through all this, there was no sign of the beautiful boy. The meal was near its end. Dishes of honey cakes, Turkish delight, nuts and fruits appeared on the table with a bottle of golden dessert wine. Then suddenly he was there, standing beside Vickery. He'd made no sound coming in and it was all I could do not to gasp at his sudden appearance, so close was he that I could have reached out and touched him. He was tall and slim, smooth complexioned as if he didn't yet need to shave, but not girlish. His hair was black and curly, his nose decisive and his lips full like a girl's. He wore plain black trousers and a loose, open-necked shirt but still had the air of an athlete in a vase painting, poised and ready to race, eyes on a distant finishing post. The other shock was that the eyes were opaque and unfocused, staring past us at the wall. He was blind.

'Georgios,' Vickery said. The boy's sightless eyes turned to him. 'We have visitors.' He introduced us, turning towards us as he named us so that the boy's head followed the direction of his voice. He bowed politely and I bowed my head back at him, ridiculously because how could he see it? 'And Father Demetrios, of course.' Another bow, less formal this time, and a smile on the boy's face. The priest was clearly a friend. 'We'll talk later, Georgios. Find Jolly and finish your lesson.' He held out a plate of honey cakes. The boy took one with perfect accuracy, bowed again to the table in general and left as noiselessly as he'd arrived. At the door he turned and for a moment – you'd have said looked if it weren't for those blank eyes – he angled his head towards Emilia Panter. Vickery missed that because he was choosing a honey cake but caught my eye as Georgios left the room.

'I'm encouraging him to improve his English. As it happens, one of my servants, Jolly, is a failed actor but a useful tutor.' A glint in his eye showed he was giving out this information, knowing very well it wasn't what we wanted to ask.

'Is he from this island?' I said, responding to the glint.

'Born and raised here.' But something about the way he said it suggested that wasn't the whole story. 'Tell me, do you find anything at all familiar about Georgios?'

A chair creaked. Emilia had turned and was looking at me, though her expression said she'd heard the guessing game before. I didn't answer immediately because something was burrowing away in my mind. There was nothing familiar about the boy, apart from sculptures in museums. I'd never seen anything like him in real life. And yet . . . Vickery laughed, a kindly enough laugh, as if pitying my puzzlement.

'You're too young, of course.'

'Too young by two thousand years or so,' I said.

'Much more recent history than that.'

A book was what my mind was showing me – the title page of a book. Poetry, I was pretty sure of that. An engraving on the page within a printed oval frame, olive leaves round it and a name under it. 'He does look rather like a younger Lord Byron,' I said, surprised at myself.

They were all looking at me now. The glint in Vickery's eye had become something more dangerous. 'You know Lord Byron spent some time here on Cephalonia?' he said. 'Five months. There were people who criticised him for staying here so long when there was fighting going on, but the politics were complicated. That was nearly eighteen years ago.'

'Are you implying that Georgios may be Lord Byron's son?' I could hardly believe I was asking the question, it seemed so unlikely.

Instead of replying, Vickery tilted his head towards the priest. Father Demetrios took his time, speaking more slowly than before. 'I was a young man here, my first parish. For an Athenian, which I am, it was a remote place to be. As a priest, perhaps I should have kept apart from politics, but I was a patriot too. Our country was fighting to be reborn, and when the great Lord Byron arrived to join our cause, you can imagine what a hero he was to all of us. I was introduced to him and was even of use in carrying messages between him and some of our leaders. He was kind enough to accept me as a friend and we spent many hours together discussing everything from ancient philosophy to modern warfare. He rented a house on the island and was well known to all the local people. In one case, as it turned out, too well known.' He raised a hand as if to check himself, and lamplight glinted on his heavy gold ring. 'You may say that I shouldn't be talking of old scandals concerning a great man who's dead.'

'You're talking anyway,' Emilia said with more animation than she'd shown all evening.

Vickery glanced at her and put a finger to his lips. 'Please go on, Demetrios. It has to be said.'

Why? I wondered, but said nothing.

'She was very beautiful,' the priest said, 'the most beautiful woman on the island. Not a peasant, the daughter of a prosperous merchant, eighteen years old and engaged to be married to a very suitable man. I'd heard the expression "mad for love" but I'd never seen it before. Some of the old superstitious women said she'd been bewitched. No power on earth or in heaven could keep her away from him. God knows, I tried. I spoke sternly to her and even risked my friendship with Lord Byron by appealing to him. He agreed with me and promised to show restraint.'

Another silence, this time broken by Geoffrey. 'But then he didn't.' The coarseness was surprising coming from such a mild man, but the priest simply nodded.

'He broke his word. But by the time that became apparent, Lord Byron was dead and a hero. Her parents disowned her, locked her out of the house and mourned her as a child dead. Only the grandparents on her mother's side showed pity and took her in, an old couple living up in the mountains. When the child was born and word spread about his blindness, the superstitious ones whispered that it was a judgement. Then the mother died soon afterwards and of course that was a judgement too. The boy grew up a long way from anywhere, minding his great-grandfather's goats, but if anybody happened to see him in the distance they'd make the sign for keeping off the evil eye. The boy was cursed.'

I'd listened, growing angry. 'Even though he was a hero's son?'

'When god and mortal meet, it isn't always good for the mortal,' Vickery said. He was watching the effect of the story.

'So why is he here?' I said.

Father Demetrios looked at Vickery, got a nod from him and carried on. 'The great-grandmother died two years or so ago and the great-grandfather not long afterwards. The boy stayed on his own in the cottage in the mountains, looking after the goats and managing to grow a few vegetables, seeing nobody. Then Mr Vickery here put in at Cephalonia on an earlier visit and was told the story. His kindness did the rest.'

'It wasn't kindness,' Vickery said. 'Not at first, anyway. I collect superstitions and when somebody mentioned a blind devil boy living up in the mountains, naturally I was interested. It was nearly impossible to find anybody who'd show me where he was. In the end, an old drunk took my money and agreed to take me there but then he stopped dead half a mile or so from the cottage and wouldn't go any further. I went on by myself, up a track so overgrown it can't have been used for months, and there was the devil boy in the devilish activity of picking tomatoes. He must have known I was there – probably heard me coming all the way up the track – but he gave no sign of it. He was choosing those tomatoes carefully, by touch and smell. When he'd picked what he wanted he stood up with the best one of them flat in the palm of his hand, came up and offered it to me like a prince giving something precious to an ambassador. And he spoke like one, welcoming me to his home, though as far as I could see the cottage wasn't much more than a heap of boulders. The grandparents had brought him up well.'

'So what did you do?' I said.

Vickery smiled. 'I ate the tomato, and very sweet it was too. Then, when I happened to be in Athens, I mentioned the boy to my good friend Father Demetrios, knowing he'd spent time on Cephalonia as a young man. Perhaps I wasn't surprised when he told me the story. He knows most things.' A smile and a tilt of his glass towards the priest. 'He very kindly agreed to interrupt the many other things he should be doing and come back to the island with me.'

So the presence of Father Demetrios was no coincidence.

'What's going to happen to the boy?' I said.

'Georgios will come back to England with me.' Vickery made it sound like the most obvious thing in the world. 'He's been living with us for some months now and, as you heard, his English is good.'

'That's what he wants?'

'Very much. What future for him is there in a place where people cross themselves when they see him? Besides, he wants to see his father's country.'

'He knows?'

'Oh, yes. His great-grandmother told him. She was proud of the connection, at least.'

Somebody changed the subject after that – I don't remember who or to what. In any case, the mood of the party had changed too. A breeze was blowing through the open windows, fluttering the lamp flames, swirling the moths around them.

'The locals said there was a storm blowing up,' Vickery remarked. 'You'll stay with us overnight, I hope.'

Robert and I looked at each other. We could have insisted

on being taken back but that would have been uncivil seeing that it was our host's boat. More than that, we were both intrigued. Robert thanked Vickery and the villa was thrown into that polite, no-trouble-at-all flurry that goes with unexpected guests. Vickery excused himself to give orders to the servants and some agitated conversation in Greek drifted in from outside the room. I looked at Emilia Panter while this was going on, thinking that as the nearest thing to a hostess she might have been involved, but she sat there, peeling a shrivelled apple, cutting it into quarters then not eating it. As the rest of us talked about the islands and sailing the storm began to gather force, rain skittering against the windows and gusts of wind rattling loose panes, the sound of the shifting olive leaves even louder than the sea. I like storms. Restless after sitting for so long, I made my excuses and found my way outside. A short corridor with one lamp glowing dimly on the wall led through a broad open door to the terrace at the front of the house. I stood in the shelter of a deep porch, watching white crests being whipped up in the harbour. The last quarter of a moon, with rain clouds racing across it, gave just enough light to see that the terrace was in a poor state, with broken flagstones and statues missing heads or limbs. Our own yacht some way out and Vickery's were black outlines. After a while the confident tread of bare feet sounded and Vickery was standing beside me.

'Well, what will London make of him?'

'Of Georgios? You're planning to take him there?'

'He has a right, don't you think?'

'I don't suppose the family will acknowledge him.'

'Nor do I. I mean wider society. The name Byron still counts for something?'

'Yes, it does.'

'I've lived a loose sort of life, neither chick nor child until now. I intend to adopt Georgios and give him a place in society.'

I thought, but didn't say, that Lord Byron's place in society had been a pretty loose one too. 'Then there's his blindness,' I said.

'I've been talking to a German doctor about that. He thinks it may be curable. There's a form of cataract that some babies are born with. He thinks that's what Georgios has and, with

luck, it could be put right by an operation. I've said nothing
to Georgios about it but that's another reason for taking him to
London.'

The olives were turning up the pale undersides of their leaves,
silver under the moon. I thought about the oddity of talking so
seriously to a man I hardly knew.

'Why did you invite us?' I said. The question came out before
I'd thought about it. He laughed, not offended.

'Wouldn't it be common politeness?'

And yet he didn't seem a man who cared about common
politeness. Was it his way of preparing a welcome in London
for Georgios? If so, he was overrating our importance.

The moon disappeared and the rain came blowing in with
more force, so we went back inside. Vickery showed us upstairs.
Like the rest of the villa, the staircase might have been grand
once but it was carpetless, the stone stairs chipped and broken,
lit by one guttering lamp. He led the way into an immense
room smelling of mould, with only a wash table and a vast
four-poster bed showing signs that it had been made up hastily
with blankets askew and a dim candle lamp on the wall. He
thought the storm would be blown out by the morning and he'd
have us taken back to our yacht. When he'd gone Robert and
I stood at the window overlooking the sea, watching the two
yachts being bobbed around on the waves. After a while, as I
was starting to undress for bed, I noticed that I'd lost my shawl.
It was a special one that Robert had bought for me in Athens,
made from the finest white wool with white silk embroidery of
waves and dolphins. I knew I'd worn it when we left the yacht
so it would probably be downstairs in the dining room. Robert
said he'd go down and have a look but since he was in socks
and shirtsleeves and I still fully dressed apart from my stockings, I said I'd go. The servants were probably clearing up after
dinner. I went carefully down the dark stairs in bare feet, making
for a vertical line of lamplight coming from the door of the
dining room. There was no sound from inside and when I opened
the door a little and looked in I thought at first there was nobody.
Then in a corner, a long fall of gold silk, the back of Emilia
Panter's dress and above it her gold hair. I wondered why
she was standing there until, over her shoulder, with his head

practically resting on her, a face looked at me. Again, it was so direct and apparently focused that 'look' seemed to be the only word to use but the boy who'd turned his face to me couldn't have seen me. Georgios, and it was obvious that as the door opened he'd had his arms round Emilia. Making a useless gesture of apology, I backed out and shut the door. Back upstairs, Robert took one look at me and asked what was wrong. I told him, realizing I'd forgotten entirely about my shawl. He put his arm round me.

'I'm sorry you had to see it, Lib, but it's no business of ours. Tomorrow we'll be gone.'

'Do you think her husband knows? Or Vickery?'

'I'd guess that Vickery doesn't know. I suspect the Panters would be on their way if he did. He treats Georgios very much as a boy but he is seventeen, after all, if there's any truth in the Byron story.'

I knew that was something we'd both want to discuss but it would keep. 'And Geoffrey Panter?'

'We both had the impression at dinner of a coolness between those two. Perhaps Georgios is the reason.'

At least he didn't say – as I'd feared he might – that if Georgios really were Lord Byron's son he was embarking quite early on a notorious part of his father's career. We went to bed and at intervals through the night I half woke, hearing the wind rattling the windows, raindrops lashing and gutters sprouting water. By the time it was light the wind had weakened and the rain had stopped. I looked out from the window at a sky that was mostly pale blue but streaked with rose-coloured clouds. Somebody was shouting down on the beach beyond the olive trees – a fisherman, I supposed. I dressed as quietly as I could so as not to wake Robert, not bothering with stockings or shoes, and went downstairs and out on to the terrace. The shouting from the beach sounded urgent now. I went down the steps, the old stones cold under my feet, into a disaster.

THREE

The shouting had stopped by the time I got to the beach. The boat we'd arrived in the day before had put out in the harbour with two figures in it and was being rowed slowly, parallel to the shore. The waves were still white-capped. At the bottom of the steps I almost collided with Vickery. He looked as if he'd dressed in a hurry, beard and hair uncombed, his face creased with worry. I asked him what had happened.

'Panter's missing, probably drowned.'

'Drowned? How?'

'Trying to rescue Georgios.' Vickery turned his head towards a clump of tamarisk at the edge of the beach. Georgios was sitting beside it wrapped in a blanket, his head bent. 'Georgios went for an early swim. He does that sometimes, though I'd have forbidden it this morning if I'd known because the sea's still rough after the storm. It seems he got into difficulties and Geoffrey went in to rescue him.'

'But Georgios is a wonderful swimmer. We saw him.'

'I know. I'm trying to make sense of it. The boy's shocked but I'll try talking to him again when we've searched the harbour. Father Demetrios has gone to the village to speak to the fishermen.'

Two rowing boats from the other side of the harbour joined the first one and combed it methodically with an occasional shouted instruction from Vickery. I went over to Georgios and at first he seemed unaware that anybody was there, the blanket drawn up over his head, only some strands of black hair showing. After a while he looked up at me with his blank eyes. I wasn't sure if he recognized my voice. He said something in Greek. Then in English, 'It's my fault. I bring bad luck.'

'No!'

I'd still no idea what had happened but had to protest at such misery. He bent his head again and after a while I sat down quite near him on the sand but not touching him. Something about him suggested that my impulse to put my arm round him wouldn't be appreciated. We stayed like that for some time. When Robert came down, looking for me, I explained what I knew then went back to sit by Georgios with Robert on his other side. After a while Father Demetrios came back and stood beside Vickery. The boats returned to the shore and Vickery came towards me, shaking his head.

'The fishermen say there's a current that may have taken him out to sea. Georgios?'

He squatted on his haunches beside Georgios and said something to him in Greek, quite gently. The boy nodded without looking up.

'I told him we'll speak English this time,' Vickery said. 'Georgios, tell us what happened.'

The boy's blank eyes turned to me as if they were focusing on my face. He kept his voice low and level. 'He swam out to me. I was in no trouble, I'd only dived down. I do that after storms. Storms shift things on the seabed. I like to feel where they've moved.'

Vickery and Robert seemed to be waiting for me to ask questions.

'You'd swum out on your own? Early?' I said.

'Very early. The storm kept me awake. I knew Mr Vickery wouldn't have wanted me to swim. I'm supposed to have a servant with me, with a bell to guide me back to the land. I don't need it. I can tell from the sound of the water where I am.'

'Did you know Mr Panter was there?'

'No. I came up from my dive and there was somebody beside me in the water, splashing and breathing hard. I didn't know it was Mr Panter till he caught hold of me and I smelled his hair oil.'

'Did he say anything?'

'He said who he was, that it was all right. But he didn't swim well and he was heavy, pulling me down. I got away from him.'

'You struggled?'

Georgios repeated, 'He was pulling me down. Then my elbow hit him – in the face, I think.'

Vickery shifted his position. 'You didn't tell me that.'

'Not enough to hurt him, or I didn't think so. He'd spoiled my swim so I went back to the beach. I thought he'd follow me. When he didn't, I swam out again and called his name but he didn't answer.'

'And that was much how things were when I came down to the beach,' Vickery said. 'Georgios waist deep in the water, calling. We've been looking since then. Georgios, go up to the house and get dressed. Don't say a word about this to anybody till I tell you.'

Father Demetrios had appeared beside us. 'Mrs Panter?' he said, his voice low.

'I'll tell her,' Vickery said. 'She won't be up yet.'

The priest nodded. Georgios was on his feet now, the blanket wrapped round him. Father Demetrios put a hand on his shoulder and went beside him up the steps. Vickery waited until they were out of earshot to speak, then it was just one word.

'Well?' Then, after a while when we didn't answer, 'He must have been too scared at first to tell me about hitting Panter with his elbow. Do you suppose he might have knocked him unconscious?'

'It's possible, I suppose,' I said. 'Or if he was struggling to get away from Mr Panter he might have pulled him underwater. Is he right that Mr Panter wasn't a strong swimmer?'

'Not strong at all. He'd rarely come in with us.'

'And he must know that Georgios swims like a dolphin, yet he went in after him.'

'He must have thought Georgios was in trouble. After all, it would have been barely light then.'

Which came to the big question I hadn't asked so far. 'Was Mr Panter accustomed to be down on the beach at first light?'

Vickery gave me a long look then shook his head. 'No. It was the storm, I suppose. It kept a lot of us awake.'

Was that long look because he guessed what was in my question? Robert didn't think that Vickery knew about Georgios and Emilia, but he might be wrong. If so, it might be in both Vickery's mind and mine what had led Panter to the beach in the early morning. Either he'd found out about the affair suddenly or the strain of living with the knowledge of it had been too much for him. Embarrassing for a man set on drowning himself to collide with Georgios on his illicit swim, but it might have happened and Georgios, not seeing, might have misinterpreted things entirely. The other possibility – that Georgios had somehow decoyed Panter into the sea – was so nearly unthinkable that I put it to the back of my mind. The Georgios of this morning had looked very much a boy, even younger than his supposed seventeen years.

'We won't discuss with Georgios whether he might have knocked Panter unconscious,' Vickery said. 'It's bad enough for him as it is. The sooner I get him away to England the better.'

'What about telling the authorities?'

He nodded. 'It's got to be done. I'll sail round later to Argostoli, but not for a while in case his body's found.'

We walked up the steps to the house. People were stirring, a servant sweeping, the smell of coffee coming from somewhere at the back. Vickery sighed, asked me to excuse him and went slowly upstairs, I supposed to break the news to Emilia. Robert, who'd thrown on clothes hastily when he'd heard the shouts, also went upstairs to get properly dressed. I waited in the corridor, wanting to get back to our yacht and away from the complexities of Vickery's household. As I was standing there, light footsteps came up behind me and paused. I turned and there was Georgios in dry clothes, wet hair sleeked back.

'Mrs Carmichael?'

'Yes. How did you know?' I was genuinely curious.

'I am not sure. I think the smell.'

'Smell?'

'Rosemary from your hair and rose water. And I think sand from sitting on the beach. They haven't found him?'

'No.'

'I killed him.' He said it flatly, like a statement that the world was round. He seemed to be continuing from where we'd left off on the beach. 'If I had not been swimming, if I had not dived down he wouldn't have come into the water. He was wearing a jacket, I felt it. He hadn't meant to swim.'

'It wasn't your fault.' I thought he was right but the blank sadness in his voice made it impossible not to try consoling him.

He shook his head. 'I'm cursed. Did Father Demetrios tell you that? I'm the bad luck boy.'

'Nobody's cursed.' I said it forcefully but he only shook his head.

'Has Mr Vickery gone upstairs?'

Something in his voice said he knew Vickery was going to Emilia. When I said yes he wished me a polite good morning and went into one of the rooms off the corridor. Robert and I took ourselves to the arbour under the vine and a servant brought us coffee, dark as tar in small cups.

'So did he drown himself?' Robert asked.

'It's possible, isn't it? Perhaps he'd just found out about it.'

'Last night, when you saw them, did you have the impression it was for the first time?'

'It was only for a second so . . .' I pictured it again and shook my head. 'No, I don't think it was. She wasn't struggling or protesting.'

'So perhaps it had been going on for some time and yesterday she decided to tell her husband, or he found out. That would account for the atmosphere between them at dinner.'

'Unless my seeing her with Georgios somehow brought things to a head,' I said.

'I very much doubt it. She probably didn't even know you were there. And, you know, it might have been an accident. Georgios' account is quite credible on the face of it.'

'Except it leaves out the question of what he was doing on the beach so early in the morning. Georgios is sure Panter was wearing a jacket. A man doesn't go swimming in a jacket. Even if he's running into the sea to rescue somebody, he'd take his jacket off.'

Robert nodded and finished his coffee. 'So we conclude that Panter was trying to drown himself and Georgios got in the way. What do you make of the boy?'

'I feel sorry for him. He's had a terribly confusing life so far.'

'And is he Byron's son?'

I thought about it. My belief, deeper than any reason, was yes. But that wouldn't do for Robert. I did my best to put it into words. 'There were better poets than Lord Byron, I admit. I'd certainly agree with you that there were better men.

But there must have been a force, a kind of magnetism about him. People wanted to know what he thought, what he'd do. He was somehow always on the interesting edge of things. Georgios has something of that. You can't help being interested in him, wanting to know what will happen.'

Robert didn't look convinced. 'I can't think Vickery's right, taking him off to England.'

'How can he leave him here, where he has no family and people cross themselves when they see him?'

We sat there for some time over the cold sludge in our coffee cups then went into the dining room. It hadn't been cleared from the night before but there was no sign of my shawl. Jolly came in with a serious expression that didn't suit his round face, wished us good morning and asked if we'd like more coffee. I asked him about the shawl and he hadn't seen it but promised to look out for it and send it over to our yacht if found. His mobile lips performed a droop like a mask of tragedy. 'Mr Vickery's up with the poor lady now.'

As the only other woman in the establishment, it might have been my place to go upstairs to Emilia, but I guessed she wouldn't appreciate my presence, even if she didn't know I'd seen her with Georgios the night before. I thought of the gold dress and how it would be two years at least before Emilia would wear anything like it again, a bleak waste of widow's blacks and greys ahead of her. We went out and lingered on the terrace, and after a while Mr Vickery appeared, full of apologies, regretting that our pleasant evening should lead to this. He understood that we wanted to get back to our yacht and the boat was at our disposal as soon as we liked. He hoped we'd meet again in happier circumstances. Father Demetrios, who'd gone back to the village, sent his respects. Vickery looked drained and tired but I risked asking him what would happen to Mrs Panter.

'I suppose we'll have to stay here for some time for the formalities, and to see if Geoffrey's corpse is recovered. After that, we'll all go back to England, except Father Demetrios, of course. It's time Georgios was there, at any rate.'

So we took the boat back to our yacht and a day later sailed for Corfu and the start of the long journey home. I thought about Mr Vickery and his establishment quite often, but told myself he'd been one of those acquaintances you make on journeys, even though it had ended more disastrously than most. In spite of what he'd said, I didn't expect to see any of them again.

FOUR

September, 1841

O nce back in London, we should have begun a proper married life with visits given and returned, dinner parties and a house rented that people might visit without getting mud on their shoes. We were both apprehensive about that, knowing how easily it could claim all our time and attention. We were by no means sure yet what we wanted to do with our lives but knew it should be more than napkins and silver spoons. In the meantime, Robert simply moved in with me at Abel Yard, to the delight of my housekeeper, Mrs Martley, who'd been trying to get me married since she'd known me. Robert and his books. Three tea chests of them arrived one day, with a note from the carrier saying the rest would be delivered shortly. Robert pointed out that in the marriage service he'd endowed me with all his worldly goods and most of them were books. We stowed tea chests in every available space, looked at various rentable houses but found some fault with all of them, rode in the park and were happy. Even my occasional apprentice, Tabby, who lived, when the mood took her, in a cabin in the yard, approved of Robert and came and went much as before. I took on no new cases. I supposed my days as an investigator were behind me and was surprised that, deep down, I regretted the loss of them. Then, after only a few weeks back, something happened to break up our routine before it had properly started. Robert was needed in Italy. The reason why has nothing to do with this story and was both secret and political. We discussed it and agreed that he should go. His mission would take several months and there was no place in it for me, so I'd be the wife waiting at home. I didn't care for that but I did approve of his reason for going, so had to accept it. He went and I was back on my own at the house in Abel Yard, stunned by so many changes in a few months. My morning rides in the park with my great friend, the groom Amos Legge, were one of the things that didn't change, and became more important with Robert away. As the days shortened to autumn we'd ride out of the yard while it was just getting light then canter over wet grass with the first leaves beginning to fall. We were walking back from one of those rides when Amos, without knowing it, dropped his bombshell.

'I've got a new young man to teach to ride.' As well as being the most fashionable groom in Hyde Park and a horse dealer on the side, Amos was an instructor. His clients were usually good riders but humble enough to learn from a master. 'Pretty much a beginner, except on mules now and again. But enough nerve for six. Jumped over the railings yesterday and stayed on, even though he'd lost both stirrups. And blind as a new-born puppy.'

'Blind? What's his name?'

'Master George was what I was told to call him. Foreign but speaks English as well as anybody. His guardian says he wants him ready to go hunting this season and he will be the way he's going.'

I asked the guardian's name but hardly needed to. Vickery. Apart from that, Amos didn't know much about him, which was unusual because the grooms in Hyde Park usually hear more about London society than the nosiest dowager. Mr Vickery was pretty free with his money and a pleasant enough gentleman and that was it. I wondered whether to tell Amos that I'd met Mr Vickery on my travels and decided against it. There was nothing I'd willingly keep from Amos but it sounded as if Vickery was determined to establish Georgios – or George now – in society and might not want his earlier life known. Also, if I talked about it I'd have to go back to that early morning and Panter's drowning, which was fading now to something like an odd dream and I had no wish to revive it. Still, I was curious about Vickery, and that was partly why I took up a long-standing invitation to visit my friend Celia Medlar for tea that afternoon.

Celia and I had been together through a bad time once, the kind of experience that might have left her scarred and defeated for the rest of her life. But she'd recovered as rapidly as a stray cat brought in by the fireside, married a man who loved her and happened to be rich and now divided her time between their country estate and their London house. I was godmother to their child. She was one of the most effective gossips I knew, picking up bright and glittering scraps and presenting them to her friends in ways that usually made sense if you followed patiently. For the first part of the visit I admired the infant, now trying to stand upright and ricocheting off furniture, then she was sent upstairs with her nursemaid and tea things appeared. Celia poured then settled into the deepest armchair, nested in cushions. It didn't surprise me in the least when she confided that she was *enceinte* for a second time.

'Isn't it positively scandalous? Philip only has to look at me, poor love. It will mean months in the country, doing nothing again, so I'm making the best of London while I can.' She reeled off a series of stories about people we both knew, then: 'I suppose you didn't happen to be at Lady Blessington's last week. No? Of course, I don't go there and Philip positively won't so I'm almost in the dark about the lion of the moment. Well, lion cub is probably what I should say, though the keeper is something of a lion too from what I hear. He presented him to Lady Blessington, almost seeking royal approval, if you see what I mean. In any case, she wouldn't have invited him if she hadn't been practically convinced, would she? I'm told she actually kissed him on both cheeks and looked as if she were going to cry, though personally I don't believe Lady B has cried about anything since she left the cradle. But then she did know his father well, very well indeed from what some people say.'

'Are we talking about Lord Byron's son?' I said when she paused to sip tea. It was true that my old friend Lady Blessington had been a friend of Lord Byron. If Vickery had gained her approval for George it was a great step.

'So you think so too? Everybody's arguing about it. They say he's even been inquired about at Windsor, if you can believe it. Have you actually seen him?'

Rather against my better judgement, I admitted that I'd met both George and Mr Vickery on Cephalonia. It was typical of

Celia's geographical vagueness that she got it confused with Sicily but we sorted that out as far as it mattered.

'And you thought he was Byron's son?'

'He is very like the portraits, apart from being blind, of course.'

'Do you think it's something about that family, a sort of curse?'

'I don't believe in curses.' I said it more sharply than I'd intended, thinking of Georgios saying he was cursed, and Celia looked surprised.

'But you've seen him close up and you think he is?'

'Probably, yes.' Lady Blessington's opinion counted for a lot.

'I've only seen him from a distance, in a theatre box,' Celia said. 'I forget what the play was but the audience were restless, turning round and whispering. Even some of the actors seemed distracted, looking up at one of the boxes. In the end, I had to turn round to see what was causing it, and there in a box was the gentleman who must have been Vickery with this beautiful young man beside him. They must have left the box before the curtain came down for the interval because there was a positive stampede of people out to the foyer, trying to catch a glimpse of them, but they'd gone.'

It struck me that Vickery was wasting no time in introducing George into society.

Celia poured more tea. 'Who do you suppose the mother was?' she said. 'Somebody told me she was a warrior princess, like Boudicea, fighting alongside Lord Byron against the Turks. Then somebody else said she was a Turkish lady from a harem he set free who fell in love with him. You'd think people would get things like that right, wouldn't you?'

Which was about as much sense as I got out of Celia on the question. Various other inquiries to friends and acquaintances produced much the same results. Vickery and his ward had been seen at plays, receptions and private dinner parties, although nobody seemed clear about who Vickery actually was. At any rate, he was spending money. He'd taken a house in Knightsbridge on a short lease, hired a carriage and was said to be restoring a country home out somewhere north of Highgate. As for George, the general opinion seemed to be that he was indeed the son of the man whose disorderly life was even better known

than his poetry. The legitimate Byron family said he was an
imposter and refused to have anything to do with him, but that
was only to be expected. Although I couldn't help being interested, it was nothing to do with me so I kept it at the back of
my mind – until Vickery's note arrived.

It was short and businesslike, delivered by penny post to Abel
Yard, with the letter heading of his rented house in Knightsbridge.

> *Dear Mrs Carmichael,*
> *You may remember that we met on Cephalonia. I should*
> *be very much obliged if you would allow me to call on*
> *you and consult you. If I may, I shall call at three o'clock*
> *tomorrow afternoon.*

Just that and his signature. At five minutes to three the next
day I was waiting in the yard as he came striding through the
gateway, cane in hand and glossy top hat on his head. Although
he was dressed in conventional clothes with his feet in shiny
black shoes, there was still something of a piratical air about
him. He'd had his hair cut shorter and trimmed his beard to an
elegant point like some Elizabethan sea captain. His face was
still almost as brown as it had been on Cephalonia. He took in
at a glance the yard with its chickens and cowshed and nodded,
approving it. I led him up the narrow staircase to my office,
deciding not to call Mrs Martley as a chaperone, settled him in
a chair at the table and took another. He asked after Robert and
showed no surprise that he was out of the country. Travelling
seemed natural to Mr Vickery.

'I had intended to call on you in any case,' he said. 'But the
fact is, I need your help. I've been hearing about you since we
came to London. You're Liberty Lane.'

'Was.' I liked the fact that he was so open about his inquiries.
Perhaps I even liked hearing my old name. 'Why do you need
my help?'

'I'll show you, if I may.' He was carrying a portfolio, very
slim. He opened it, took out two pieces of paper and put them
on the table. The handwriting on both was the same, quite small
but decisive, with diagonal crossings on the letter 't' and
closed loops on 'g's and 'y's, in blue ink on good quality white

notepaper. The heading was simply a day of the week and the signature one word.

Monday

Dear Mr Vickery,

I want to speak to you and to see the boy for whom you are acting as guardian. I shall be waiting in my carriage outside the banqueting hall in Whitehall tomorrow between 2.30 and 3 in the afternoon. I have a particular reason for the request. Please do not fail me.

    Helena

The other one was headed Wednesday.

Mr Vickery,

I find I must insist on what I previously requested. You chose to disregard my first message. I shall wait again at the same place, at the same time, tomorrow. Please do not fail me again and force me to measures we should both of us regret.

    Helena

He watched me while I read.

'When did these arrive?'

'Last week. I did nothing. It seemed to me all part of the excitement George's arrival has caused. I'll admit to you, I was surprised that the Byron name has such force still. I'd assumed that I could show George a little of London society in our own good time then retire to the country to continue his education. As it is, it's hard to go out without being mobbed and women are writing the boy letters they should be ashamed of. Naturally I don't tell him about them. He's puzzled by the attention – a little alarmed, even.' He gave me a rueful smile. I wondered if he could possibly be so unworldly.

'So why did these two letters concern you particularly?'

'It's hard to say. The first one didn't. But after the second one I've had the uneasy feeling that people are watching George.'

'Half the town is, as far as I understand.'

'I mean, watching particularly – a man standing on the other side of the street a little too long, a woman staring at the theatre, a face as we get into a carriage. I've believed my nerve to be more than usually good but sometimes I think of Helena and *measures we should both of us regret.* Perhaps it's this weakness in my nerve that worries me most. If I knew who she was – just some other deluded woman – I'd be on an even keel again. So I decided to consult Liberty Lane.'

'I'm sure you could find plenty of competent investigators.'

'No other women that I've heard of. Surely another woman would understand this Helena better than a man.'

'You're sure this is a woman's writing?'

'I think so, don't you?'

In fact, I did, though not to the point of being certain. 'What exactly were you hoping I might do?'

'Find her, and let me know why she thinks she has some sort of claim on us.'

'Then you should have come to see me last week and let me meet her carriage.'

'I know. It's only over the last few days that I've thought about it more, and worried.'

'As it is, we only have the letters to go on. All they tell us is that she's educated, has some means and a fair amount of freedom, but lives with people who wouldn't approve of what she's doing.'

'Yes, I thought of that, otherwise she'd have given an address.'

'How does she know where you live?'

'If you go about in society I suppose it's not difficult for people to find out. So, will you do it?'

I sat back and thought about it. It was an unpromising business, but then I had nothing else to do. Also, I was as interested in the Byron case as anybody.

'George has quite taken to you,' Vickery said. 'He would like to meet you again before we go to the country.'

'You're going?'

'Quite soon. I've taken a house out near Muswell Hill but it's being renovated at the moment. As soon as it's ready I'll take George there along with a tutor and somebody to read to him. He's to go to Cambridge, like his father did.'

'I'll do what I can,' I said. 'I don't promise results.'

The look of relief on his face showed how badly this business was affecting him. 'Naturally I'd expect to pay you. A retainer . . .'

'I'll take nothing until I see whether I can make any progress. And I want your permission to speak to two other people about this – my apprentice, Tabby, and the groom, Amos Legge.'

'Legge, from the livery stables on Bayswater Road? George rides with him.'

'I know. Mr Legge is one of my oldest friends. If people are watching George it would be a good opportunity to do so when he's out riding in the park and Amos would notice.'

I could see no snobbery, or even surprise on his face, that I should claim a groom as an old friend. He nodded and said I could keep the two letters.

'And if you get any more like them or anything else happens, you'll tell me at once?'

Another nod. I promised to report to him at the Knightsbridge house in a few days. As we went down the stairs I asked him how George was enjoying London.

'Very much, on the whole. He's young enough to enjoy being feted and I try to make sure it doesn't turn his head. But he has nightmares still.'

I wasn't surprised. Few young men under the sun could have experienced the changes George had in less than a year. I escorted Vickery to the yard gates then went back upstairs for my bonnet and walked across the park to Amos's stables.

'Whitehall's next door to impossible,' Amos said. He was picking out the hooves of a bad-tempered hunter, persuading it in a low and gentle chant to be reasonable, only half his attention on what I'd said. I was so used to his solving any problem on four hooves that it was like stepping on a stair that wasn't there.

'Too busy, I suppose?'

'Nobody owns it – that's to say, nobody looks after it. Most streets, you get somebody who knows the comings and goings. With all the world coming and going through Whitehall, it's too big for that. Still, I'll see what I can do.'

I watched him finish the job and clean the hoof pick with a handful of straw. He seemed less responsive than usual, not

sulking quite, but distant. 'It's to do with your pupil,' I said.
'The blind one.'

'I thought it might be.' He came out of the box and bolted
the door.

'Why?'

'When Tabby was here with him I knew it was something
to do with you.'

'Tabby was here with George?' I was amazed.

'Yes. She comes here quite a bit, on and off. She was here
the first time he came and somehow they must have got talking.
Now as soon as Mr Vickery goes, she's here. They talk and
laugh together like good friends. I thought you knew.'

No wonder he'd been hurt. As far as I knew, Tabby and
George had never met. A friendship between the street urchin
and the lord's son – even from the wrong side of the blanket
– seemed as unlikely as the hunter growing wings.

'No, I didn't. The woman with the carriage in Whitehall
wanted to see George. We've no idea who she is.'

I went to visit Rancie and Amos and I agreed to ride as
usual in the morning. I got back to Abel Yard determined to
ask Tabby how she'd become acquainted with George, but there
was no sign of her.

Over the next three days I did some serious thinking about the
two notes and got precisely nowhere. The ink and paper gave no
clues. They could have come from any good stationer. The letters
had been posted at a busy central London office. Helena kept,
or at least had access to, a carriage but that would apply to several
thousand women in London. She knew enough about the city to
choose a busy place where she could wait without being particularly observed, but so did tens of thousands of others. As for
women obsessed with the memory of Lord Byron, the current
excitement over his possible son showed there were plenty of
those around. On the fourth day Amos arrived for our morning
ride at Abel Yard on a nervy grey with that look on his face that
showed he had news to tell. As usual, he drew it out.

'No luck from Whitehall. Full of carriages waiting half an
hour or more and the cab drivers shuttling around, picking up
fares so quick they don't notice much else. Might as well look
for a particular salmon in the Wye.'

'And yet you have a trace of our particular salmon?'

He grinned, drawing rein to let a phaeton into the park gate. 'Sometimes if you wait it'll swim up to you. Maybe it did yesterday. George came for his lesson. Your Tabby knew he was coming because she was in the yard beforehand. They talked after Mr Vickery had gone but if you want to know what they said it's no use asking because I wasn't listening. So we saddled up and I took the lad towards Kensington, a good gallop and him happy as a robin on a branch. There was a carriage or two trying to keep pace with us, mostly women in them, but we were too fast for them. He pretended not to notice when they called out to him – at least, I think he did. There was one carriage, though, not like the rest. It was waiting outside when we got back to the stables and stayed there until Mr Vickery came to collect him. Closed carriage, it was, quite plain, ordinary dark bay cob, driver on the box and blinds down most of the time, only I noticed when we rode past that one of them went up a little bit at the corner as if whoever was inside wanted to see and not be seen. When I next looked out, it had gone. I'd have told your Tabby to follow it, only she'd gone by then.'

'Did you recognize the carriage?'

'No, nothing special about it. Hired by the day, I'd say, and not one of the best yards. The bay's off-fore shoe was getting thin and I'd have had words to say to the boy who was supposed to polish the harness buckles. A hundred like it in London.' An escaped greyhound ran across our path with a servant lad following it, shouting. The grey thought about shying but a slight movement of Amos's hand made it think again. 'But I reckon she'll be back now she knows for sure the boy comes here,' he said.

'Today?'

'Could be. The boy's coming this morning to try out a horse Mr Vickery might buy. He wants to take a couple of hunters with him when he moves to the country.'

So instead of going back home I went on with Amos to the stables at the end of our ride and waited in the tack room. When a carriage drove in soon after eleven and Mr Vickery and George got out, I stayed where I was. I didn't want to see Mr Vickery before I had something to report to him. From the window, I

watched as a sensible-looking chestnut cob of about fifteen
hands was led out to the yard. Amos was obviously explaining
his good points to Mr Vickery and George. George listened and
ran his hand over the animal's chest and shoulders, managing
to look as knowledgeable as if he'd spent his life with horses.
Mr Vickery gave the cob a glance but apart from that his eyes
were on George all the time. George nodded and Amos cupped
his hands and threw him up into the chestnut's saddle where
he settled as easily as a jockey. Mr Vickery said something to
him, got into his carriage and drove off. Through all this I'd
seen no sign of Tabby, but that didn't mean she wasn't there.
A stable lad led out Rancie and I went out to the yard and
mounted.

'Good morning, Mrs Carmichael. Are you riding with us?'

George's voice was becoming more English by the week,
with almost nothing to distinguish it now from any other young
gentleman. He was smiling, those blank and unchanging eyes
turned towards me.

'How did you know it was me?'

'Your scent, of course.' Then he laughed. 'Legge mentioned
you might come out with us. What do you make of him?' He
nodded down at the chestnut.

'Useful. Probably a schoolmaster.'

He pursed his lips, pretending annoyance. 'Another one. You
know Mr Vickery's engaged a tutor for me?'

'I mean he seems a horse to look after you, out hunting.'

'I have enough of being looked after.' There was something
like real annoyance in his voice now. 'On a horse, swimming
in the sea, you're free, equal to everybody else or better. Will
he give me that?'

'Ride him and see.'

The petulance – arrogance even – made the resemblance to
Lord Byron sharper than I'd seen it before. He really was a
very good-looking young man and the blankness of the eyes
didn't detract from that. If anything, it added to it. It was hard
to escape the feeling that he could see out without letting
anybody else see in. Amos rode up to us on the grey and kept
close beside George as we went out of the gateway on to the
Bayswater Road. Many carriages were coming and going and

I could see Amos's eyes sweeping them but he shook his head. We had a long ride, along Rotten Row to Kensington and back. The chestnut behaved perfectly but when Rancie overtook him easily at a canter – although I wasn't pushing her – I knew he wasn't going to join Vickery's stables. George demanded that Amos should find him something livelier next time. All the time I could see Amos looking around for the coach. A sudden jerk of the shoulders told me he'd spotted something. I let George get ahead and pushed Rancie up beside the grey.

'Something?'

He moved his head slightly to the right. 'That one was behind us along the Row and turned when we turned. Could be the same. We'll give it a bit of a dance.'

For the next twenty minutes or so he led our trio across the grass or on tracks only wide enough for ridden horses. All the time, though, he was making sure that we could be spotted from the roads where the coaches were. After a while he turned towards the Ring, an area he usually avoided because it was congested with the carriages of the fashionable who came out to see and be seen. Sure enough, when we came out to a carriage road, the plain vehicle he'd noticed wasn't far behind us. We walked on very slowly but the carriage's progress was slower because of the press of vehicles in front of it. Eventually it came to a complete stop because the passengers in two open carriages on opposite sides of the road were having a conversation as comfortably as if they were in their own drawing rooms, blocking the way for a few dozen others in both directions. Coachmen were getting restive, some of them shouting, but the talkers seemed oblivious. Amos called to George and the three of us turned back at a walk, going towards the plain carriage. As we got nearer to it, I saw the blinds were down – an odd thing for somebody taking the air in the park. Amos pressed ahead, leaving me riding beside George. He'd given the grey a long rein and was sitting slumped in the saddle like a bumpkin. The coachman on the box of the carriage, a plump man with a pockmarked face, gave him a hostile look. It turned to outright anger as Amos turned the grey so close to the carriage that his stirrup scraped it below the driver's box, leaving a scratch in the brown paintwork that showed pale undercoat beneath. It

wasn't much of a scratch and the paintwork hadn't been very
good in the first place, but the driver yelled at him and struck
out with the butt end of his whip. Amos avoided the blow and
came out with a muttered apology in his slowest Herefordshire
accent, very much the countryman. He said he'd pay for the
damage. Yes, he would pay, the coachman said, five sovereigns
for repainting. The charge was clearly ridiculously high but
Amos didn't argue, just asked meekly where he should bring
the money as he had none on him. Perkins' Yard, east side of
Covent Garden, the driver said, and Amos had better be there
because he knew what stables he came from. While this was
going on George and I had held back, out of view from the
inside of the carriage even if the blinds had been up. When
Amos rode on, head bent, we followed. I let George ride nearer
the carriage and kept to the outside. Sure enough, as we went
past the bottom of the blind went up diagonally, as if somebody
were pushing it with a finger rather than using the cord. There
was a woman inside. All I could see was part of a dark bonnet,
a black glove and a flash of white cheek before the blind dropped
again. Not an old woman, I thought, but not so young either.
George, of course, noticed nothing. We rode back to the stables
where a carriage was waiting to collect him with Vickery's
driver but not Vickery himself.

When he'd gone, Amos and I conferred.

'Do you know Perkins' Yard?' I asked him.

'No, but I know the kind of place it'll be. Farm carts for the
market and a couple of carriages for hire like that one. I'll go
there after we've done evening stables.'

I'd have liked to go too but knew his methods. He'd watch
where the grooms or drivers went to drink at the end of the day
and discover they had common acquaintances in the network
of horse people across London. That would be genuine too. I
asked him if he intended to pay five sovereigns, thinking it
would be a serious jolt to the petty cash, but he said a sovereign
would cover it and to spare. I went back home to write an
advertisement.

FIVE

It's the sorriest resource for an investigator, advertising in a newspaper, but one most of us try when we can't think of any other way. It wasn't that I mistrusted Amos's efforts – I knew he'd get all there was to be got from the stables at Perkins' Yard – but I was frankly ashamed to think I'd contributed so little. So I wrote that if Helena wished for a reply to her letters of the previous week she should write to Miss L. Lane at Abel Yard. I walked to Fleet Street and paid for it to go into the *Times* and two other newspapers the next day. When I got back, Mr Vickery was waiting for me. He must have charmed Mrs Martley because he was in the parlour, sitting in the best chair by a fire much livelier than it usually was at this time in the afternoon, with a cup of tea beside him and the cat on his knee. He started trying to stand up as I came in but I told him to stay where he was for the good of the cat. I'd more than half expected the call because he hadn't struck me as a man used to waiting patiently. I decided not to tell him anything about the carriage in the park until I had results from Amos to report, but let him know about the advertisements. He said did I think they'd do any good and I said probably not, but it was worth trying. I asked him if he'd been aware of anybody watching George over the last few days and he said no. He seemed in no hurry to go.

'I'm planning to ask Amos Legge to come out to my country house for a week or two. Do you think he will?'

I thought about it. Amos did occasionally take time out from his duties to buy or sell horses but usually for no more than a week. 'I suppose it would depend on what you wanted him to do.'

'Set up a stables for me. The buildings are there and a pony and cart, and a man who calls himself a groom, but if George is to hunt we'll need three or four good horses and staff.'

'The house has been out of commission, then?' I was fishing shamelessly for anything about him.

'Since the owner died and that's more than five years ago. I'm renting it from the son on a cheap rate if I pay for repairs and improvements. I've had men working on it every daylight hour. The sooner it's fit to get George out of London, the better.'

'You seemed to be enjoying London.'

He made a face. 'It was necessary. I never thought the family would acknowledge him and I wasn't wrong there. The important thing was that society should accept him for what he is. I've shown him to the people. Now it's time to live quietly and carry on his education. Next year he'll go up to Cambridge, as I said before. I've already engaged a well-recommended tutor and a reader is on his way down from Scotland, mostly for Latin and Shakespeare.' He paused, then, 'Perhaps if all goes well he'll have his sight by the time he goes to Cambridge.'

'You've consulted doctors?'

'I had the best eye doctor in London come to visit without letting George know who he was. He couldn't give a definite verdict without a proper examination but he thinks the blindness is indeed from cataracts and it may be possible to operate. I haven't spoken to George about this yet.'

I thought what a terrifying thing it would be to grow up in darkness, then, quite suddenly, acquire a new sense. All the visible world would surely come rushing in like a storm tide, crushing and unmanageable. I felt almost scared for George with yet another strangeness to face. Vickery left soon afterwards and I promised to let him know if there was any reaction to the advertisements.

'It's about the most secretive stable yard I ever met in my life, apart from racing,' Amos said. We were out on our morning ride. 'I reckon that's how they make most of their money – hiring out carriages for gentleman and ladies doing things they don't want talked about.'

He'd spent most of the previous evening in and around Perkins' Yard. He said it had been pretty much what he expected: a shoddy sort of place with a dozen carriage horses and cobs of no particular merit, two closed carriages, a phaeton and several carts. The pock-marked driver who seemed to manage the place, name of Simmonds, had grudgingly accepted a sovereign and five shillings for the scratch to his paintwork but been about as chatty as a deaf adder with lockjaw when it came to any discussion of his clients.

'So I noticed this little fellow doing most of the work, buckets and haynets – and the hay not good enough to use as a dog's bed – with one withered arm. I waited outside the gates for him. He came out as it was getting dark and turned out to be quite receptive when I suggested a pint of porter at the public house on the corner. Turned out that he'd been a jockey at Newmarket, had a bad fall and was rolled on, ended up at Perkins' Yard as the best he could get and didn't like the pock-marked one any better than a rabbit likes a stoat. So I bought him a drink or two and got him talking. Your Whitehall woman gave her name as Mrs Shilling. The boss drove her out four times, the first two the dates on the letters. My man didn't know where but they were away a short enough time for it to be Whitehall. When they got back the boss said something about her man not being there. The second couple of times fitted with her being in the park.'

'What did she look like?'

'Ladylike, not young. Thirties, perhaps. Well dressed. Dark haired. Quite good looking for her age, he said. Kept her gloves on so he couldn't see if she was wearing a wedding ring.'

'And the driver didn't collect her from home?'

'No. Each time she came to their yard on foot and went away on foot, and the jockey didn't particularly notice in what direction. Seems to be part of their service not to be too inquiring about customers.'

'Are they expecting her back?'

'No telling, he says. The boss might know.'

'I don't suppose they keep an account for her with the address on it.'

'No such luck. It's usually cash on the nail but my man didn't know how much she paid or when. She can't be poor, any road. Their rates are high as the West End.'

I said it sounded like a job for Tabby and Amos said that was what he was thinking too. I had to wait the best part of the day before she arrived at the yard in the evening, looking even more dishevelled than usual. She hated any prying into her private life but George was business, so I told her outright

that I knew she'd been with him at the stables. She gave me a
nod and a look that said, so what about it?

'How did you meet him?'

'In the yard at Mr Legge's stables. He hit me on the nose
with an apple core.'

'He's blind.'

'I know that now but I didn't know it then, otherwise I
wouldn't have tumbled him over in the muck heap.'

'You did what!'

'It was a fair fight, considering. He bit me, look.' She peeled
back a frayed sleeve and showed me a crescent-shaped scar on
her forearm. 'He said he was sorry. He didn't know I was a
girl till I spoke. He'd thought I was one of the stable lads
watching him.'

'The start of a fine friendship.'

'We laugh. I describe people to him and we make up stories
about them. My friend Plush taught him to pick pockets but I
told him he's not to do it because he can't get away fast enough.
The man who's going to adopt him doesn't know about us.'

I said I supposed not, thinking that Vickery's plan to make
an English gentleman out of George hadn't reckoned on Tabby
and her gang. I asked her about Perkins' Yard and she knew it
at once. She'd done some of her growing up in the streets around
Covent Garden. I gave her Amos's description of Mrs Shilling
and said I hoped she'd be back there within a few days. The
task was to follow her on foot when she left the yard and find
out where she lived. Tabby nodded, this being much easier than
A-B-C to her. She had only one question.

'If it's a few days, can I use Plush and one of the others as
well?'

I nodded, knowing she had her gang well in hand, and gave
her a few shillings for expenses.

Two days passed. As I expected, Mr Vickery got tired of
waiting and came to call on me again. I told him about Perkins'
Yard but not about Tabby and George. It seemed to me that the
young man had precious little freedom and if he managed to
escape for an hour or two, good luck to him. Tabby would
do him no harm. He said the name Mrs Shilling meant nothing
to him. I promised that when Tabby found out where she lived,

I'd tell him and we'd plan the next step. It took another two days. On Thursday evening Tabby appeared with a grin on her face.

'Chandos Street, house with the dead geraniums.'

She reported the details. Plush had been watching the stables in Perkins' Yard that afternoon when a woman appeared on foot from the direction of Covent Garden. It was drizzling at the time and the woman wore a black cloak with the hood up. She was quite old, Plush said, but in his world that could mean anyone over thirty. He only caught glimpses of her face but it was pale and her hair dark. Under the cloak she was dressed all in black, apart from a pink neck scarf and matching trim to the bonnet. She'd gone straight to the room next to the carriage shelter that did duty as a tack room and office, knocked briefly on the door and went inside. After a few minutes she came out, no particular expression on her face. When she left the yard Plush had no difficulty keeping her in sight to Chandos Street, to the south-west of Covent Garden, where she'd unlocked the door of the house with dead geraniums on the step and gone inside. Plush had kept the house under observation for some time, with no further appearance of the woman, then come back to report. By the time Tabby had finished it was getting dark so we decided to postpone our visit until the next morning. We walked there soon after nine o'clock. Chandos Street is not fashionable but not a slum either, mostly the living and working place of small tradesmen, printers and engravers, statue carvers, a coachmaker, a bookbinder – all in narrow houses crammed tightly together. Also, for quite a short street there were a lot of public houses – at least four of them. Tabby stopped outside one of the printers, looking across the street.

'That one.'

It was next to one of the public houses, respectable but shabby. The pots of geraniums on either side of the three steps leading up to the front door hadn't been watered since summer and paint was peeling from the green shutters that were partly closed across the ground-floor windows. In such an industrious street with everybody else chipping, carving or type-setting it looked inert and deserted, no nameplate on the nondescript pillars that flanked the black front door. Net curtains, none too clean, were drawn over the two windows on the upper floor. We moved on so as not to attract attention.

'Shall I go round the back?' Tabby said. 'There's an alleyway.'

Trust her to know. I nodded and she was gone as quietly as a cat. I stood looking at views of Wales in an engraver's window, thinking that the simplest thing to do was knock on the front door and ask whoever came to it if he or she knew of a woman named Helena. I crossed the road, rapped on the doorknocker that was showing ridges of rust from under its black enamel, waited and knocked again. No answer. When I looked up there was no sign of a twitch to the net curtains. I gave it five minutes, knocking occasionally and waiting with no result, then found the alleyway a few doors along and joined Tabby. She was waiting by the back door of the house. It was brown painted, shabbier than the front, with a simple latch. The two windows either side of it were thickly curtained with sacking and cobwebs. Tabby raised her eyebrows and glanced at the latch.

'It's probably bolted inside,' I said. Tabby replied by putting her hand on the latch. It lifted and the door opened a few inches, grating on concrete. We looked at each other.

'All right, I'll go first,' I said. The door opened directly into a scullery with a copper for washing clothes, orderly enough with a big mangle standing by, but everything so covered with dust that it couldn't have been used for months. An old towel hung from a hook on the back of a door opposite the one from the alleyway. I opened it and went through into a small kitchen, followed closely by Tabby. Again, neat enough but the cooking range was covered with dust, the ashes in it long cold. The next door led to a narrow hallway, the bottom of a staircase and the back view of the front door, lit only by a rectangle of dusty daylight from a small window over the door. I called, 'Hello, is anybody here?' and my voice echoed. No reply. There were two doors to the left and right. After calling again and waiting I opened the one on the right. The gap between the shutters let in a dim, underwater light. At last, there were signs of recent occupation. A length of carpet covered bare boards to one side of the room. A pine table with two plain chairs held an inkstand and a blotter. When I took the lid off the inkstand I found about half an inch of ink inside, still liquid. The blotter had been used. I carried it over to the window and found blue handwriting with diagonal crosses and closed loops. Impossible to make out the words in this light and without a mirror, but it looked very similar to the handwriting of the Helena letters.

Tabby had been standing by the open door, watching me. Suddenly her head jerked towards the stairs.

'Somebody.'

The steps were slow, as if pausing between each stair. I put the blotter back on the table and moved out to the hall, followed by Tabby. The person coming down the stairs was no more than a hunched shape in the dim light.

'Good morning,' I said. 'I'm sorry, we let ourselves in.'

The shape took another cautious step down. 'I can't hear you.' The voice was old, male and gentle. As he came on down he took shape as a thin man, round shouldered, long white hair mingling with an untrimmed beard. His clothes seemed mostly shapeless corduroy. He negotiated the last stair and came up so close he was almost touching me.

'We're looking for a woman named Helena.' I had to repeat it twice before he mouthed the name after me, but in a tone that said it meant nothing to him. 'Dark hair,' I tried. 'Not young, not old. Wears black.'

He shook his head. 'There have been so many women and men. I seldom know names. I am mostly upstairs, doing my work. They don't disturb me, or not often.' He kept giving me puzzled glances, as if trying to place me.

'Your work?' He seemed too old to do anything but breathe.

'The Etruscans.' As he said the word his face broke into a smile like a child's watching a butterfly. 'I've been studying them since university. Another year or so and I may be ready to publish.'

From behind his back, Tabby caught my eye and made a face.

'So the rooms downstairs are rented out to people?' I said.

'Indeed. I suppose they must be or people wouldn't come here.'

'But you don't know who rents them?'

A shake of the head. 'If you'll excuse me . . .' He gave me a nod and, surprisingly lissom, twisted past Tabby and started going back upstairs. She gave me a look, asking if she should stop him, but I shook my head. I asked if he'd object if we looked in the downstairs rooms and he turned at the top of the stairs to say not in the least, then opened a door on the landing and disappeared. Tabby and I went back to the room on the right and I folded the top sheet from the blotter and put it in my pocket. Then we opened the door on the left. After the plainness of the other room it came as a surprise because it had clearly been used as a temporary bedroom. Blankets and a bolster were heaped in disorder on a not-very-comfortable-looking couch, a woman's black jacket was hitched over the back of a dining chair and a plain black bonnet hung from a hook on the wall. Apart from the couch, the only furniture was a small table, a dining chair and a large cupboard built into the wall. I opened the cupboard and found various pieces of clothing on hooks inside, a skirt in blue wool, plain but well cut, and a newish jacket in dark green velvet. We went back to the first room. Two sheets of screwed-up paper were under the table. I pocketed them as they were, guessing they might be rough drafts for Helena's letters. We found nothing more of interest so we went out through the kitchen and scullery. I supposed I'd committed theft as well as house-breaking in taking the blotting paper with me, but whatever was going on in the ground-floor rooms in the house with the dead geraniums, I didn't think the occupant was likely to call the police.

I settled with Tabby that she and Plush should keep the place under observation. Back in my office, I spread the blotting paper out on the table and uncrumpled the first of the letters I'd found on the floor. Phrases leaped out at me . . . *on what I previously requested. You chose . . . not fail me.* They were from one of the Helena letters sent to Vickery. So, as I thought, this had been a discarded attempt. Only I wasn't right at all. I smoothed it out quite flat and found none of the things you'd expect in a discarded attempt – no blots or crossings out. The few lines it contained were flowing and confident but in quite a different hand from the reversed lines on the blotter. Quite different too from the letters Helena had sent Vickery. I took those letters out of my pigeonhole for comparison. The reverse letters on the blotter and the letters sent to Vickery were the same, but the crumpled letters had clearly been written by somebody different. So Helena had been copying out letters written by

another person. Who? I decided that this deserved reporting to
Mr Vickery and was about to put on my outdoor things when
I heard Tabby's whistle from down in the yard. I went down
and opened the door. A woman in a black cloak was standing
beside her.

'She says she wants to talk to you,' Tabby said.

Under the pink-trimmed bonnet the woman's face was hard
and pale.

'Helena Shilling?' I said.

The merest of nods. Without any more words, she followed
me up the stairs to my office.

SIX

The question in my mind as we went upstairs was whether she'd come in response to the advertisement or followed us from Chandos Street. In the study, I swept the blotter and papers off the table and into a pigeonhole, but if she were quick she might have seen them. I sat her down in a chair by the table. She kept on her bonnet but took off her gloves and folded them, staring at me as if she wanted to be sure of recognizing me again. Her only ring was a plain wedding band.

'You're very young,' she said. Then, after a pause: 'You are connected with Mr Vickery?'

'I'm working for him, trying to trace a woman named Helena who wrote to him. It seems I've found her.'

A nod.

'Is Helena Shilling your real name?'

'That doesn't matter for now. Why wouldn't he do what I asked?' It was a pleasant enough voice, low and controlled. Her skin was so pale it seemed almost colourless apart from a little artificial pink on the cheekbones, her eyes very dark and features well shaped. Small lines around the eyes and mouth suggested she was nearer forty than thirty.

'Mr Vickery is very protective of George,' I said. 'Why do you want to see him?'

'Because the boy he calls George is my son.'

I daresay my mouth fell open. 'Your son?'

'By Lord Byron, eighteen years ago.' She looked me in the face, unblinking.

'But Mr Vickery found George on Cephalonia, the son of a woman from the island.'

She moved her head once from side to side. 'That's his story, is it? It's a lie. However much he's paying you, I'll pay more. I want to see George.'

'Mr Vickery has not paid me anything,' I said. It was true, but her look said she didn't believe me.

'Then why are you helping him steal George?'

'The boy's with him perfectly willingly.'

'He's not of age. He's only eighteen. He can't give his legal consent to anything.'

'I believe Mr Vickery plans to adopt him,' I said. 'Both his parents are dead.'

'I'm alive.'

I stared at her, not believing what she said but thrown off course. 'You say you are his mother. You were on Cephalonia with Lord Byron?'

'No, it happened in Genoa, before he went to Greece. I was there with my father. We had a house in England but my father spent part of the year abroad for his health. My mother had died a long time before. My father became friends with Lord Byron. We met. I could see he admired me. I was young, my head full of nonsense about poets and artists. And he was beautiful. People don't understand how beautiful he could be. So – it happened. I had his child. My father was not a conventional man. He didn't cast me out. I think he would even have let me keep the baby, told some story. But after he was born I was ill, very ill. I didn't know what was happening to me. By the time I came to my senses, the baby was gone. My father said he'd died but I think he was trying to protect me. I think Lord Byron took him with him when he went to Cephalonia and abandoned him there.'

Her voice had quivered when she talked about Byron's beauty, but by the end of it she'd got herself in control again. She wanted me to believe it. I didn't, though I tried not to show it. The idea of a group of men going off to war, taking a baby with them, was too absurd. From what I knew about Lord Byron, I couldn't believe he'd care so much for the baby as to take it, or so little as to abandon it. The story we'd been told by Father Demetrios and Vickery seemed much more likely. I might believe that she'd had a child eighteen years ago, though without evidence even that was uncertain. It was a fact that Byron had lived in Genoa before sailing for Greece, but she could have known that from any account of his life. Even if I stretched a point and accepted that there had been a child, and that Byron had been the father, why disbelieve her father's account that he'd died?

'Is your father still alive?'

She shook her head. 'He died several years ago.'

'Did you ask him about the child?'

'After that first time, no.'

'Have you been looking for the child all these years?'

'No. Most of the time I tried to forget it had happened. It wasn't difficult. It was as if it had happened to somebody else or in a dream. I married one of my father's friends, much older than I was but a kindly man. He's dead too, quite recently.'

'Did you have children?'

Another headshake.

'Had you known the baby was blind?'

'No. Until I saw him at a concert one evening, I hadn't even known he was alive.'

'You saw him and decided he was your son by Lord Byron in that instant?'

'Yes.'

I closed my eyes and thought about loneliness and the different ways of being mad. When I opened them her expression hadn't changed – it was still terribly watchful.

'So you wrote that first note to Mr Vickery? Did you expect him to do what you asked?'

'If he were an honest man, he would have.'

'But you gave him no address to write to.'

'It didn't need an address. All he needed to do was bring the boy to me.'

'And then?'

'Simply, I'd claim him. He'd know. I have a house of my own and more than enough money. We might travel abroad if he wanted. Anything. But Mr Vickery is not honest.'

'Because he wouldn't bring the boy?'

'What does anybody know about him? He appears out of nowhere and suddenly people are talking about him, inviting him. It's because of George. Without Lord Byron's son, he'd be nothing.' There was some justice in that but Vickery had been right in not responding to Helena. I imagined George being taken to that waiting carriage, embraced by an unknown woman who claimed to be his mother. Unthinkable.

She sighed like somebody who'd been wasting time. 'So,

double whatever he's paying you. All you have to do is bring the boy to me. There'll be a bonus of a hundred pounds in your hand as soon as you manage it.'

I shook my head. 'But suppose I could persuade Mr Vickery to meet you, would you see him?'

'If he came with George, yes.'

'And without George?'

Her pause wasn't so much hesitation as thinking things over. 'Perhaps. I'd consider it.'

I hadn't much hope of convincing her but it seemed worth trying. I asked how I should let her know if he agreed and she said I should put a message in the *Times* again. So she'd seen the advertisement. I went downstairs with her and saw her out of the yard gates. She'd get a cab easily in Park Lane. Tabby was waiting by the water pump and asked if she should follow her. She might try, I said, but by now it was the busy time of the afternoon with people going home from offices or paying calls so she shouldn't worry if she lost her. Tabby had something black in her hand.

'Her gloves. She dropped them on the stairs. If she sees me I can say I wanted to give them back to her.'

She ran off. I went upstairs for my cloak and bonnet and walked across the park to Knightsbridge.

'No.' Vickery's response was instant and absolute. 'I'm not seeing her. She's obviously a madwoman. You did well to flush her out, but that's it.'

I told him there was more to it than that and showed him the blotter and the two letters. That silenced him for all of half a minute.

'So she's being used,' he said at last.

'Yes, I'm afraid so. For all I know, she might sincerely believe that George is her son but there's at least one other person involved in this. And nobody lives in those rooms at Chandos Street. They were rented especially.'

'Kidnap then?'

'It looks like it.'

'Well then, we'll leave London. The day after tomorrow, at any rate. I'd intended to wait another week or so for the house to be got ready but we'll have to take it as it is.'

'You think he'll be safer in the country?'

'Fewer people, at any rate. I'll have somebody with him all the time. You'll come, of course, and I believe Amos Legge will.'

It was like being hauled along by a steam train and I resisted as best I could. If I agreed to come out to Muswell Hill I certainly couldn't be ready by the day after tomorrow and I was by no means sure I'd be any use to them. He said at least I'd seen the woman, which was more than anybody else could claim.

'Wouldn't it be a good idea for you to meet her before you go?' I suggested.

'She's a madwoman being used by kidnappers. What's the point in seeing her?'

'She seems quite rational in other respects. Perhaps if you told her about finding George on Cephalonia she'd be convinced, so no help to whoever's using her.'

'From what you tell me, I'd be wasting my breath.'

I tried to persuade him but privately I agreed. Helena's seemed the kind of stubborn delusion that not even proof could shift. Our talk ran on into the evening and he invited me to stay for supper, completely informal, no need at all to dress. He'd send me home in his carriage afterwards. By then I seemed to have agreed to join his household out at Muswell Hill within a few days so it seemed best to get to know it. The tutor was there and the reader had arrived and he wanted to introduce them to me.

'Will they know why I'm there?' I said.

'They'll have to, yes. They'll be part of our line of defence. But George is not to know anything about it. We shan't talk about it at supper. You're simply the friend from Cephalonia who's coming to stay with us.'

We walked out to the hall, Mr Vickery intending to show me a room upstairs where I could tidy up, and found the main staircase blocked by two men and a trunk. One of them was Jolly, the other dark haired and in his early twenties with a broad forehead and full, well-shaped lips.

'Jolly, for goodness' sake, why didn't you take it up the back staircase?' Vickery said.

'We tried, sir, only it got wedged. Main stairs or nothing.' Jolly's reply was cheerful rather than deferential.

'What's in it?' Vickery asked.

'Books and manuscripts mostly, sir. A few clothes.' The voice was Scottish and polite, but again, not overly deferential. Its owner was introduced to me as Hamish McCloud, come from the University of Edinburgh to be a reader to George. Eventually, the two of them got the trunk upstairs and I was shown into a bedroom to tidy up for what turned out to be a pleasant enough if unconventional dinner, myself being the only woman there. Apart from Vickery, George and Hamish McCloud, the only other person present was a mild, middle-aged man named Mr Ridgeway, George's tutor. As promised, I was taken home in Vickery's hired carriage. Tabby was waiting in the yard to tell me that Helena had taken a taxi cab in Park Lane and driven away southwards. Tabby hadn't been near enough to hear what instructions were given to the driver and was annoyed with herself for that, but it would have been too much to expect. She was still clutching Helena's gloves and gave them to me. I asked her if she wanted to come to the house at Muswell Hill with me. Vickery had said I could bring a maid and, although Tabby in that role was a hopeless prospect, it would be good to have her company. She agreed more readily than I expected, perhaps at the thought of being in the same house as George.

As he'd intended, Vickery and his establishment left London two days after I'd seen him. Tabby travelled the day afterwards, on the servants' coach along with Jolly, a housemaid and my trunk. Amos and I went two days later because he had things to do at the stables. After discussing it with me he'd accepted Vickery's request to spend two weeks at his country estate building up the stables, and since Muswell Hill was an easy day's ride out from London, he suggested I take Rancie too. So on Wednesday we rode up Primrose Hill together, Amos on a chestnut hunter he'd bought for Vickery's stables, plus a lad on a pony he'd recruited as one of the grooms. The lad was a good worker, he said, and a pony was always useful. We came to a stretch where we could have a long canter, then stopped and waited for the lad. In the clear autumn light we could see all of London stretched below us, with the sun glinting on the dome of St Paul's and the Thames silver grey.

'I hope he's paying you,' Amos said.

'He offered to pay me at the start. I've taken nothing yet.'

'He's not short of money; he's given me a free rein for the stables. Where does it come from, do you know?'

'I don't. In fact, there are a lot of things about him I don't know.'

Away from Vickery's magnetism, I knew there were questions to be asked about him. His rootlessness and lack of a past were disturbing and I didn't much care for the way he'd been showing George to society. But what clinched the decision to join his house party was George himself. I couldn't get out of my mind the way he'd come to me on Cephalonia saying in that desolate, accepting way that he was cursed. Far more than the glamour of being Byron's son, that made me want to do what I could for him. Also, I instinctively liked Vickery and his determination to go his own way. I liked too the way he regarded me as a professional. Most people of my own class, faced with the reality of how I'd earned my living, reacted with embarrassment. Vickery simply took it for granted. He also took it for granted that I was professional enough to move in with a household that consisted almost entirely of men without fussing about reputation. To be fair, I'd accepted from the start of my professional life that my reputation was as good as lost as far as some people were concerned. It was odd that the same people tended to be the ones who nagged at me to preserve it. Apart from a housekeeper, newly engaged, and the other female servants, I'd be the only woman at the house. Northlands, it was called, and he said it was a mile or so out from the village of Muswell Hill. We rode on through the village, a larger place than I'd expected with some quite impressive houses and fine trees. People who'd made their fortunes in London moved out here for the clean air and countryside, with the financial heart of the City still reassuringly within view. A mile further on we turned left as instructed up a side road that would be muddy in the rain but was still wide enough to take a two-horse carriage. After a while it turned right through a pair of open gates into a drive leading uphill. The gates hung from two sandstone pillars and looked neglected, with stems of bindweed climbing halfway up them. The drive would have been broad once but grass had crept up on it from either side. In some places it was scored with new ruts as if heavy carts had passed recently. It wound for half a mile or so between clumps of rhododendrons, occasionally opening up to a view of stubble fields and copses. Then we turned a final bend and the prospect changed to a building site. A gang of gardeners was attacking the weeds on either side of the drive, spreading barrowloads of fresh yellow gravel. More were working on a flat area of newly dug earth beside the house. One side of the building was almost invisible under scaffolding and ladders with workmen moving up and down. The other side was in the Gothic taste and probably not more than thirty or forty years old, sprouting turrets here and there, narrow pointed windows and a steeply pitched roof covered with slates in a pattern of grey, green and purple. A broad flight of steps led up to the front door, newly painted dark green. A smell of fresh paint hung over everything. We picked our way over the new gravel and Amos noted a broad track leading off to the right. He decided it would lead to the stables and told the lad to take the pony down there while he and I made our way to the bottom of the steps, where he dismounted and helped me down. By then the front door was open and Vickery was coming down the steps. Amos saluted him with his riding crop.

'Good afternoon, sir. I'll take the horses down to the stables.' I noticed that he was speaking in his broadest Herefordshire as he often did in a new situation. I think it was his way of claiming territory. As he vaulted on to the hunter and rode off, leading Rancie, I felt very alone among all the activity but Vickery was shaking my hand warmly, asking about our journey, leading the way up the steps. The housekeeper was waiting inside, a tall, good-looking woman in her thirties in a black dress. Mrs Cole, Vickery said, introducing us. I noticed she wore both a wedding ring and a mourning ring with a lock of dark hair, so was widowed. The hallway was high, with an octagonal dome at the top and windows of alternate plain and stained glass throwing rainbow colours on the black-and-white tiled floor. Mrs Cole led the way upstairs and opened the door on a large bedroom overlooking fields and copses to one side of the house. She asked if I needed anything, said tea would be downstairs as soon as I was ready and left me to myself. I walked round, opening the wardrobe and drawers. Somebody – though certainly not Tabby – had unpacked my things and stowed them neatly away. The smell of new paint was strong in here and when I touched the windowsill my finger came away white. I opened the window to let in fresh air, along with the noise of the builders. Leaning out, I could see roofs that were probably the stables and beyond them, some way downhill, the chimney stack of a cottage. I washed at the marble-topped washstand in cold water, changed out of my riding habit into the plum-coloured wool dress and was just arranging my hair when the door opened and Tabby walked in without knocking. She was wearing her grey dress – tolerably neat – clean shoes and a dissatisfied expression.

'Mrs Cole said you wanted me.'

I didn't particularly, but a housekeeper would naturally assume that a lady needed her maid. Tabby perched on the edge of a chair while I went on doing my hair.

'It's a madhouse here.'

'Oh?'

'None of the servants knows any of the others, the kitchen's half built, the cook's Italian and Mr Vickery has meals when it suits, all odd times. I've been walking round outside mostly, watching the workmen. George knows I'm here and he came out to see me, only he had to go back in again for a piano lesson. With Mrs Cole, that is. She can play the piano. There's a Scottish man who walks around talking to himself in foreign languages.'

'Mr McCloud, that would be.'

'George says he's all right. But George didn't want to leave London. He says he only agreed to come when he heard Mr Legge would be here with horses.'

I thought George would have had no choice, but he was obviously not above trying to impress Tabby. I finished doing my hair and Tabby said she might as well go down to the stables and see Mr Legge, naturally without asking my permission. We parted on the landing, she going through the door to the servants' staircase, I down the main stairs. A door was open to the drawing room with tea things on the table inside. Mr Ridgeway the tutor was alone at the table. He stood up when I came in, said it was a pleasure to meet me again and poured tea neatly with no fussing.

'George and Hamish are reading *Macbeth*, Mr Vickery's been called out to deal with some building crisis and Mr Astley never takes tea.'

'Mr Astley?'

'An old friend of Mr Vickery's – a solicitor. I believe he wants to consult him about adopting George.'

I drank tea, very welcome after the ride, and we talked about George. Ridgeway seemed genuinely impressed by him. 'He has one of the fastest minds I've ever encountered in a young man and an excellent memory. If Hamish reads him a passage a couple of times he can quote it back perfectly. And he has a real gift for languages.'

I asked how he came to be working for Vickery and learned that he'd been recommended by his previous employer, whose son had gone up to university. He'd recruited Hamish McCloud as a reader through an old friend who lectured at the University of Edinburgh because, in his opinion, educated Scots spoke some of the purest English. Hamish fancied himself as a poet but was a good young man for all that.

'Of course, you'll be interested in all of our backgrounds. I imagine that a kidnapping gang would love to introduce one of their own into a household.' This was said over a second cup of tea, quite casually and with a smile.

'So Mr Vickery's told you?'

'Yes, all of us and the servants. Everybody except George himself. He doesn't want the boy disturbed. From my observation, George is a stronger character than Mr Vickery imagines but that's his decision. Mr Vickery's very pleased that you agreed to come here.'

It was a relief that I didn't have to pretend to anybody except George. I asked a few questions and it became obvious that Vickery hadn't told his household the full story. They knew that he suspected an attempted kidnap but nothing had been said about Mrs Shilling. We finished our tea and Mr Ridgeway went back to his tutorial duties. I walked outside and watched as gardeners planted dozens of rose bushes in the expanse of freshly dug earth to one side of the house. Mr Vickery came up beside me, his hands covered with stone dust and a smear of clay on his cheek.

'I've been talking to the builders. They mostly lodge down in Muswell Hill and drink in the public house there. They'd notice any strangers curious about this place. Nobody so far.'

'Wouldn't anybody be curious?' I said. 'You're transforming the place.'

'It needs it. I've taken a five-year lease. That will be the longest I've spent in any place for quite a while.'

I hoped for more about his travels, but that was all. He excused himself to go and interpret between the cook and the housekeeper about dinner, which he thought would be around seven. I walked on to the back of the house where there was no work going on. A roughly cut lawn sloped down to a flight of broad steps. Below them was a kind of water garden, a small pond with a pair of mallard on it, willows and the seed pods of irises. A cast-iron seat in a pattern of intertwined ferns, with rust showing between flaking paintwork, stood on a flat-topped hillock overlooking the pond. It was all overgrown and obviously too far from the house for Vickery's improvements to have reached it yet. I sat on the seat for a while watching the ducks, thinking about Robert and wondering what I was doing there. It seemed a long way from London and the threat of further measures from Helena. I thought Vickery had reacted too strongly, but then he was a man who made quick decisions. It seemed a pleasant enough place to be for a while and quiet country life would do George no harm. Or Rancie either, come to that. I'd stay until his fears died down then go back to London and, just for my own curiosity, pursue the case of Helena Shilling.

Six of us sat down to dinner. Alwyn Astley, the solicitor friend, was plump to the point of being fat with a round face, bald head, body shaped like a seal with a fleshy torso dwindling to short legs and small feet like flippers in their patent evening pumps. When we were introduced he said he was delighted to meet me but with a look that made it clear he thought I shouldn't be there. He had a ravenous appetite for meat, taking second helpings and munching it in teeth that looked so white and regular they must be false. In spite of that, it was a lively occasion. The talk was mainly of the theatre. Vickery mentioned a particular Shakespeare performance he and George had attended in London (not, I noticed, the one when they'd been forced to flee at the interval). Hamish McCloud had been in a college production of the same play and told a story against himself of theatrical disaster that brought laughter from all round the table. He was more confident than you might have expected from a young man at his employer's table. Vickery encouraged him but it was clear Astley hadn't taken to him. My story of an operatic fight with a collapsing dagger seemed to go down well. That was one of the good things about the evening – it was taken for granted that I'd join in along with the rest. And Georgios – or George as I must now think of him? George was simply perfection. As the youngest there he naturally did more listening than talking, turning always towards the person speaking. His hair was shorter than I remembered, the dark curls sleeked down. The candlelight emphasized the fine contours of his face. Sometimes Vickery or Mr Ridgeway would put a question to him directly or give him a conversational prompt and he'd respond with good sense and, occasionally, an anecdote of his own from his short time in London. Never anything about Greece. Altogether the perfect model of a young gentleman, no connection at all with the boy who'd lived with goats in a hovel.

Except he was as fragile as a Venetian glass that a sound might shatter. He was sitting diagonally across from me at the table and I tried not to look at him too much, but you hardly needed to look. Vibrations were coming from him like that glass when you run a wet finger round the rim, spiralling higher and higher into something that can only be felt, not heard. It makes the fine hairs on your arm lift like the filaments on a stinging nettle leaf. He sat, smiled sometimes, ate a little and sipped moderately at his wine. Between the rare smiles his expression didn't vary from polite attentiveness. I noticed that several times he tilted his head across at McCloud. After dessert, when Vickery suggested that he might go upstairs because he'd be up early for Mr Ridgeway's first session in the morning, he stood up, bowed politely and asked me to excuse him. When he'd gone there was a general feeling of relaxation round the table. I asked them to excuse me too. It was the point in a more conventional dinner when the ladies would have withdrawn in any case and I needed fresh air. The front door was unlocked so I let myself out and went down the steps, breathing the good country air. A quarter of a moon was rising in the dark sky and a few clouds were blowing across in a wind from the west. I stood watching them then heard steps on the gravel coming from the side of the house. The person came quite close before I realized it was George. He'd been walking with his head down but seemed to sense that I was there and stopped a few yards away.

'Mrs Carmichael?'

'Yes. I thought you'd gone to bed.'

'I don't go to bed just because I'm sent there. I'm not a schoolboy, even if Vickery treats me like one. He asked you to come here because of me, didn't he?'

The directness took me by surprise. 'He's concerned about you,' I said.

'I think you should leave.'

'I beg your pardon?'

'Leave tomorrow. You can tell him your family are concerned about you. You have a family?'

It was intolerable rudeness. 'I don't think it's your place to give me orders.'

Silence. He seemed surprised by the anger in my voice. Then, apologetically: 'I'm only saying it because I like you. Bad things happen to people around me. I told you so on the island when Panter drowned.'

'It wasn't your fault.'

More silence, and when he next spoke his voice sounded older, a man's rather than a boy's. 'Well, I've warned you. I can't do more.'

I wished him goodnight and went back inside. Upstairs I lay awake for a long time, hearing people coming upstairs to their beds, Mr Ridgeway and McCloud talking, then some time later Astley's heavy tread and harsh breathing. After him, the light steps of George. If Vickery came up it must have been later when I was asleep. Once, half waking, I heard footsteps outside on the gravel path and wondered if he was outside, keeping guard. He'd virtually fled from London and yet I sensed he was less at ease here, waiting for something to happen. The boy had told me to go because, he said, he liked me. That guaranteed I'd stay.

SEVEN

For two weeks, we settled. It rained every other day or so. Gravel was laid all the way down the drive and some of the scaffolding taken down, showing newly pointed brickwork and clean stone. The smell of fresh paint still hung over everything but mealtimes became more regular. Amos got the stables into some order and bought a cob, a light carriage and another useful hunter. He was planning to move back to London, his work done. I walked a lot, played modest card games with Mr Ridgeway and missed Robert. George seemed to relax a little and spent most of his day with Mr Ridgeway or Hamish McCloud, or occasionally at the piano with Mrs Cole. He seemed to get on especially well with the young Scotsman, which wasn't so surprising given that McCloud was nearest to him in age. I heard them laughing together once at some private joke, a rare unguarded reaction from George. On one of my walks I saw McCloud unexpectedly. He was in the lane that went down from the stables to the main road, talking to a girl whom I recognized from the back view as one of the maids. She was a pretty girl, the daughter of a foreman from the village who helped out in the kitchen and went home with him in the evenings. I was nearly sure that I saw McCloud hand her something, possibly a book or small package. She walked away hastily towards the house and McCloud saw me and looked embarrassed. I smiled to myself, thinking that the young man was a fast worker if he was already giving poetry books to a servant girl but it was hardly my place to intervene. I wished him good afternoon, said nothing about the girl and went on with my walk. Vickery, though, didn't relax. I knew from hearing his footsteps on the stairs that he came late to bed every night and was always the first person down in the mornings, apart from the servants. He spent some time closeted with Astley but was mostly with his workmen and would report to me almost daily what they told him about strangers in the village, or anybody asking questions about him or George. Invariably, they seemed innocent – travellers passing through or local people naturally curious about the transformation going on at Northlands. Amos and I would ride down to the village sometimes and I knew he spent some evenings at the public house, made friends there and missed nothing that was going on. Tabby kept mostly close to the house itself, having no enthusiasm for fields and woodlands, but was soon part of a gang made up of some of the workmen's more unruly apprentices. Mrs Cole's efforts to make a lady's maid out of her resulted in an occasional appearance asking if I wanted anything and a swift exit when I said no. Quite often Vickery invited me to go with him on walks in the grounds and delighted in explaining that here would be rose arches, there the nuttery, over there strawberry beds. Once he confided that George would bring back friends for the holidays when he went to Cambridge and he wanted the place to be pleasant for them. He made no mention of Helena. For most of the time George had been kept too busy at his studies to go riding, but at dinner on Friday evening two weeks after I'd arrived Vickery suggested that we might go riding in the morning as a reward for his hard work. The boy's delight was as spontaneous as the laughter I'd overheard.

'You'll come, won't you, Mrs Carmichael? We can try your mare against my chestnut.'

'Not everyone wants to race,' Vickery said.

'I do,' I said. 'Rancie loves being in the country.'

In the morning George, Mr Vickery, Hamish McCloud and I walked together down the back lane to the stables. Hamish had no great opinion of horses and wouldn't be riding, but I guessed he and Mr Ridgeway had been instructed not to let George out of their sight. Vickery was to ride the cob, a placid and useful animal that would go in the shafts or bridle. He saw my eyes on him as he clambered ungracefully into the saddle and smiled.

'As you can see, Mrs Carmichael, I've spent more time at sea than on horseback.'

I sometimes wondered if he was deliberately handing me these small scraps of information about himself. He must know I was curious. By then George was in the saddle of the chestnut Amos had brought from London, his hands light on the reins. Amos handed me up on to Rancie then vaulted into the other hunter's saddle. As we went through a gate into a bridle path George looked almost as happy on horseback as he'd been in the sea, instinctively responsive to the animal's movements, turning his head from side to side as if the horse's own sight was feeding his. Amos went first to manage the gates, then Vickery on the cob, George, Rancie and I. We came into a long field, bounded by hedges. Rancie's head came up, sensing a race, and I patted and spoke to her to calm her. George's chestnut began circling round and I saw concern on Amos's face. The horse was quite a handful and George was promising but inexperienced. Amos told me later that he'd had it in mind to get horse and rider gradually acquainted before anything ambitious, and I was annoyed with myself for having talked so eagerly about racing. I tried to repair it.

'Shall we just have a canter, George? I'll go first.'

The grass felt springy underfoot, wet with dew, the sky was blue with a scattering of white clouds and the air an invitation to stretch out. After the first few strides George and the chestnut came flashing past me, George's hair blowing in the wind and an intense happiness on his face. I advised him to slow down but I might as well have talked to the wind. After a few strides I stopped trying to fight Rancie and let her follow. George and the chestnut rounded the far corner of the field more by luck than anything because George, naturally, hadn't seen it coming and adjusted his weight too late. He lost a stirrup but regained it down the far side of the field and settled back in the saddle. A trimmed hawthorn hedge about four feet high closed off the end of the field. I was sure the chestnut would swerve sideways when he came to it. Almost certainly George would be thrown off but with his youth and the softness of the grass probably no great harm would result. Instead, however, the chestnut went straight on at the hedge, failed to stand off to give it a fair chance at the jump and somersaulted over it and out of sight, but not before we'd seen its rider parting company like a stone from a catapult. Horrified, I followed, Rancie taking the hedge like a bird. A few strides after we landed on the other side I checked her and slid down from the saddle, leaving her to her own devices, sure she wouldn't run off. The chestnut was on his feet, reins broken and flanks heaving but apparently unharmed. George was face down, insensible. I ran over to him, hitching up my riding habit. He was breathing at least and his neck and limbs seemed to be lying normally. I was wondering whether to turn him over when Amos arrived at a run. He gave a glance at me, ran his hands over George and then signalled me with his eyes to help turn him over. As we did it, very carefully, an expression of puzzlement came over the boy's face. When we got him on his back his ribcage was rising and falling fast. A raw whooping sound came out of his mouth.

'Winded,' Amos said.

A rustling in the hedge and Vickery was beside us, his face twisted with anger and anxiety.

'He'll be all right,' Amos said before Vickery could say anything. 'Just give him time.'

But Vickery was down on his knees. 'Georgios.'

A few more whoops, lessening in severity, then the boy's face relaxed and he smiled. 'Here. I'm here.' He tried to get up but Amos told him to stay where he was for a while and took him gently through a list of checks – could he move his arms, his legs, his fingers? Yes was demonstrated to all. Did his head ache? No. Once it was clear that he'd come to no great harm, Amos said we'd get him home. He helped George stand up and supported him through a gateway into the field where the cob was grazing peacefully. I picked up Rancie's reins and saw that Vickery had got hold of the chestnut. He was yanking at the reins and it was trying to rear so I went over to calm things.

'Don't worry, just give him more rein and . . .' I stopped because Vickery was holding a pistol, a short barrelled one, foreign probably. His eyes looked mad and he was trying to drag the horse's head down so that he could put a bullet through it. 'No.' I pulled the reins out of his hand and the chestnut went off at a gallop. For a moment it looked as if Vickery intended to use the pistol on me instead.

'The animal's mad. It could have killed George.'

'It wasn't the horse's fault,' I said. 'George will be all right.'

He looked at me and slowly the madness in his eyes faded.

He tucked the pistol into whatever part of his lower clothing had been holding it. I collected the mare and we went back to the other two. By now George was on his feet, supporting himself on Amos's shoulder and talking happily. He seemed disposed to regard the thing as an adventure and, after a glance at me, Vickery followed his lead. Amos suggested that George should ride the cob back and Vickery accepted without argument. He was quiet and almost passive, recovering from shock. George wanted to know where his horse was. I told him it would find its way home and not to worry. In fact, by the time we got back to the stable yard it had fallen in behind us, reins trailing and saddle awry, limping but entirely unrepentant.

'Do you always carry a pistol when you go out riding?' I said.

It was mid-afternoon and I'd been thinking about it all day. After the ride, Vickery had disappeared, George had gone to his studies and I'd had nothing much else to do. If Vickery had been simply my host I might not have said anything more about what had happened in the morning. I'd told Amos, of course, but that didn't count because he was as discreet as the stone posts at the bottom of the drive. But Vickery was, after a fashion, my employer and it was something I should know. He came to find me as I was sitting and reading in a summerhouse on a bank overlooking the new rose garden and I put my question before he could say anything.

'I carry a pistol when I'm likely to be under attack.' He looked strained, not recovered from the anxiety of the morning. He glanced at me for permission to sit down. I nodded and he took his place on the far end of the bench. The wood was silver with age, pitted with holes and covered with pigeon droppings.

'And you feel you're under attack?'

He nodded, preoccupied. 'George seems remarkably undamaged, I'm glad to say. Mrs Cole has put arnica on the bruises.'

'He's young and strong,' I said.

'He still has nightmares about what happened on Cephalonia.'

'Mr Panter?'

He nodded. It was the first time we'd spoken about it on English soil. I asked if he'd seen anything of Mrs Panter and he said that she'd gone to her family when they got back to England. He didn't sound very interested and I wondered if he knew about her and George. We sat in silence for a while before he spoke again.

'I've been careless. I've decided that from tonight we'll mount guard inside the house. Jolly and I will take most of the responsibility with some help from Astley.'

It surprised me, after the quiet routine of the last two weeks. I'd come to believe that we'd left the threat of Helena and whoever was working with her behind us.

'Has something happened?'

'One of the bricklayers said this morning that he'd heard there were a couple of strange men in the village asking about a blind boy. He didn't know any more than that but it was a reminder to me. I've been letting my guard slip.'

Amos had reported nothing from his friends in the public house and I thought this sounded nothing more serious than usual village chat. Vickery was probably still unsettled from the morning's accident, seeing threats everywhere. Still, I'd come here to work, although so far there'd been no necessity for it. I said I'd be happy to take my share of the night watch.

He shook his head. 'I don't think we need to disturb your rest at this point. Your usefulness will be to identify the Helena woman if she's seen here. We might go to church in the village tomorrow and you can make some discreet inquiries.'

That amused me because we'd not gone near the church in the time we'd been there, but I nodded, thinking I'd get Tabby cleaned up and take her with us.

'And George is not to set foot outside without at least two of us with him,' he said.

'Have you told him?'

'No, and I'm not going to. He can think it's just happening naturally. George mustn't know any of this.'

I thought George probably knew more than he guessed but there seemed no point in protesting. That evening, after dinner, Vickery sent George off with McCloud for some Shakespeare reading and told the rest of us his plans. Mr Ridgeway, whose bedroom was next to George's, should leave his door half open throughout the night, alert for any sounds, with McCloud on the other side. From midnight to four in the morning Vickery would be in the hall by the front door with the servant Jolly by the back door with a bell to summon help if anybody tried to get in. At four another servant would take over from Vickery and Astley would replace Jolly for the last two hours before the rest of the servants were stirring at six. Astley looked unenthusiastic about his part in the guard. He usually slept late and invariably had breakfast in his room. I wondered if Vickery happened to be making a point about his friend's idleness, but if so he gave no sign of it.

'And Legge will be sleeping with his window open at the stables in case anybody tries to come up from the back road,' Vickery said.

I wasn't convinced that any of this was necessary. I didn't believe Mrs Shilling would try a direct assault on the house. As for the two men in the village, even if they'd existed they might be no more than hopeful burglars. Did I even believe Vickery when he said they'd asked about a blind boy? After his performance with the horse that morning my confidence in him was badly shaken.

I went to bed at about eleven but couldn't settle. The house had a variety of clocks that chimed the hour at slightly different times, one of them on the landing just outside my room. I'd deliberately left my door a little open, not wanting to be out of things if anything really did happen, and at midnight I heard Vickery's and Jolly's voices down in the hall, then the gentle thud of the servants' door closing, presumably as Jolly went to his post by the back door. I slept for a while but woke at intervals to hear Vickery pacing in the hall – all night, it seemed. Then, just before four came the slow footsteps and heavy breathing of Astley making his way downstairs. I thought he could hardly have repelled a kitchen maid armed with blunt scissors and wondered again why Vickery had chosen him. Then there were three quiet voices in the hall – Astley, Vickery and presumably the male servant who was taking over the guard by the front door. I expected to hear Vickery's footsteps coming upstairs to bed, surely exhausted by now, but instead the front door opened and footsteps sounded on the gravel before it closed again. Vickery was still keeping up his guard. As I went to sleep

I thought his protectiveness of George had become an obsession, then after what seemed like a very short amount of time
I was woken harshly while it was still dark by a hand bell
clanging.

It came from downstairs, at the back of the house. My room
was pitch-black and I scrabbled for the candle holder and flint
lighter. By the time I got the candle alight feet were thumping
down the wooden stairs from the servants' quarters. Vickery's
voice from the hall called sharply up to somebody to stay where
he was and not come down. To George? I dressed as fast as I
could in whatever was nearest, not bothering with corsets and
cursing buttons that slipped from my fingers. When I looked
down from the landing on the hall it was bright as a stage set,
all the lamps lit and the front door wide open. The clock on
the landing said it was twenty minutes to six. The housekeeper
was standing in the hall with two woman servants, all hastily
dressed as I was. I asked her what was happening.

'Burglars. Mr Vickery's got the men out looking for them.'

'Where's George?'

'Upstairs with Mr Ridgeway and the Scottish gentleman.'

I went out of the front door and found Vickery on the steps
outside, talking to Amos. The air was cold enough to make me
shiver. Vickery had his pistol sticking out of his pocket, not
bothering to conceal it.

'Somebody was trying to get in at the back door,' he said.
'Astley heard them. Come and see.' He picked up a lamp from
the steps and Amos and I followed him round the side of the
house. He shone the lamp on the back door and sure enough
there were fresh score marks in the paintwork and a long
carpenter's chisel lying abandoned on the ground.

'A very amateurish attempt,' I said. 'It looks like a local
burglar and not a very good one.' But would even an incom-
petent local burglar make his attempt less than an hour before
the household would be up and about? From the look Amos
gave me he was puzzled as well. I asked if anybody had seen
the man or men trying to break in.

'No. Astley heard them and quite rightly rang the bell so
they'd have run off,' Vickery said. 'I've got the men out looking
for them.'

'How did you get here so quickly?' I asked Amos.

'I was up already. The chestnut's given himself a strain and I wanted to change the poultice. I heard people shouting and ran up here.'

'An hour to daylight,' Vickery said. 'Legge, you go back to the stables. As soon as it's light get mounted and ride around the copses. They can't have got far.'

'How would they have got him away without rousing the household?' I said.

Vickery didn't answer. He was looking towards the garden where light from a lantern was glowing faintly through rhododendrons. The servants were searching but surely by now the men would be further away than that. I said on impulse that I'd go down to the stables and ride out on the hunt with Amos. Vickery just nodded, his attention on the lamplight. Now that something had almost happened, some of the tension had gone out of him. He seemed drained, almost at a loss.

Amos and I walked down the back lane together, stopping to let a badger cross our path. A couple of times he took my arm to save me from walking into potholes. I believe he can see in the dark.

'Does he really think it was kidnappers?' His voice, casual as if commenting on the weather, proved that our minds were moving in the same direction.

'I don't know. On almost everything he's quite rational but when it comes to George he sees threats everywhere. I can't think that this was anything to do with Helena. Whatever she was doing somebody had planned it, spent money on it. This was no more than a nonsense.'

'And yet he predicted it,' Amos said.

'Are you thinking . . .?'

Because I'd been thinking it too, I let the question die away.

'Easy enough for him to arrange,' Amos said.

'But why?'

'Two reasons I can think of. One is to keep the boy close to him; the other is to keep you here.'

'No! He's been the perfect polite host, not a question of anything out of line.'

'I just mentioned it,' Amos said, and was silent all the way to the stables.

When we got there he made me sit down in the tack room with a horse blanket around my shoulders while he started the morning stable round. By the time it was fully light the boy who'd come with us from London and the older resident groom had joined him. The clanking of water buckets and the murmur of Amos's voice as he saw to the chestnut were soothing after the tensions of the house.

When Amos came in, I said, 'I'm wondering whether to go back to London after all. I don't understand what Vickery is doing. I wanted to help George but I don't see how I can.'

He nodded. 'I've told him I'm going the day after tomorrow. We'll ride together if you like.'

I thanked him and asked if we were really going to ride out and search the copses as Vickery had ordered. He shook his head.

'Waste of time. But we might ride down as far as Muswell Hill, see if anybody in the village knows anything. If it was just a local burglar trying his luck somebody will know.'

So he saddled up Rancie and the cob and we rode down the lane. After a while the roof of the cottage came into view. I'd passed it on some of my walks and knew it was unoccupied. Beside it, the lane turned a sharp bend with a clump of ash trees on the other side. As we rounded it Amos gave a whistle of surprise.

'Well, I'll be . . .'

A carriage stood there, more or less facing the road but dragged to one side because the horse in the shafts was grazing on the bank. A plain, closed carriage of the sort a none-too-choosey yard might put out for hire. The reins were hitched loosely on the rail in front of the driver's box. The blind on our side was pulled down. I'd so nearly convinced myself that the kidnap attempt had been invented by Vickery that I could hardly believe what I was seeing. Amos swung off the cob, gave the reins to me and went up to the horse, an ordinary-looking bay. Several piles of droppings in the lane showed it had been there for some time.

'He's all right, anyway.' He knocked with his fist on the carriage door. No response. 'So they'd left it waiting here after all.' He turned the handle of the door, pulled it open then just stood there.

'What is it, Amos?'

He ducked inside but was out again in a moment. 'Stay where you are.'

But something in his face had already brought me sliding out of the saddle. I left our horses where they were and went to stand beside him at the open door. There was somebody inside the carriage – a woman. Her clothes were black except for a white triangle where her skirt had been pulled up over a petticoat. She lay with her head and upper body on the seat and her legs on the floor. Her face was white, her eyes open. One leg was bent back and the other stretched forward showing an expanse of white stocking, splashed red. Blood had poured from her head over the seat and on to the floor, so much so that it was now dripping out of the door on to the lane. Some of it had started to coagulate in a ridge where the carriage door had been closed. Amos stepped up into the carriage, trying to shield me from the sight. I think he must have lifted up her head because he said one word.

'Shot.'

'Where?'

'Back of the head.' He stepped out backwards, closing the door. There was blood on his riding boots and although his face was too weather-beaten to go pale it had a tight, stretched look. 'Not a lady I recognize.'

'I do,' I said. 'It's Helena Shilling.'

EIGHT

Amos stared at me. I tried to make my mind move. All I could think of was her white face.

'So they really were trying to kidnap George. She was waiting here for them and . . .' I let it trail away, looking at the blood that had pooled on the muddy ground. Rain had started to fall.

'What's become of the driver?' Amos said.

He stepped round the blood and closed the carriage door, shutting in the view of her.

'Perhaps he was one of them trying to break in.' My mind started moving again, slowly. 'They're scared off and come back without George, but they still want paying. She refuses and . . .'

Amos was looking closely at the paintwork of the carriage. 'It's the same one from Perkins' Yard. So if they shot her, why wouldn't they just turf her out of the carriage and drive off?'

I had no answer to that. Amos suggested that if I felt well enough we should have a look at the cottage. The hedge between its garden and the lane was high and unkempt, tangled with brambles, and large blackberries shining in the wet. We found a gate and walked up the overgrown path. It looked as if somebody had walked along it quite recently, brushing the long grass aside, but when Amos knocked on the brown-painted door the noise was hollow, empty. Thin cotton curtains were half drawn over the window beside the door. I looked in and saw only the outlines of simple furniture, no lights or sound of life. We walked back down the path.

'We'll get her up to the stables,' Amos said. 'Can't leave the horse stuck here.'

He had to unhitch the horse and manoeuvre the carriage with his own strength to get it pointed up the lane. He wouldn't let me help and I was glad of it, seeing how he had to trample in pools of blood and mud. Once the carriage was clear of it, I helped him re-harness the horse and he took his place on the box and gave me a hand up beside him. The pace was slow, more from the weariness of the horse than respect for what we were carrying. The boy from London was mucking out one of the boxes when we got to the stable yard and was wide-eyed at the sight of a strange horse and carriage. Amos told him and the old groom to get the horse into a box, rub him down and give him water and hay. That left the two of us standing by the carriage.

'I'll have to stay with it,' Amos said. 'The lad'll go with you up to the house. You'll be all right?'

'Yes.' I didn't feel all right; I felt sick and Amos probably knew it.

'What will you tell Mr Vickery?'

'How we found her and who she is. What else can I do?'

'You reckon he might have shot her?' From his tone, he might have been asking when I thought the rain would stop.

'He's been carrying a pistol. I think there's nothing he wouldn't do to protect George. But he was on guard in the hall most of the night until four, then outside afterwards for a while, and there when Astley rang the alarm bell. That was probably around half past five.'

It was a relief to be talking about times and Amos knew it.

'I'm nearly sure I'd have heard him if he went past the stables,' he said. 'That means he'd have had to go across the fields in the dark and that would have taken longer. I didn't notice any mud or blood on him.'

'No, neither did I. So he'd have had to go upstairs and change as well. Could he have done all that in not much over an hour?'

We looked at each other. 'Possibly, maybe,' Amos said. 'Difficult, though. On second thoughts, you stay here with the lad. I'll go up and talk to him.'

'No. Don't worry, I'm not going to march up there and accuse him.'

But he looked worried as I set off for the house, the lad walking respectfully behind me. It was raining harder now, the cart channels in the lane running with brown water. When we came to the house I sent the lad round to the kitchen door to get something hot to drink and went up the steps to the front door. I opened it without knocking and at once found myself face-to-face with Mr Vickery, standing inside the hall as if waiting for me. He blinked and took a step back. I suppose I must have looked a sight, hair wet and flopping down, skirt muddy and stuck with burrs.

'She's dead,' I told him, watching his eyes. They seemed blank, puzzled.

'Who?'

'Mrs Shilling, or Helena if you prefer. Amos Legge and I found her in the lane. He's with her at the stables.'

'Dead in the lane? How?' His voice was level, no alarm in it, just mild surprise. Nothing to be guessed from that. He was a man who could control his emotions most of the time. If he'd killed her, he'd had time to decide how to play his hand.

'Shot in the head.'

'And you found her. I'm very sorry for that.' The look in his eyes was now concern for me. 'I'll call Mrs Cole to look after you then get down to Legge.' He moved towards the bell inside the door.

'I don't need looking after,' I said. 'It's not the first time I've seen a murdered body.' The thought of the first time – my father – still cut through me, but that was nothing to do with him. 'What do you think happened?'

He looked at me for what seemed like a long time then moved away from the bell. 'A falling out among thieves. She'd hired kidnappers, criminals. The woman probably thought she was controlling them. When they reported failure, I suppose they argued. Did you and Legge get any sight of the men?'

'No. We'll have to tell the authorities. I suppose there's a constable at Muswell Hill.' I didn't know if Northlands was in the Metropolitan Police area and thought it was probably just over the border, but somebody must represent the law.

'All in good time. I need to speak to Legge first, then Astley. Don't tell anybody yet. As far as the household is concerned, you've just been out searching for the men. Understood?'

This time I let him ring the bell. When he turned, I noticed there was no pistol in his pocket. A maid answered the bell, her eyes wide at my dampness and untidiness, and was sent to find the housekeeper. In the short time before the housekeeper

appeared, Vickery was out of the front door. Mrs Cole asked
no questions beyond whether I preferred tea or coffee sent to
my room. She said she'd send up my maid to help me change.
As I went slowly up the stairs I thought about the tone of
Vickery's '*Understood?*' It had been a command as much as
an inquiry. He was taking charge of events and expected me to
do what he said. In my room, I'd drunk two cups of tea and
changed into clean clothes before Tabby appeared. She walked
in, glanced at my face and the pile of wet clothes on the floor.

'Who's dead?'

It was by way of being a businesslike query. I stared at her.
'How do you know someone's dead?'

'George says so.'

Surely the last person in the place Vickery would tell. In any
case, George was supposed to be under somebody's eye all the
time, so how had he come to have a conversation with Tabby?
She answered one question at least, scuffing the toe of her shoe
on the carpet.

'The Scotsman had to come out to the place on the landing
for a piss, so George had to go too. It's by the servants' door.
George was waiting outside when I came out and he whispered
it to me then. He was nervy, strung-up.'

'Did he say who was dead?'

'He didn't know. Wanted to know if I knew, then the Scotsman
came out and I had to go. So who is it?'

No point in keeping things from Tabby and she'd hold her
tongue. 'Helena Shilling. But for goodness' sake, don't tell
anyone, not even that there's been a death. I don't know how
George knew.'

'We talked about it once, back in London. He says it's all
round him – he can smell it.'

Was that George talking for effect or did he know something?
I pointed to the heap of clothes on the floor and told Tabby to
carry them down to the laundry room. She gathered them up
in her own good time, looking closely at the hem of the skirt.
There was blood as well as mud on it but she said nothing.
When she'd gone I did my hair and went downstairs. Breakfast
things were still laid out in the dining room so I ate toast and
coddled eggs and wondered how much to tell the constable

when he arrived. I was still wondering when Mr Vickery put his head round the door. His hair was sleeked down from the wet and there were drops of water on his beard.

'Mrs Carmichael, I wonder if you'd join Astley and myself in the library.'

Astley was deep in a leather armchair by the fire, a coffee cup and a brandy glass on the table beside him. He made a token effort to get to his feet then subsided, but his eyes were on me and looked hostile.

'Vickery tells me you identified her. You're sure of it? The light can't have been good and you were naturally shocked.'

'I'm not easily shocked. The light was adequate. She was Helena Shilling – at least, that's what she called herself. Where have you put her?'

I was sitting in an armchair opposite him, Vickery at right angles to us. When it was clear Astley wasn't going to, Vickery answered my question.

'Legge and I brought her up from the stables. She's in the old game larder outside the scullery.'

'And you'll have confirmed that she was shot in the back of the head?' I knew it well enough but it was important to have it acknowledged. He did so with a nod.

'Suicide,' Astley said. 'The woman was clearly unstable. The kidnap attempt failed and she destroyed herself.'

'People who kill themselves with guns don't usually do so in the back of the head,' I said.

I could see from Astley's eyes that he wanted to argue but Vickery spoke first. 'It's more likely that one of the kidnappers shot her after an argument.'

'In any case, the inquest will be looking into that,' I said. Silence, apart from the fire crackling and the slopping of a mop out in the hall. We'd brought in a lot of mud between us.

After some time, Vickery spoke. 'It's the inquest we want to talk about. Did Mrs Shilling have a family?'

'None that I know of. She said her parents and her husband were dead and she had no children.'

'So if it were not for the coincidence of your being here when she died there'd be nobody to identify her. And how well did you know her?' Astley said, his cold eyes boring into mine.

'I met her once when she came to my house. But I know very little about her.'

Astley took a sip of brandy. 'The point is that you were hardly intimate with the woman and, as you admit, you know very little about her. So just how valuable would your identification be at any inquest?'

I saw where this was heading and didn't try to hide my anger. 'The first business of an inquest is identification and then the circumstances of death. I know who she is and I was with Amos Legge when we found the body. That makes me a witness on two counts.'

'It's George I'm worrying about,' Vickery said after another silence. 'If you identify the woman at an inquest then the story of how you knew her, the ridiculous claim of George being her son and all the rest of it will come out. The newspapers will get hold of it.'

'Not necessarily,' I said, although the newspapers usually did find out most things sooner or later. 'Besides, why don't you just tell George?'

'No.' Just the one word from Vickery, but it was absolute.

'Legge could give evidence of finding the body,' Astley said. 'You needn't be involved at all. I'm sure you'd find an inquest intrusive and distressing.'

'Not particularly,' I said, giving him stare for stare.

'Perhaps there's another way,' Vickery said. 'If you, Mrs Carmichael, were to return to London, with your investigative skills you might discover some friend or relative of Mrs Shilling who could identify the body. Then you wouldn't need to appear at the inquest and none of what we know need come out.'

Even Astley looked surprised at this. I wondered how Vickery thought the inquest would regard the violent death of a London woman in a country lane. Both of them were inviting me to join a conspiracy to hide the facts. Surely Vickery knew I must suspect him of shooting Mrs Shilling. Was I supposed to keep quiet out of friendship – not even that – acquaintanceship? But every word they said made me want to get away from the place and decide what to do without their influence.

'They open the inquest as soon after death as they can,' I said. 'Even tomorrow.'

'Today's Sunday,' Astley said. 'I don't suppose they can get an inquest together before Tuesday at the earliest and then it will have to be adjourned.'

'Very well, I'll go back to London today,' I said. 'There's still time. Amos Legge will escort me.'

A moment of surprise on Vickery's face at having won his point so easily. 'And you'll look for friends or family?'

'Yes.' Did he guess that wasn't all I'd be looking for? 'Is Amos Legge still up at the house?'

Vickery thought he'd gone back to the stables and offered to have him sent for but I said I'd go down and speak to him. Vickery got up to open the library door for me but Astley stayed where he was. I went behind the servants' door to find Mrs Cole in the housekeeper's room, and told her I was leaving so would she kindly tell Tabby to retrieve my riding habit from the laundry room. In my room I put on my cloak and heavy shoes and walked down to the stables. The carriage was standing in the middle of the yard with a pool of water around it and a smell of carbolic on the damp air. Amos was shining the door handle with a cloth.

'Still no sign of the coachman?' I said.

'None.'

'Do you think it was the usual driver, Simmonds? I suppose he ran off and left the horse and carriage. Wouldn't that be like a sailor deserting his ship?'

'For a good driver, yes, but I didn't notice much good about Perkins' Yard.'

'Did you find anything in the carriage when you cleaned it?' I knew he'd have had a good look.

'Not much to the purpose. A lot of mud underneath her but no clear prints.'

'No reticule?'

'No. I don't know if she had anything in her coat pockets. Maybe I should have looked.'

Maybe he should. I should have done but there was a decency about Amos that would prevent him from rifling a dead woman's pockets.

'He locked up the game larder we put her in,' Amos said, seeming to follow my thoughts.

'Can we get back to London today?'

He thought about it. 'If we have to. We'll leave the carriage here and I'll ride the big hunter. Tomorrow I'll go round to Perkins' Yard and see what I can find out about the driver. I won't say why I'm asking until I know whether he's turned up there.'

'I'd like to take Tabby with us, if we can.'

'She can ride pillion with me if you like. A featherweight like her won't be any odds. An hour from now, say.'

Vickery agreed that Amos should go with me to London but wanted him back by Tuesday in case he were needed to give evidence about the finding of the body. He and Amos walked around on the gravel drive together for some time before we left, around midday, Tabby perched easily behind Amos in a borrowed waterproof coat and myself on Rancie. As we went, he told me about his talk with Vickery.

'Mainly, he was making sure I wasn't going to tell an inquest who she was. He doesn't know you and me discuss most things and I wasn't going to tell him. So I said I couldn't swear to who she was – which is true. And he suggested I shouldn't say you were with me when I found her, so that you weren't dragged into it.'

'Oh, Amos.'

'So I'm riding down the lane when I come across the carriage and find a lady I've never seen before dead inside it. Makes sense, as far as it goes.'

'What about the attempt on the house?'

'Mr Vickery gives evidence that there seemed to be an attempt at burglary. So she got shot because there was a falling out of thieves. That way, nothing about kidnappers, nothing about Master George and no reason for the newspapers to be interested.'

'The police won't just leave it at that.'

'Mr Vickery thinks they might. He says according to Astley we're just outside the Metropolitan Police area here and the local constabulary won't be so sharp.'

'Is all this Astley's idea?'

'He's certainly been discussing things with Mr Vickery.'

I thought it odd behaviour in a solicitor. I didn't like the part

I was being asked to play – or not play – in concealing facts about Helena's death. My hope was that back in London I'd find somebody who could identify her and that would take the whole thing out of Vickery's hands.

'Of course, we could go to the police ourselves,' Amos suggested.

He'd touched on a sore point. In a recent case of mine the police had behaved badly – in my opinion, at any rate. They'd included an officer I'd trusted. Besides, what would we tell the police? With anything like the whole story, even a not especially sharp officer would be suspicious of Vickery. I was, too, especially after my conversation with him and Astley, but there was just enough uncertainty to make me play for time.

'Not yet,' I said. 'Not until we know more.'

By the time we came to the outskirts of London, in a wet half-light with no view of the Thames, we'd settled that Amos should ride back to Northlands the following day after talking to somebody at Perkins' Yard. He dropped Tabby and myself off at Abel Yard and took Rancie with him, across the park to his stables.

I was tired but something was nagging at me, so I changed out of my riding habit, made myself as presentable as possible and walked the short distance to a house in Brook Street. It was the home of a solicitor who'd employed me on what turned out to be a more complicated case than expected and taken him closer than he liked to a scandal. He was grateful to me for rescuing him from it and had paid promptly. I think he liked me well enough but was downright alarmed at the way I made my living and wouldn't have thanked me for walking into his chambers, probably carrying smells of sulphur and pitch with me. I arrived on his doorstep in that sinking Sunday evening time between dinner and supper and sent in my old name since he probably didn't know about my marriage. He came out into the hall dressed in a velvet jacket and Turkish cap, looking more alarmed than welcoming. The children were in the sitting room, he explained as a reason for not inviting me in. Goodness knows what he thought I'd do to them.

'This won't take long. I just wanted to ask if you knew of a solicitor named Alwyn Astley.'

He put a hand to his mouth and considered. 'Not somebody I've met in the course of my work. I'm almost certain I've never met him. And yet there is some recollection of the name. It is in my mind that somebody may have mentioned him to me, but some time ago.' His voice and the look on his face told me he was remembering more than he admitted.

'If you do think of anything, could you please let me know? I could call at your office tomorrow if you like.'

He positively shuddered. 'Oh, I don't think that will be necessary. If I think of anything that may be helpful, I'll send a note to you. You're at the same address?'

I told him I was, we wished each other good evening and he scurried off to join his children. I walked home and called Tabby upstairs for a consultation in the parlour since Mrs Martley was away visiting. We talked over cups of tea and hunks of bread and cheese. I said the main aim was to find anybody who knew Helena Shilling. There must be somewhere she lived, apart from the temporary lodging in Chandos Street. One line of inquiry could start from there, finding the landlord who'd rented the property to her. The other place we knew about was the stables at Perkins' Yard but we'd leave that to Amos. I went to the pigeonhole and brought out the only things we possessed of Helena's: the two letters sent to Vickery and the pair of gloves she'd dropped.

'We know the letters were originally written by somebody else but I think we can take it that it's her handwriting,' I said. 'Not a lot to be guessed from that. It's a decent, educated hand but that would fit tens of thousands of women in London.'

Tabby, uninterested in writing, was spreading out the gloves. 'They're not even.'

At first glance they looked perfectly even to me – black silk gloves of good quality, buttoned at the wrist, such as any lady might order by the dozen. Tabby pulled the cuffs of them tight to show me.

'The right-hand one's got three buttons and the left hand only two, with a big space between them. And it's not because a button's come off. There's no bits of thread or needle holes.'

She was right. They'd been carefully and deliberately made like that. The label inside was from a well-known glove-maker in New Bond Street. I sometimes used the same establishment myself when in funds.

'We'll go there in the morning,' I said. 'After Chandos Street.'

We agreed to meet downstairs at nine and I suppose Tabby retired to her cabin in the yard. In spite of it all, I slept well. It had been a long day.

NINE

I hadn't expected to see Amos on Monday morning, knowing that he had a full day ahead of him, but there he was on the hunter in the yard at about the time we'd usually have been going for our ride. It turned out that he'd gone round to Perkins' Yard on Sunday evening.

'Just as well too, because the little fellow with the withered arm was worn nearly to a shadow trying to look after the place with nobody there except him and a lad. The boss hadn't come back since Saturday morning. So I gave him a hand and got what story there was. The woman, Mrs Shilling, came to the yard early on Saturday morning and Simmonds drove her out – just her, nobody else. He didn't say anything to my fellow about when he'd be back but my fellow thought it would be well before it got dark because he'd never been out longer than a few hours with Mrs Shilling before. Then Saturday evening comes and he's not back. My fellow sleeps in the hayloft overnight to keep an eye on the place, but all of Sunday, nothing from the boss. He's worried, of course, thinking they've had an accident.'

'You didn't tell him?'

'No, but I wished I could have said something to put his mind at rest about the horse. He seemed more worried about that than his boss or Mrs Shilling.'

'And he knew nothing about where they were going?'

'Nothing at all, and I believe him. All he's interested in are the horses and his beer. He says he's got used to not seeing things. I reckoned mostly he meant hiring out carriages for husbands who don't want their wives to know where they're going and the other way round sometimes, but he could have meant anything. There's something not right about that yard and I'll keep an eye on it. I'm on my way back to Muswell Hill. I'll look after the horse and carriage for now. They're comfortable enough in Mr Vickery's yard and, if the driver doesn't show up, I'll take them back when it suits me.'

Chandos Street on Monday morning was in a bad temper because of a hold up to the traffic. A stonemason's wagon and a tub-like thing piled with old clothes drawn by a donkey, going in opposite directions, were both held up by an open cart with a bony horse standing outside the house with the dead geraniums. A man was hunched on the driving seat and the front door of the house was open. Two more men were in the hallway struggling with the frame of a double bed, turned sideways. It looked as if they'd got it wedged in the corridor. Tabby and I stood on the other side of the street and watched, as you do when men are having arguments with furniture. It took them some time to get it into the downstairs room on the left and it made a graze on the wall of the corridor that showed raw plaster. Then they came out to the cart and shouldered in a double mattress which was none too clean.

'Moving new tenants in,' I said. 'We'll have a word when they come out.'

After ten minutes or so the men emerged and one of them locked the door. He was a working man in an overcoat and muffler, with a battered brown hat. When I crossed the road and asked if he was the landlord he looked at me, narrow-eyed.

'What if I am?'

'I'm looking for rooms to rent in this area. Somebody mentioned that there might be some available here.'

'They've been taken.'

'I'm sorry about that. A friend of mine was staying there, a Mrs Shilling. Do you happen to know what became of her?' I unclosed my hand to let him see the two half-crowns I'd put there ready. His eyes went from them to my face.

'Owes you, does she?'

'Did she give a name and address?'

'I don't remember. The name was Black or White or something and she never had to give an address because she paid cash down for a month like I asked. I gave her the key and that was that.'

The two half-crowns had found their way from my palm to his pocket. Bad value so far.

'Who brought the key back at the end of the month?'

'The month was up last weekend and nobody did. So I had to use my key and now I'm out of pocket for getting another one cut.'

'Did you talk to the woman at all?'

'I only saw her the once, and that was when I looked in to see about a window that got broken. She was on her own. I said I'd come to see the window and she nodded and that was it.'

'What did she look like?'

'You said she was a friend of yours.'

'Just tell me.'

'Ordinary. Dark hair, not bad looking but not young.' He shook his head and glanced towards the cart. The donkey-owner had turned and gone away but the stonemason and the driver of the furniture cart were shouting at each other. I watched my man climb up on his cart and be driven away. Tabby joined me from a few yards away, having heard everything.

'Was he lying?'

'Why should he be? He had his money, in any case. I don't think that gets us any further.'

We went to the glove-makers in New Bond Street and Tabby waited outside. The sales clerk summoned the manager who handled the gloves gently, like a lost lap dog come home.

'I don't even need to consult our ledger for these. There's only one lady who has her gloves made like this. But may I ask why you want to know?'

When I said I'd like to reunite the gloves with their owner he nodded and gave me a name, Mrs Whitbourne, and an address in Dover Street. He added that he believed she was still in town because her maid had come in with an order only a week before. We went across to Dover Street and Tabby waited again while I knocked on an elegant front door with clipped bay trees on either side. It looked a prosperous and very respectable house, not likely to be connected with violent death in a hired carriage. I felt far from confident, knowing I was probably bringing bad news to it. The speed and simplicity of finding where Helena Shilling lived had taken me by surprise and I knew that when the door opened there'd be questions to ask and answer, and incomprehension. The simplest possibility was that Helena

Shilling and Mrs Whitbourne were the same person, in which case her servants would surely be worried by her absence for the past two days. If so, I hoped there'd be a butler or house-keeper I could talk to and break the news as gently as possible. Perhaps Mrs Whitbourne was a relative, or even a mother, although Helena had claimed her parents were dead. If so, did she know about Helena's obsession with Byron's child? If not, breaking the news would be even harder and much more compli-cated. The door was opened by a maid, middle-aged and neat in a newly starched cap and apron. Her face was gloomy and her eyes red, but perhaps she was always like that. She sniffed and I realized she had a head cold. She kept me waiting on the doorstep with the door pushed nearly but not quite shut while she went to see whether Mrs Whitbourne would receive me. So the first question was answered. Mrs Whitbourne was not Helena Shilling. I'd given the maid one of my old cards with my maiden name on it because I'd had no time to get new ones printed. The maid came back and opened the door wide enough to let me in. The walls of the hallway were papered in stripes, with cut-out silhouette portraits in oval frames and a severe arrangement of chrysanthemums on a low table. Their smell mingled with beeswax polish. The maid opened a door on the left, into a salon decorated in tones of pink and grey, the furni-ture elaborate eighteenth century. The woman sitting upright in a winged armchair was obviously from the eighteenth century as well, as elderly and elegant as the Georgian silver vase on the table beside her that held one white rose bud on a perfectly straight stem. Her back was straight too and she sat on the edge of her chair, not slouching against it, probably as taught by a strict nurse six decades or so ago. Piled up silvery hair and eyes like cold pewter completed the effect. She was old enough to be Helena Shilling's mother but I could see no resemblance. She didn't invite me to sit down.

'Miss Lane? I've heard of you, haven't I?'

'Possibly, yes. I'm an investigator.' No telling from her eyes whether what she'd heard had been good or bad. Some of my investigations had involved old families and old feuds and I'd made enemies simply by acting for one side or the other.

'So what's your business with me?'

'I've come to return your gloves.' I produced them. After a pause she stretched out a pale hand and took them. The reason for the oddity in the buttons was clear. Her left wrist had a bony lump on it, the result probably of a long-ago break, badly set.

'Yes, they're mine, but three years old. May I ask where you found them?'

'A visitor left them at my office.'

'And you've gone to this trouble to return a pair of old gloves?'

'They were left by a woman who called herself Helena Shilling,' I said, looking her in the face. Something in her eyes changed and I thought it was anger but her posture didn't shift. 'You know her?'

'Go on.'

'I'd like to find anybody who knows her.'

'I never knew a Helena Shilling. To my regret, I did once know a person who called herself Helena Claremont. But then she was the kind of woman who probably changed her name as often as she changed her bonnets. What has she done now?'

At least I wasn't having to break bad news. 'I'm afraid I'm not free to discuss it,' I said. 'But anything you can tell me about her would be helpful.'

She sighed. 'Very well. But you should warn your client to have nothing to do with her. Two years ago Helena Claremont, so called, was engaged to a nephew of mine. He is a somewhat nervous character, not easy with women, and he became besotted with her. I found out afterwards that he'd actually seen her playing some small part on the stage and approached her. He's wealthy and she took advantage of him, told him a pack of lies about being a clergyman's daughter fallen on hard times. He was of age so we couldn't stop him. I suggested he should move the woman in with me before the wedding, knowing I'd smoke her out. She was no more a clergyman's daughter than the queen of the fairies. My nephew was starting to have doubts. She realized that and moved out smartly, taking all she could carry of my things with her, including fifty pounds in money, some jewellery and a box of gloves. So what is it?'

'She's dead,' I said, having no reason to hide it.

'Good.'

'Have you any idea where she came from?'

'The theatre world, I suppose. She was a good actress, I'll say as much for her. She came very near to fooling me – for a couple of days.'

I thought how she'd convinced me that she believed the George story. Certainly a good actress. Although I stayed for some time and asked more questions, I found out nothing of any purpose. Helena had gone and since the jewels were not of great importance – the good ones being in the bank – the family had made no attempt to find her. The nephew had married a bishop's widow who was dull but perfectly presentable and that was that. Tabby and I discussed it as we walked home.

'Where would you look for an actress?'

'A playhouse,' Tabby said promptly.

'Imagine an actress growing older with no prospects. She uses her talents to try to catch a rich husband and fails. The Whitbourne family might even have been one of many she robbed. Whoever's plotting against Vickery knows she's available for playing a part.'

'So we go round all the playhouses asking if anybody knows anyone who looks like her?'

'Hopeless. There'll be dozens of dark-haired unsuccessful actresses. And the inquest is probably tomorrow, so we've no time.'

Back at Abel Yard, a message had been delivered from my highly respectable solicitor friend – five lines of precise penmanship. It informed me that he had made inquiries about Alwyn Astley and he was no longer a solicitor. He had been struck off the roll eight years ago. My friend was not aware of the circumstances but advised me to have nothing to do with him. He remained my obedient servant. I was tempted to try his obedience by presenting myself at his rooms and demanding more information, sure he'd know more than he told me, but decided to spare him after all. So after soup and tea with Mrs Martley – who kept asking if I'd heard from Robert as if I'd somehow carelessly mislaid him – I walked on my own to Fleet Street. My old friend Jimmy Cuffs was usually to be found in the early afternoons dining off toasted cheese and a pint of porter at his favourite public house. As usual, I had to send a boy in to let him know I was there, Fleet Street public houses not being welcoming to ladies. He came out brushing toast crumbs from his coat front. Jimmy is one of the most intelligent people I know but scrapes a living reporting inquests for the newspapers. He also has various friends in the legal profession, none of them rich. I apologised for interrupting his breakfast and asked if he knew of a struck-off solicitor named Alwyn Astley.

He wrinkled his forehead. 'I've some rag of a memory about the name but no more than that. I'll ask around. Could you be back here after first edition time?'

I said I could. I wondered whether to ask him if he'd heard anything of another inquest which might be taking place the next day at Muswell Hill, but it was outside his usual area. In the early evening, just as the light was going, I arrived back at the public house as he came out with a couple of closely written sheets for the copy boy waiting at the door.

'It will make the late editions. Would you care for a coffee?'

Politely, he offered me his arm. I took it, though adapting my pace to his was difficult because he limped and wasn't tall. There was a coffeehouse not far away, with a back room where men and women might drink together as friends of the proprietor. Some of the women scraped a living writing for the more radical of the newsheets and magazines that clung like barnacles on rocks to the side alleys and courtyards of the important newspapers. A few of the others scraped a slightly better living in more traditional ways but loved the talk and gossip they shared with the journalists. I remembered a woman with dyed chestnut hair and a scar on her cheek taking on a barrister in a debate about the philosophical writings of Bishop Berkeley and scoring a few palpable hits. Early in the evening it wasn't yet crowded, with only half-a-dozen or so people at the tables. Jimmy led the way to the corner where a middle-aged, paunchy man with glasses and an attractive smile was sitting over a glass of port. He stood up and Jimmy introduced him as a barrister named Gregory Cleggs. He had the air of a man who was beyond being surprised at anything. I guessed from the carefully brushed but not new appearance of his jacket and his friendship with Jimmy that he probably made a practice of defending hard and not very profitable cases.

'You were asking about Alwyn Astley. It's eight or nine years ago and I have no experience of him personally, but a senior person in my chambers was concerned in the case. It was of some general interest at the time.'

His voice was high and light, his eyes amused. I supposed Jimmy had told him something about me. We sat down and the waiter brought cups of coffee.

'What did he do?' I said.

'Forged a letter. The case concerned a financial fraud, complicated as these things usually are. As far as I remember, the defendant was claiming that a certain banker, recently deceased, had given him permission to carry out a particular course of action and the prosecution disputed it. Then, at the eleventh hour, Astley, the solicitor for the defendant, produced a letter purportedly written by the banker supporting the defendant's case. My colleague was representing the defendant but he suspected that the letter had come altogether too pat. He made inquiries and it turned out that Astley had written it himself. Naturally he refused to produce it in court. His client was found guilty – almost certainly the correct verdict – and sentenced to seven years' transportation.'

Jimmy leaned forward. 'Wouldn't the solicitor have been guilty of a criminal offence?'

'Certainly, if the letter had been produced in court, but my colleague stopped it before it got that far. It was glossed over as an accidental error, which it certainly wasn't. But Astley was struck off. Do I gather you've encountered him, Mrs Carmichael?'

'Yes.' From his face, he'd have loved to know where, but I wasn't going to tell him. 'Can you remember the name of the defendant?'

'Peters. I think it might have been George Peters.'

'What was he like?'

'I only saw him a couple of times when he came to our chambers. Fairly ordinary clerk type, I'd have said. Quite young. Self-assured, but then fraudsters usually are.'

'Not striking to look at?'

'Not in the least. You could have found a dozen like him in Threadneedle Street.'

He was looking at me with his head on one side, guessing there was a story here. At least his answer had laid one thing to rest. The defendant in the case had not been Matthew Vickery. Even eight years younger, he'd have stood out anywhere. But it still left the question of why, with so many solicitors to choose from, he should have allied himself with a disgraced man.

'If any of your acquaintances has dealings with Astley, I'd advise him to be very careful,' Cleggs said.

We were standing up and Jimmy Cuffs was helping me into my coat when I remembered that he was a keen theatregoer, especially where Shakespeare was concerned. I mentioned to him, not expecting anything from it, that I was trying to trace a dark-haired woman in her thirties who sometimes went by the name of Helena Shilling and who might once have been an actress. I added as an afterthought: 'She used the name Claremont at least once, two years ago.' A sudden movement came from the next table. A sharp-faced man was turning round in his chair, looking at us.

'Did you say Helena Claremont? I saw her earlier this year, lying herself out of all hope of salvation on a breach of promise case. The judge threw it out with some very harsh words about being lucky he wasn't committing her for perjury. It was pretty obvious the plaintive had paid her.'

'Dark-haired, pale-faced, late thirties?' I said.

'That sounds like her.'

'Do you know where she was living?'

He grinned – not a pleasant grin. 'If you're thinking of employing her, I'd advise against it. The lady has a reputation.' It was obvious he was more than half drunk and Jimmy Cuffs and Cleggs were uneasy, feeling he'd exceeded the free-speaking traditions of the place.

'So where was she living?' I repeated.

'A lodging house off St Martin's Lane, I believe – the church end of it. Don't say you weren't warned.'

I let them hustle me out and Jimmy Cuffs insisted on walking some of the way home with me but had to turn back at Piccadilly for a meeting with an editor.

Back at Abel Yard, at last I had something to tell Tabby. The church end of St Martin's Lane wasn't very far from Chandos Street. Now we knew Helena had been living there up to a few months ago, under another name, Tabby would have the exact place pinpointed in twenty-four hours or less. She'd have started there and then, in the dark and rain, but I persuaded her to wait until morning. I warned her to come back and tell me when she found the address and not go in on her own. Altogether it had not been a bad day's work, but there were two things that worried me. We knew more about Helena and were close now to finding out much more, but we were as distant as ever from the man or woman who'd written the letters for Helena to copy. Helena had been no more than a tool, and an unlucky one. What worried me even more was Astley. He'd been introduced to me, by Vickery, as a friend as well as a solicitor. The forgery that had cost him his living, and might have put him in prison, had happened eight years ago so surely Vickery would have known about it. When it came to the question of arranging things at the inquest, Vickery had obviously been relying on Astley. When I thought of that I wished I'd insisted on staying to give my evidence, whatever the result. But it was too late now. With luck, the inquest would simply be adjourned and perhaps by this time tomorrow I'd have found somebody who could positively identify Helena. Vickery might not like it but he had something else to explain now.

I was about to undress and get ready for bed when I heard somebody knocking on the outside door to the main staircase. I looked out and saw a large dark shape in a waterproof coat and hat so wet it was almost shapeless. A face turned up towards me.

'Amos, what are you doing here?'

He looked as exhausted as I'd ever seen him and worried, which was rare for him. I hurried down and took him into the parlour. I got the lamp going, stirred up the fire and put the kettle on. He stood there in his coat, dripping, hat squashed between his big hands.

'Mrs Martley's up there?'

'Yes. Can't you hear her snoring?'

To me he was family and it didn't occur to me to call Mrs

Martley down for respectability's sake, but Amos had some conventional instincts. Still, he gave a nod which seemed to accept her snoring as chaperonage. He took off his coat and hung it on the door. His tweed jacket was damp in patches and his hair was soaked, clinging to his head.

'What in the world have you been doing?'

'I could only get an outside place on the coach. It rained heavy out there.'

'Coach?' This was new. In all the time I'd known Amos he'd never had to pay for travel. 'For goodness' sake, sit down and I'll make some tea.'

He fitted himself awkwardly into an upright chair. The teacup looked as small as a thimble in his hand and I refilled it a couple of times.

'There's a problem,' he said.

'Why? Is it about the inquest?'

He shook his head. Usually he liked drawing his stories out for effect but this time he still seemed to be trying to get something clear in his mind. 'It won't happen.'

'You mean they'll adjourn the inquest? But we expected . . .'

Another headshake. 'There'll be no inquest on account of there being no body.'

'What?' I nearly dropped the teapot. 'Of course there's a body.'

'Not now. It's gone. Down by the pond, I'd say, though I don't know for sure.'

I sat down heavily on the armchair. 'Tell me.'

He did, slowly, sometimes pausing to make sure I'd got it clear. 'You remember I went back this morning? When I'd seen to the horse I went straight to the house, expecting orders to take all of us to the inquest the next day, wherever it might be. I sent word in to Mr Vickery and he came out, looking like a man who hadn't slept much. I said would we be going to the inquest and he said there'd be no inquest because somebody had come and taken the body away. I asked him who and he looked for a minute as if he was going to tell me to mind my own business, then he said it turned out she came from a family out Muswell Hill way. They'd sent for the body and they'd be seeing to the inquest.'

'That's total nonsense. You don't see to inquests like that.'

'I wondered whether to take him up on it but I said nothing, just waited to hear whether he'd say anything else but he didn't, just turned and went back inside. I was still standing there when out came the housekeeper in her bonnet and outdoor things saying would I bring the trap round to take her and her trunk to the main road to catch the coach. I said was she leaving us and she said yes, she was, so I went and got the trap. When I left her at the coach stop I said it was a bad business and she said, "The worst, Mr Legge. I want no part of it, wages or not, and I don't care what he says. The boot boy says their shoes were clotted with fresh mud this morning, all three pairs".'

'Three?'

'Vickery, Astley and the servant, Jolly.'

'Astley!' I couldn't imagine him as a gravedigger, though it was quite possible that it had been his idea. Perhaps Vickery had insisted. 'So where did you say they buried her?'

'In the rough bit of the garden, where the pond is, I reckon. They wouldn't have carried her far. I'd have looked only I thought I'd better let you know.'

By that time, my head was in my hands. Vickery and Astley had made no attempt to go to the police or the magistrates. Helena Shilling would be left to rot by the pond and it would be as if she'd never existed.

'Vickery must know he can't get away with it,' I said. 'You could go straight to the police.'

'He thinks he thought of that. Before I left the stables there was a paper package with ten sovereigns in it sent down by a servant and a note from him thanking me for my hard work. I left them on the tack-room table. He might have found them by now.'

'What sort of world is he living in?' His own world – that had been clear from the first time I'd set eyes on him. He'd take what he wanted and everything in the way of it was to be bought or destroyed. 'What about George? Does he know what's going on?'

'I don't know. He hasn't been seen outside all day. The housekeeper said he's been kept upstairs with the tutor and the Scotsman. So what are we going to do about it?'

We stared at each other, knowing what the answer should be: tell the police. A woman had been killed. The problem was that I didn't trust the police. I didn't know what sort of influence Vickery could bring to bear but would put nothing past him.

'We can't just leave George with Vickery, knowing what we know,' I said.

'But he won't have much of a life otherwise, will he? You said the Byron family don't want anything to do with him.'

'So we say nothing and let Vickery get away with killing the woman? In any case, I'm sure George will know something of what's going on. He knows more than Vickery imagines.' I thought that if he knew he'd probably be blaming himself for another death.

'So I'll go back and have it out with Vickery,' Amos said.

'Accuse him to his face of murder? No. You do realize he has a very good reason for wanting you dead?'

'You too,' Amos said, looking as sombre as I'd ever seen him. 'He must be wondering if we've gone to the police yet.'

'I should tell somebody and let him know we've told them?' But who did I know well enough to trust with this? Amos and I would be committing a crime in concealing a murder and the disposal of a body. In the end we settled that I should write it in a letter to an MP of my acquaintance, Mr Benjamin Disraeli, who lived just round the corner facing Park Lane. I'd enclose it in a covering letter and mark it not to be opened unless he heard I was dead.

'And I'll stand guard in your yard tonight,' Amos said.

'No, you won't. You've had a long enough day already. Besides, I don't really think Vickery would do it.'

'He killed the woman.'

'If so, she was a problem to hand and he solved it the shortest way. That's how his mind works. I don't think he looks very far ahead.'

We argued but in the end he gave way. I told him that in the morning I might be finding out more about the Helena woman. On the way out, he paused.

'Another thing – the horse and carriage have gone. The lad at the stables said a man arrived early this morning, said they were his and drove them away. The boy didn't know any better than to let him – it's not his fault. I asked what the driver looked like and he said his face was all pock-marked, so it sounds like Simmonds.'

Normally this would have been important news, but we were both so shaken at what Vickery had done that I simply said we'd discuss it in the morning. After Amos had left for the stables I fetched a pen and ink, wrote as concise an account as I could manage, enclosed it in a sheet addressed to Mr Disraeli and sealed it. I went to bed and slept better than I'd expected, but woke up just as it was getting light with my mind on the letter. I decided to deliver it myself, got up and dressed. Outside the cloud made a low, grey ceiling over Mayfair, not raining yet but getting ready for it. I went round the corner, handed my letter to the maid who came to the door with ashes on her apron and her hair tied up in a scarf, and walked back to Adam's Mews. The place was waking up, grooms raking out stables, carrying baskets of soiled straw to the midden and cows being walked towards Park Lane for the first milk round of the day. Tabby had already left, presumably for St Martin's Lane. I wished her luck but couldn't see how finding out more about Helena would help us much now.

TEN

T abby's whistle sounded in the yard around midday and I went down to her.

'Found her. Just behind the church. There's an old woman she shared a room with, chatty as a parrot. You'll want to see her.'

She was so pleased with herself that I hadn't the heart to point out that I'd told her to come back and talk to me before going in anywhere. As we walked quickly towards St Martin's Lane I asked her if she'd told the old woman that Helena was dead but she said she'd left that to me. There's a narrow road called Dawson's Alley off the southern end of the lane, crammed with mean little houses. Tabby went to one in the middle of the row and shouted up that she was back with her friend. An elderly voice, more cultivated than I'd have expected from the surroundings, shouted down that we were to come up. The narrow stairs were dark and littered with bits of torn ballad sheets, as if a street-seller had dumped his stock-in-trade there. A door stood open off a landing of bare boards.

'Come in, whoever you are. I'm Elsa.' The speaker was a woman with orange hair, obviously dyed, and a face as brown and wrinkled as a raisin. She was probably small in any case, but her upper body was tipped forward almost parallel to the ground and she had to raise her head to look at us. Her eyes were grey, ringed with white and bright as a bird's. Her clothes were like something from a pantomime – striped woollen tights and a tunic decorated as a playing card, the three of clubs. Various costumes hung from hooks around the walls: a gauzy ballet skirt, a black velvet cloak with tarnished gold embroidery, a crown of tin stars. A tray with a teapot and several cups, all of different patterns, stood on a rickety-looking table. 'I do fortunes,' she said.

I suppose I must have said yes because she sat us down on a sagging sofa and lit a spirit lamp under a small kettle, talking non-stop about the predictions she'd made, mostly of great successes with the occasional foreseen disaster. I put down a shilling on the table, drank an atrociously weak cup of tea and let her interpret the pattern of leaves in the cup. Great success for my husband, it seemed, travelling to foreign parts and with several healthy children. If the tea had been stronger there'd probably have been a whole tribe of them. Tabby watched, her mouth open. She has a tendency to superstition and had firmly resisted having her own future told. At the end of it, Elsa put down the cup, drew a deep breath and peered up to look me in the eye again.

'You've come about Helena?' The fortune telling had been her way of getting some money, modest enough as a ploy for keeping herself with a roof over her head and much needed from the look of the place. From her tone, she guessed the news wasn't good. 'She's not here. If it's work for her, I'm expecting her back any day now.'

'She lives here with you?'

A nod.

'When did you last see her?'

'She went out Saturday morning, early.'

'Did she say where she was going?'

Her head moved fractionally from side to side. 'It was work, that's all. I didn't ask. She said she'd probably be back on the Sunday.'

Tabby and I looked at each other. 'I'm afraid she may have had an accident,' I said.

Her eyes closed then her head went down. 'Bad?'

'I'm sorry to say she may be dead.'

Silence, then: 'Who was it who killed her?'

Tabby looked impressed, as if it were more fortune telling.

'You knew she was taking risks, didn't you?' I said. 'She'd do things outside the law.'

'What's outside the law and what's inside it? How do you expect people like us to know? If somebody came to her and said there was money in her hand for pretending to be this or that, it was just like any other acting. She'd have gone on doing it on the stage if she could have but she couldn't and she had to live. She had a talent for it. She was the best Desdemona I've ever seen and I've seen a dozen of them. Acting's acting, whether you do it on a stage, in the witness box or in a drawing room.'

'Yes, she was good,' I said, thinking that she'd convinced me that she believed the Byron story. 'She was on the stage?'

'Born to it, actors from way back. In Birmingham that was, and all round the Midlands as far out as Hereford and up to Stafford. I was costumes – born to that as well. When her mother died I suppose I was a mother to her, as far as you could be with all the travelling round.'

'What happened?'

'Desdemona happened. She fell head over heels for her Othello and had his baby, only it died. Othello's wife said she'd make sure she'd never work in the theatre again, and she meant it. She knew a lot of people and could do it. So there was Helena, sick from having the baby and no work. We moved to London. Now and again she'd get a bit of work, only she wasn't much of a dancer and that was what was on offer, mostly. So the other things started. A gentleman wanted a lady he could present as his wife now and then, or a lady wanted a woman to put temptation in her husband's way, to see if she could trust him. Always something like that. Harmless, most of it.'

Give or take the occasional piece of perjury, I thought. 'Did you hear of her meeting somebody in Chandos Street, just round the corner, quite recently?'

'I told you, we never talked about things that much.'

'Or a livery stables at Perkins' Yard?'

Another headshake, then: 'You're asking a lot of questions but you haven't answered mine, have you? Who was it who killed her?'

I hesitated. Even if I'd said the name it would probably have meant nothing to her. In any case, suspicion wasn't certainty. 'I don't know. It seems she was working with a gang trying to kidnap a boy.'

'She wouldn't do kidnapping.' But she didn't sound quite certain about that. 'Where is she now?'

'We think the person who killed her may have buried her.'

'Just like that? No ceremony?'

'No.'

'And how do you come to know about it?' The question was angry rather than puzzled.

'I was working for the boy's guardian. I'm sorry I can't tell you more but there's a lot I don't know.'

'So she's gone.' The words hung in the air of the room among the dejected costumes. At least somebody was grieving for Helena. 'She had no luck. Whatever she did, she never had any luck.'

I took out my card, left it on the table beside the teacups and promised I'd come back if I had any more to tell her. Outside, Tabby asked why I hadn't wanted Elsa to go and identify the body. When I said that there was no body above ground to identify and told her Amos's story she seemed impressed rather than shocked. Her moral outlook probably wasn't a world away from Vickery's and she had no use for inquests or any other kind of officialdom. She simply asked whether we were going to do anything about it.

'I don't know and that's the truth.' Part of me wanted to walk away from it all. Helena hadn't deserved what happened to her but she'd involved herself in something criminal. Vickery was probably a murderer, but without him what would happen to George? Why not leave him to whatever fates might, sooner or later, avenge a killing? 'I'll discuss it with Amos,' I said, and she nodded as if that settled the question.

I had to wait for him because he was riding in the park with two ladies, one of them on Rancie. It was fair enough because occasional work paid for her keep and I knew he'd only let the best riders on her, but it contributed to the gloom of my mood. I waited by her loose box until he clattered into the yard with the two ladies, the mother on a grey and her daughter on Rancie. She rode well and Rancie obviously liked her, which didn't help. I watched as Amos helped them down and saw them into their carriage, then led Rancie across to where I was standing.

'Thought I'd find you here,' he said.

I followed him into the box, helped untack her and watched as he rubbed her down with a hay wisp.

'I've been thinking about it,' he said. 'What I can't get clear in my mind is how he did it in the time he had. For one thing, there's his shoes.'

'Shoes?'

'That housekeeper was a clever woman. When the three of them buried Mrs Shilling on Sunday she noticed mud on their shoes on Monday morning. She didn't say anything about mud on Vickery's shoes on the Sunday morning and there would have been, whether he'd gone across the fields or down the lane.'

'He might have cleaned it off himself.'

'But that would take time and time was what he didn't have. You're certain he was in the house from midnight to four?'

'I heard his voice several times. I'm nearly sure. And I definitely heard it around four.'

'The other question is how he knew she was there.'

'Yes, I've been asking myself that too,' I said. 'I suppose she might have sent a message to him but I don't know when or how.'

'Why, if they'd decided to kidnap the boy? And if he wouldn't meet her safe in Whitehall, why do it in the middle of the night in a country lane?'

'There's Jolly,' I said. 'He's been with Vickery a long time. I didn't see him there when the alarm was raised.'

'You think Vickery just told him to go down and shoot her, and he did?'

'I don't know what to think. Suppose the carriage had been up nearer the house when she was shot?'

'Then I'd have heard it. As it is, I'm surprised I didn't hear the shot, but if it was inside the carriage with the pistol against her head it would have muffled it.'

He finished his wisping and threw a rug over Rancie. I helped him with the girth. It was a relief, as always with Amos, to get to the practicalities of things.

'But he buried her, we're agreed on that,' I said.

'Burying's not killing.'

'So now you think he didn't kill her?'

'All I've been thinking is there's a doubt about it. I suppose we could ask him. He strikes me as a direct sort of an individual. He might even tell us.'

I believe that if I'd said the word he'd have saddled up there and then to do it. Instead, I told him what I'd found out about

Helena. The problem was that she was only part of it. Another person had written the original letters and I could think of no way of finding him or her. Something else was nagging at me and Amos couldn't help with that because he'd only seen Astley from a distance. I couldn't see how Astley and Vickery fitted together but whatever had happened on the Saturday night, he'd have known about it. Something between them went back a long way.

I said goodbye to Amos and walked to Fleet Street. Newspapers keep their old copies and for a small consideration will allow people to search them. I'd done that in a couple of my past cases and knew the routine – a word with the clerk in the outer office, a few shillings passed over then down to a basement with walls that rocked from the sound of the presses thundering overhead. It was like being in the cabin of a steamship. A young man as pale as if he'd never seen daylight asked what dates I wanted and I asked for seven and eight years ago. He raised his eyebrows, perfectly arched and fine as a girl's, fetched two heavily bound volumes and put them on an inclined desk by the wall. The archives room closed at eight o'clock, he said. It was then only just past two so he obviously expected a long search. So did I, with the probability that it would be fruitless. I sat on a high clerk's stool at the desk and began turning pages that were already fragile and musty smelling. Going through two years of papers wasn't as bad as might have been expected because the law reports were always in the same part of the paper. Fraud cases appeared quite frequently and were reported in some detail. Glancing through them, I was struck by the sheer credulousness of the victims: emerald mines in India, railway schemes in America, a chalybeate spring in Derbyshire that would rival Bath or Cheltenham – there seemed to be no project so farfetched that people wouldn't part with large sums of money to finance it. And these were the ones that had ended in clear failure, with the originators of the schemes in the dock and sad or angry people tramping in and out of the witness box with their stories. The country must be full of people selling such schemes, not yet found out or with victims too embarrassed to go to the police. All the time I was looking for the name of the defendant – George Peters or something like it. Cleggs

hadn't been certain. In fact, it turned out to be Gerald Peters
and I almost missed it. It was there, on a Friday in November
eight years before, with the prisoner Peters found unanimously
guilty by the jury. There were some harsh words from the judge
about unprincipled extortion on the basis of a well-known name
and the sentencing of Peters to seven years' transportation.
Obviously the case in which Astley had been involved, although
there would have been no mention of Peters' solicitor. No
mention either that the solicitor might have been in the dock
himself on a perjury charge if his forged letter had come into
court. The report was only a paragraph, crammed in at the
bottom of a column, clearly the end of a story that had been
reported in a previous issue. I turned back a day and found the
story I'd missed. It was, in many ways, a repetition of the other
fraud stories. Gerald Peters had been twenty-nine years old at
the time, formerly employed as a clerk by a firm in the city of
London that specialized in financing trade between English
firms and various parts of Europe. Evidence was given by his
former employers that he had been dismissed for trying to set
up a scheme of his own with one of the firm's clients. Then he
embarked on his fraud and the list of witnesses suggested that
Peters must have been very convincing indeed, persuading
people, including a clergymen, the widow of an admiral, a
retired professor plus several dozen others who did not appear
as witnesses, to contribute to his money-raising scheme. The
beauty of it was that he had not been greedy, in most cases
taking only a few hundred from each victim with the highest
loss being a thousand pounds. Still, it had added up to a very
respectable sum. The investors had been led to think they were
part of a small, carefully chosen group rather than a wide sweep.
He'd been honest, up to a point, letting his targets know that
the thing was a risk and success could not be completely guaranteed. He'd even made a virtue of the risk. I guessed there'd
been something adventurous about it, making these respectable
people feel their money was sailing off on a treasure hunt with
a chest of gold at the end of it. And it really was a chest of
gold. It took me some time to find out what the bait had been,
there in a short sentence among the various testimonies, and
when I did the gasp I gave must have been audible above the

sound of the presses because the pale man turned round with a question mark on his face.

'Found it, madam?'

Yes, I'd found it. The accused had represented that a chest crammed with gold coins had been buried on an island off the coast of Greece ten years before. The money had been raised to help the fight for Greek independence, taken to Cephalonia and buried. The accused claimed to have knowledge from a friend who had been there at the time of the burying. The treasure had never been spent because the man who'd buried it for safety, and died before he could arrange to have it delivered to the Greek freedom fighters, was Lord Byron. I sat staring at the paper but in my mind seeing Vickery as I'd first seen him, on the beach under his rented villa. The connection was there – Byron's island, Byron's probable son and Astley. But then I thought it seemed not so much a connection as another tangle. Vickery was not Gerald Peters. The description I'd had of Peters wasn't a good one but he didn't fit it at all. Peters had spent most of the past eight years in Van Diemen's Land and, given delays to the convict ships, he might not be back yet. Meanwhile, Vickery had been in Greece long enough to meet Father Demetrios and find George. But Vickery regarded the solicitor who'd come to grief trying to defend Peters as his friend. It was quite possible that Vickery had been behind Astley's fraud. Was his decision to adopt George part of another and more ambitious attempt? If so, it only made it more likely that he'd kill anybody who got in the way of it. I closed the book, thanked the clerk and walked out into the dusk.

ELEVEN

I t was dark by the time I got back to Abel Yard, with Mr Grindley's workshop closed and just one window of lamplight showing upstairs from our parlour. My head was aching from thinking and I wanted tea, so perhaps I wasn't as alert as usual when I turned in at the gates. I was halfway across the yard before I was conscious of steps behind me from the street, not light enough for Tabby. They came fast. I got to the door and put my hand on the latch then turned. A tall figure came out of the darkness and took shape as Vickery, hatless, hair disordered. I'd thought he was still out at Northlands and in the surprise of seeing him there I hardly took in what he was saying. He was repeating it over and over, like a threat.

'Where is he? Where is he?' I thought at first he meant Amos and started asking why he expected to find him here, but he added something: 'Legge took him away, didn't he? He brought him here.'

'Who?'

'You know who. George.'

'George has gone?'

'He's here, isn't he? You're hiding him.'

'Of course I'm not.'

'I don't believe you. I'm going to search this place.' His face was white and pinched with anger. I took a deep breath.

'Well, in that case you'd better come in and start.'

I led him up the main staircase and into the parlour. Mrs Martley was knitting in a chair by the fire with the cat on her lap. They both jumped up. I tried to stay calm. I didn't know if Vickery was still carrying the pistol but I didn't want to give him the excuse to use it.

'Mr Vickery is going to search the house,' I said, trying to sound matter of fact about it. 'Will you make us some tea, please.'

She stabbed the needles into the wool, leaving it in the middle of a row, and bent down to the kettle, keeping a nervous eye on him, flinching as he disturbed pictures and trinkets. He searched methodically, looking behind the door, removing shawls from chairs, opening the piano. He even glanced at the fire, checking that it would be too hot for anybody to be up the chimney. I said nothing, calmed the cat and put scraps of meat down for her. He opened the door to the staircase.

'Our bedrooms,' I said, and followed him up the narrow stairs.

He made the same thorough business of Mrs Martley's room, pulling back the counterpane, getting on his hands and knees to look under the bed and opening her clothes chest. I had to bite my lip when he did it to mine, putting his head up the cold chimney then leaving a soot smear on the pale dress hanging in my wardrobe. I said nothing, just stood there watching. By then, Mrs Martley was up beside me.

'What is he? Police?'

'Anything but.'

She went back downstairs, giving me a look that said this was my fault as usual. I followed Vickery through the small doorway to my study. There weren't many hiding places in the room and when he'd opened my chest of books and looked up the chimney he seemed at a loss, then decided to search the whole yard and charged downstairs. In the dark, with Colley's cows in their byre at the far end, Mr Grindley and his family interrupted at supper above the workshop and hens cackling in their coop, it became pandemonium. Mr Grindley, puzzled, stood by while Vickery investigated every nook and cranny of the workshop as well as he could by lamplight and I explained that the gentleman thought somebody might be hiding there. The cows mooed and shifted in their stalls and even Vickery decided against going in with them, though he found a stick and prodded at the hay in the manger. Tabby had come out of her cabin at the first disturbance and was standing outside it, her arms folded. She didn't want to allow him to look in but gave way reluctantly at a nod from me.

'What's happening?' she asked me as his head and shoulders were inside and the rest of him sticking out.

'He's looking for George.'

She looked longingly at his backside and shifted her feet. 'Well, he won't find him in there, will he?'

At last, Vickery had to accept that he was nowhere on the premises and stood at a loss, like a terrier that's run out of rats.

'He's never been here,' I said. 'Do you propose searching Amos Legge's stables? You might not find him as patient as I've been.'

'Legge left in a hurry,' he said. 'What am I supposed to think?'

'I know why he left. We spoke when he got back to town.'

Some shift in Vickery's expression showed he knew what I was talking about but he said nothing. I suggested that we'd be more comfortable indoors and led the way back up to the parlour. Mrs Martley served tea, stewed to a mahogany colour, and I signalled with a look that she should stay with us. She'd be unreliable as a witness to whatever was said but I didn't want to be alone with Vickery. She took her place on a chair by the bookcase, along with her knitting and the cat, and I offered Vickery an armchair by the fire. He sank into it, as if the ride from Muswell Hill and his anger had taken some of the energy out of him. I sat opposite.

'So when did you know George was missing?' I said.

'Yesterday morning – Monday. He was supposed to be with Mr Ridgeway for Latin. We couldn't find him. McCloud's gone too.'

'When were they last seen?'

'Sunday night.'

'Did George say anything about wanting to go away?'

'No.'

'Did he seem disturbed about anything?'

'Not especially, no.'

'Are you sure? After all, a lot had been happening since Saturday night. But then, you had a lot to do on Sunday and you may not have noticed.'

'I'd have noticed.' He didn't rise to the bait.

'Mr Legge came here on Monday evening,' I said. 'He was alone. Wherever George and McCloud have gone, it's nothing to do with him. I suppose you've looked for them thoroughly round the estate.'

'All round it. I had the workmen round the woods and barns, gardeners turning out every shed. No sign of them.'

'Does Mr Ridgeway know anything?'

'He says he last saw them on Sunday evening. He's half frantic with worry. He admits George was much more inclined to confide in McCloud than in him.'

'And he heard nothing out of the way on Sunday night or early Monday morning?'

'No.'

'Could anybody have come into the house and taken George?'

'No, and in any case, why wouldn't McCloud have raised the alarm, unless he was the one who took George away? It has occurred to me that he might have been working with the kidnappers, but when would he have met them? He came straight down from Edinburgh.'

'Did George take anything with him?'

'His boots and top coat are missing. Also, I think, a little money. I'd given him a few pounds when we were in London and he hadn't spent them all.'

'So he put on his boots and coat, picked up his money and walked out with McCloud. Can you think why he might do that?'

He shook his head.

'Could it be because he knew you'd buried Helena Shilling in the garden?' I said.

Mrs Martley jumped at that, sending the cat flying.

He looked at me, frowning but not as surprised as I thought he should be. 'You knew about that? Legge, I suppose.'

'You don't deny it?'

'No. Astley and I talked it over after you'd gone and it seemed the best thing to do in the circumstances. You knew I didn't want an inquest.' He made it sound like a thoroughly reasonable course of conduct. 'Even if George had somehow found out about it – and I can't believe he did – why should he run away because of that?'

'He already thought he was cursed. If he knew you'd shot a woman because of him, he couldn't have borne it.'

'But I didn't shoot her. It had nothing to do with me.' He said it as if more than half his mind were still on George. 'I was at the house all night. You know that.'

'You could have slipped out.'

'I didn't even know the woman was there. Was it you that put the idea in George's mind that I killed her?' His eyes were angry again, his fists clenched. Mrs Martley was looking scared.

'No. I haven't talked to him about it at all. But he knows more than you think.'

'If he thinks I killed her, he knows something that isn't true. You're telling me that's why he left?'

'I'm saying it's a possibility. You had a pistol. You thought she was trying to kidnap George.'

'And I was right about that, wasn't I? The falling out of thieves, that's what killed her. All I did was bury her. I'll swear on anything you like – I'd never even set eyes on the woman before I saw her dead body.' He was on the edge of the chair now, his eyes looking into mine from what seemed only a few feet away.

'Then why not tell that to the inquest?'

'What you don't understand, you people who've never seen a battlefield, is why some of us don't have this reverence for bodies. She was alive and now she's dead and no amount of police or inquests or official reports can make any difference. That's all there is to it. I can tell you, that wasn't the first grave I've dug.'

'You've been in battles?'

A nod. 'And shot men. But I've never shot a woman. Even if I'd come across her that night, I don't suppose I'd have shot her.' He sat back in the chair and unclenched his fists. It looked hard work, like straightening out a pair of rusted gauntlets. 'In any case, it doesn't matter if you believe me or not. Just take my word for now that I didn't kill the woman, I'll take yours that you and Legge had nothing to do with George disappearing and we can get on with finding him.'

He made it sound as reasonable as buying a pound of rice. I looked at him, wondering whether to ask about Astley and the fraud case but decided I wanted more time to get it sorted out in my mind. I thought of Amos's doubts and took the plunge.

'Very well, for now. Only for now.'

He nodded. 'So where's he gone, then?'

'You say it was Monday morning he disappeared, a day and a half ago. Do we assume they were making for London?'

'It's the only other place in England George knows. McCloud too, as far as I know. But how would they get here? We made inquiries in Muswell Hill, of course, but nobody there can remember seeing them and George would be conspicuous. That's why I thought of Legge spiriting him away in a carriage.'

'Wrongly. Is he friendly with anybody in London?'

'No more than social acquaintances. When we were here, if we went anywhere he went with me, except when he was riding with Legge. You're the investigator. You must have some idea.'

'Only that the trail starts back at Northlands. Whether he went of his own accord or not, there must have been some preparation. I think I should go back there tomorrow.' In spite of what he'd said, I was still doubtful that George could have got far away from the house. I had a picture in my mind of him wandering out in the country on this dark night, now even more convinced that a curse was on him. It was that, more than anything, that made me prepare to cooperate with Vickery – for now.

'It's not just to do with George, is it? You're going back there to find out if I'm telling you the truth. I am. I didn't kill her and if you can find out who did, I want to know it.'

'So that you can congratulate him, I suppose.'

'Perhaps.' He smiled but there was no warmth in it.

I suggested that one thing he could do while he waited for news was to visit some of the people he and George had met in society, without saying anything about the reason. It was a long shot but worth trying and would keep him occupied. He told me that Astley had been left in charge at Northlands and wrote a couple of lines for me to give him, explaining that I was there to look for any clues as to where George had gone. Soon afterwards, he left.

By then it was after ten at night and I was bowed down with tiredness and worry about George. I kept getting pictures in my mind of him lifeless in the pond at Northlands or curled up under a tree. I slept badly and was at Amos's stables while they were still mucking out and filling water buckets. It turned out that Amos couldn't get free until the next day, Thursday, and I was impatient to get back to Northlands. We settled that he'd put me on the morning coach to Muswell Hill and there I'd hire a fly from the inn to Northlands. I'd wanted to take Tabby with me as she'd be invaluable in harvesting gossip from the servants, but she was nowhere to be found so I had to travel out on my own. I took a place on the coach from the Sovereign in Oxford Street and spent some time before we left questioning the bookings clerk and various grooms and drivers. None of them could remember a young blind man travelling into London on Monday or Tuesday but it was a busy place and I hadn't been hopeful. I had to wait more than an hour in a cold side room at the inn before they found somebody to drive the fly, so I arrived at Northlands in the afternoon. With Vickery away and the housekeeper gone, the place already had a neglected air. I had to knock on the door several times and was on the point of walking round to the back when it was opened at last by one of the maids. When she saw me, she said 'Oh' and just stood there. I explained that I was there at the request of Mr Vickery. I'd go up to my room and she would kindly tell Mr Astley that I was back and would meet him in the drawing room in half an hour. At least she stood aside to let me in and watched, mouth open, as I went upstairs. I found my room was pretty much as I'd left it, with the trunk still in the middle of the floor. Obviously with the housekeeper gone nobody had thought of sending it on, but it was useful to have some spare clothes. I washed in the few inches of water left in the jug on the toilet table, changed into my plain mulberry dress and went down to the drawing room. Astley was there, standing over a maid who was making up the fire. She looked no older than twelve and so cold or nervous that her hands were shaking. Astley was wearing a quilted velvet dressing gown over his day clothes, monogrammed slippers on his feet and, from the redness of his face, I could tell he'd been drinking. He half turned when I came in, frowning.

'Well?'

I'd decided in advance not to talk to him yet about the fraud trial and being struck off. I wanted to find out more first. I handed him Vickery's note. He read it at a glance, stuffed it into his pocket and sat down heavily in an armchair. The maid succeeded in getting a few flames licking at the kindling, glanced up at him and got a nod and another frown. As she walked sideways to the door he informed her that he'd have two chops up in his room in precisely one hour and she was to make sure the cook didn't burn them this time.

'So why precisely have you come back? The boy's not here.'

I sat down in the opposite chair, taking my time. 'Somebody in the household must know how he went or was taken. I want to speak to everybody here, you included.'

'You're wasting your time with me. He was here and now he is not. That's all I know.'

'When did you last see him?'

'Sunday night, I suppose.'

'Suppose?'

'Or perhaps the day before that. I've better things to do with my time than keep a boy under observation, unlike Vickery, it seems.'

I wondered what those better things might be. 'I thought you were here to arrange for Mr Vickery to adopt him?'

'To try to talk him out of it, more like. The boy's obviously an imposter, though Vickery won't hear of it. Now he's taken himself off, Vickery may come to his senses.'

'Did you accuse George to his face of being an imposter?'

'No. I said nothing to him, beyond perhaps an occasional good morning. Perhaps he guessed what I thought. Vickery said he had a quick understanding, for what it's worth.'

'You think George may have left because you thought he was an imposter?'

'It's possible. He'd have gone off in any case sooner or later, probably with some of Vickery's money in his pocket.'

'You said that to Vickery?'

'I tried to. He wasn't listening.'

'And you have no idea where George has gone?'

'I told you, no. So you're going to waste some more of Vickery's money quizzing the servants?'

'I'll talk to whoever I like. And he's not paying me.'

'More fool you.'

We glared at each other. There were a lot of things I wanted to ask him but didn't expect answers. I tried just one of them.

'That break-in attempt, early on Sunday morning – you were closest to it. What did you hear exactly?'

He blinked. That hadn't been the question he expected. 'A scraping sound. I assume it was a malefactor trying to break the lock with a chisel.'

'A very feeble attempt, wasn't it?'

'I have no information on the comparative efficiency of kidnappers. Unlike you, it appears.'

'And you didn't open the door to look?'

'Why should I? Vickery had told me to ring the bell if I heard anything and that's exactly what I did.'

I wasn't sure why the question bothered me among so many others, but it did. I thanked him sarcastically and went to find Mr Ridgeway.

TWELVE

Mr Ridgeway was out on the lawn at the back of the house, in overcoat and hat, peering into the distance as if the missing ones would suddenly reappear.

'McCloud's gone to look for George, I'm sure he has. It's the only explanation, don't you agree?' he said.

'You don't think they went together?'

'Not unless the kidnappers took them away together. But McCloud's a strong young man so I think they managed to decoy George away somehow and McCloud found out and followed.'

'Without telling Mr Vickery?'

'Perhaps there was no time.'

It seemed unlikely to me, but he was in such a nervous state I decided not to argue. I asked when he'd last seen George and McCloud.

'Sunday night at dinner, both of them. I became drowsy and McCloud said I should go to bed and he'd wait up with George. You know one of us had to be with him all the time, even indoors? When he didn't come to me for Latin on Monday morning I thought he'd gone to bed late, looked into his room and he wasn't there. The bed had not been slept in and neither had McCloud's. I looked for a note but there was nothing.'

'On the Sunday night, did George seem disturbed at all? A lot had happened.'

The look Mr Ridgeway gave me was almost pleading. 'The poor woman, you mean?'

'George knew about it, didn't he? Knew that she'd been shot and Mr Vickery had buried her.'

He looked away from me and nodded once, sadly.

'How did he know?'

'I think from McCloud. They were very close, almost from the start. I suppose it was to be expected. George has not met many people his own age.'

'You didn't know McCloud before he came to work for Mr Vickery?'

'Not personally, no, but he was highly recommended. A professor at Edinburgh is an old friend of mine. We correspond regularly. When the question arose of finding somebody to read Latin and Shakespeare to George it seemed natural to consult him. He recommended McCloud unhesitatingly. He'd just taken a good degree and had a particularly fine speaking voice. He wished to be in London, or at least as near to it as possible. I accepted the professor's recommendation and appointed McCloud without an interview. It seemed an especially happy appointment. And now this.'

'Did he come straight here from Edinburgh?'

'Yes. I met him off the stagecoach. He didn't know London at all and hardly went out while we were there. To the theatre a couple of times perhaps and bookshops, but that was about it, as far as I know.'

'Suppose he and George went willingly – have you any idea where they might have gone?'

A slow shake of the head. I left him as I'd found him, staring out at the woodlands.

I went indoors and asked one of the maids where I'd find Jolly. In the yard, she said, chopping wood. He was there, ruddy-faced and cheerful, with an axe in his hand and a pile of split logs beside him.

'Good afternoon, Mrs Carmichael. It's a pleasure to see you back. Any news?'

'None of George. Mr Vickery's still in London. I was talking to him about burying the woman's body.'

The cheerfulness stayed on his face for a moment out of sheer surprise and was then replaced by a look that wasn't very guilty, like a child detected in some minor wrong.

'He told you about that, did he?'

'Yes, and I know you and Mr Astley helped him.'

'Astley wasn't much use – it was just that Mr Vickery wanted him there.' He leaned the axe against the chopping block.

'You do know it's a crime, disposing of a body?'

'So's kidnapping. Mr Vickery's ways aren't everybody's but he usually comes out on the right side.'

'He told me he didn't kill her.'

He gave a long whistle. 'You asked him that, did you? He couldn't have. He was on guard in the hall all night.'

'You know that for a fact?'

''Course I do. I was mostly in the kitchen at the back and now and then he'd come through and ask if I was all right. I could hear him through the servants' door, walking up and down in the hall.'

'He went out at four.'

'Only to walk around outside. I heard his steps on the gravel when I went to bed up in the attic. Kept hearing them when I was trying to sleep.'

Whether it was true or not, he'd make a convincing witness.

'You and Mr Vickery go back a long way,' I said.

'A long way, yes.' He turned away, picked up a large log and poised it on the block. 'You'll excuse me.'

There seemed no more to be got out of him for the while so I spent most of the afternoon questioning the other servants, the cook, three maids, two male servants and the boots and knives boy. Apart from the cook they were all local people and pretty much demoralized by what was going on, although nobody mentioned the burial. It was even possible they didn't know about it but all the rest of the happenings were enough to unsettle any staff. Two of the maids said they'd give notice as soon as Mr Vickery came back. None of them knew anything about where George and McCloud might have gone, though several mentioned that the two of them had been close, spending a lot of time together. Talking and laughing, one of the maids said. Laughing at what? She didn't know.

Mr Ridgeway and I ate dinner together, just the two of us facing each other at the end of a long dining table lit by five guttering candles. The dinner was badly served by the scared maid and worse cooked, a sort of Irish stew with potatoes boiled to a mush and mutton to soaked leather. Somehow the onions, thickly sliced, had contrived to stay mostly raw. We'd reached the cheese stage and were demolishing quite a lot of Stilton, something that a drunken or demoralized cook couldn't spoil, along with another glass each of passable claret.

Mr Ridgeway sighed. 'You're suspicious of McCloud, aren't you?'

'I think George went with him, voluntarily. Perhaps because of what happened to the woman.'

Delicately, Mr Ridgeway poised a morsel of cheese on a piece of biscuit and stared down at it. 'Mr Vickery said there'd been an accident and a woman had died, but I was on no account to mention it to George.'

'But you heard more from other sources?'

'I could hardly avoid it. I don't gossip with the servants, of course, but Jolly said she'd been trying to kidnap George and had been shot.'

He picked up the piece of biscuit and cheese, looked at it and put it back on his plate.

'George had everything here. Mr Vickery thinks the world of him. He could have had anything he wanted.'

I said nothing. He ate the cheese, broke the piece of biscuit in half and then into smaller pieces.

'George really is remarkable. I've had few students so quick-minded and his mind is mature for his age. I never met his father. I can't say I approved of his way of life, though as a young man I loved his poetry. George has something of him, I'm sure of that. He has a way of making hearts go out to him.'

I tried to imagine Mr Ridgeway twenty years younger, an enthusiast for wild poetry, and failed. Life was rarely kind to tutors. We finished our wine in silence and I found a bell and rang it for the servants to clear the table. We both went to our rooms and I don't suppose Mr Ridgeway slept any better than I did. In the morning Astley left, abruptly. The first Mr Ridgeway or I knew about was when the pony cart arrived at the front door, driven by the boy from the stables. We found out later that Astley had sent the boot boy down the evening before to demand it. He ordered Jolly and one of the other servants to load his trunk into it and was bowled away down the drive to meet the London coach, not bothering to say goodbye.

Amos arrived by coach and his own two feet later on the Thursday morning and reported on his visit to Perkins' Yard. He'd arrived late, he said, after finishing for the day at his own

stables, and found the one-armed jockey still hard at work by
lamplight, doling out hay to the horses still in the yard.

'He wasn't in the best of moods because he'd pretty much
been left on his own. The coachman, Simmonds, brought the
carriage back in on Monday afternoon without a word of where
he'd been since Saturday and wouldn't answer the jockey
when he asked. He looked as if he'd been sleeping under a
hedge. He took the two best horses – not that they were much
good – out of the yard straight away in their head collars, said
he was going to sell them to a man he knew and that the
jockey could look after the others until he heard from him.
He gave the jockey a couple of sovereigns in small change
for expenses but the jockey reckons he's owed more than that
in back pay. He asked Simmonds where he could find him if
there happened to be an emergency and Simmonds said he
shouldn't try because he'd be out of London. He was in a
hurry, the jockey said – he wouldn't even unharness the
horse from the carriage, just left it standing there. Tired,
the horse was, with harness galls as if it had been driven too
long and hard. Then Simmonds came back and drove the
carriage away. I said to the jockey I was surprised he'd go off
and leave his property just like that but he said there wasn't
a lot to leave. The yard's only rented on a short lease and the
horses that are left would hardly make ten pounds put together.
I asked whether Simmonds had a family and he said not as
far as he knew, except for a niece that looked in a couple of
times but wasn't interested in the stables. "Not that sort
of horsewoman" was what he said.'

I reported to him what little I'd found out from Astley and
Jolly and we considered what to do next. It bothered him that
Vickery's investigations had found no trace of George and
McCloud on the road. In a country area like this anybody should
be conspicuous, especially a blind boy.

'Another thing I was thinking of – we should have a proper
look at that cottage in the lane. We only looked in through
the window on Sunday morning, which is not surprising with
a lot else to think about, but somebody could have been waiting
in there.'

Somebody who might have shot Helena. I could see the way

his mind was working, still looking for somebody other than Vickery. We walked down the lane to the cottage. There were still wheelmarks on the grass verge that the carriage had made and I didn't look closely at the colour of the mud. As before, the front door of the cottage was latched shut with brambles growing round it.

'Broken off, that's been.' Amos pointed to a length of bramble that looked as if it had recently been pulled aside and put his hand on the latch. It gave but the door had fallen on its hinges and he had to push with his shoulder to open it. It gave straight on to a low-ceilinged room almost empty of furniture apart from a rough table and a broken chair. A couple of blankets were roughly folded on the floor. They looked good quality for the place but felt damp to the touch. An empty wine bottle, two used glasses, a heel of stale bread and the bone from a ham hock, chewed by rats, stood on the table.

'Looks as if somebody spent the night here,' Amos said. 'Or two people, judging from the glasses.'

'Perhaps George and McCloud on Sunday night. They might have left the house in the dark and stayed here till it was light enough to move.'

'Dark and light's all the same to George. It could have been somebody who knew Helena was coming here, waiting for her on the Saturday night.'

Drinking wine with her then following her out to the carriage and killing her. I looked at the glasses. A little red wine had been left in one of them, almost evaporated and leaving a dark crust on the glass. We left everything as it was, latched the door and started walking back up the lane. Amos went back to the question of George and McCloud.

'You think the boy was scared of what was happening here and decided to go. So why did McCloud go with him? The boy's not of age. McCloud could be accused of kidnapping him.'

'Perhaps he just wanted to help George.'

Amos looked at me sideways. 'Do you believe that?'

'No.' My answer came so quickly that it surprised me. 'There's more to McCloud than that. I can't see him giving up his whole future for a boy he's only known a week or two. He had at least one secret too. He's been seeing a girl from the village.'

Amos whistled. 'A fast worker. Still, no great harm in it.'

'But it was something he was keeping from the rest of the household. As far as Vickery was concerned, his job was to be with George all the time.'

'So if it's not just wanting to help George, why did he do it?'

'Suppose he was being paid?'

We looked at each other. 'She's dead,' Amos said.

'But Helena Shilling wasn't acting on her own. There was the other person who wrote the letters. For some reason, there are people who want George.'

We went round to the kitchen door of the house and I went inside and stirred up the cook to produce bread and cold beef and a bottle of ale for him. Nobody made any objection when I insisted on carrying them out to him through the kitchen. He was waiting by the back door, scraping mud off his boots with a workman's spade. We settled that he'd come to the house first thing in the morning and we'd ride down to see what we could find out in the village. Dinner with Mr Ridgeway was much the same as the evening before, only this time it was overdone chops and underdone potatoes. Later, in my room, I was on the point of undressing and going to bed when something struck me. Why was Amos scraping mud off his boots when he'd only get more on them walking back down the lane to the stables? Come to think of it, what was a workman's spade doing near the kitchen door? As far as I'd seen, the workmen brought their own food and drink and never went near the kitchen. The answer was both so obvious and shocking that I gasped and sat down. Amos was a practical man. He might be nearly certain that Vickery had buried Mrs Shilling's body in the neglected garden by the pond, but if proof was available, he wanted it. No wonder he hadn't said anything to me. I opened the trunk and changed into a plain black dress and boots, then got out my burglar's lantern and checked it was working. It's small and easily carried, with a shutter that slides round to cut off the light. I let myself out of the side door, walked on the grass so as not to make a noise on the gravel and went down the lane to the stables. Lamplight was showing in the window of the room above the tack room where Amos slept. I watched for a few minutes, then it went out and soon afterwards a door on the ground floor opened and Amos came out, carrying a lamp. The spade clinked on the cobbles as he picked it up from where it was leaning against a wall, walked out to the lane and turned uphill. I followed him and swung the shutter round so that the light of my lamp was showing. He turned.

'I'm coming with you, Amos.'

He swore, which was unusual for him. Then: 'How did you know? Any road, this isn't one for you.'

I walked up beside him. 'It's logical, after all. You want to be sure.'

'I am, as good as. I'll tell you in the morning.'

I said nothing and tried to match his pace over the rutted ground of the lane. We came to the path that turned round the side of the house and took it, turning our lanterns away in case anybody happened to be watching from the windows. The path came out on the back lawn and we followed it carefully down a broken flight of steps into the fernery with the pond. It looked much as I remembered it, with the cast-iron seat standing on the flattened hillock. Amos shone his lamp on to the ground under the seat. It was clay, about six feet by three feet of it, recently disturbed and shining in the lamplight where spades had cut it smoothly into clods. He put the lamp down, lifted up the seat as if it were no heavier than a milking stool and carried it down to a flatter area.

'You keep back now,' he said to me. 'I'll tell you.'

This was Thursday. She'd been in the ground since Sunday. I stood back while he dug. It didn't take him long, though they'd buried her quite deeply. The smell made him cough a couple of times and drifted over to me. I gave up trying and held my handkerchief to my nose.

'It's her, right enough.' He stood up, his legs silhouetted against the lamplight. 'So what do we do now?'

'Cover her up again. It took us enough trouble the first time.'

The voice, sounding amused, came from behind us. I turned my lantern and made out Jolly standing on the steps, grinning down at us with something long in his hand. Amos went tense.

'You'd guessed anyway,' Jolly said. 'If you were going to

go to the police you'd have done it three days ago. Mr Vickery said you wouldn't.'

'We still could,' I said. My voice sounded firmer than I felt.

'You do that and they'll most likely hang him for a murder he never did. Me too, probably.' He walked towards us, looking taller than he was from his place on the steps, and I saw the thing in his hand was another spade. 'I guessed what you'd be doing, Mr Legge, but I never thought you'd take Mrs Carmichael with you.'

'He didn't want to. I came,' I said. 'It will come out in the end. You know it will.'

'Everything does, but some ends are longer than others,' Jolly said.

Amos kneeled down by the grave. I thought at first he was praying, unlikely though that would have been, then saw his hands in the lamplight tucking handfuls of earth carefully round her face. He'd made his decision. It certainly wasn't for fear of Jolly, because though he'd probably be good in a fight, Amos would be better. I honestly don't know if I'd made the decision too by then, but I was with Amos. He began using the spade and Jolly went over to join him. Together they lifted the seat back in position.

'If we do delay going to the police, we want some answers from you,' I said.

'Fair enough.'

Jolly, still sounding unworried, scraped clods of clay from his boot soles on the spade. The three of us went back along the path and down towards the stables.

THIRTEEN

We had our discussion in the tack room by candle-light. I sat on the only chair, Jolly on the table and Amos leaned against the wall, smoking his pipe. Normally he wouldn't have dreamed of doing it with me in the same room but I practically begged him to because of the smell that had seemed to cling to us all the way down the lane and beyond.

'You're deep in it now, past helping,' Jolly said, not sounding too concerned. 'If you were going to the police you should have done it as soon as it happened.'

My mind went to Robert, far away in Italy. By the time he came back, this affair might have dragged Amos and me into cells. Time to go on the attack.

'We have proof now,' I said. 'We could still do it.'

'Proof of who killed her?' He looked at each of us in turn, politely interested. 'No, I didn't think you had.'

'Of course, it's quite possible that you did,' I said. 'Mr Vickery could have gone on talking to you when the two of you were on guard, even if he knew you weren't there.'

'So he orders me to shoot her and I go off and do it, calm as delivering a message to somebody? I'm loyal, but not as much as that.'

'You told me that you and Mr Vickery go back a long way. Does that mean you were with him at the time of the Peters fraud case?'

Up to then he'd seemed completely at ease but now a shadow came over his face, though his voice was as steady as ever.

'What case would that be?'

'Were there so many? A man named Peters was transported for persuading people to finance him to find Lord Byron's treasure. Mr Vickery had met Peters when he was a clerk with a financial firm. It might have been doing some under-the-counter deal for Mr Vickery that cost Peters his job. Mr Vickery had told him the story of Lord Byron's treasure and Peters constructed a fraud out of it. Mr Vickery knew about it but I don't know how deeply involved he was.'

Since some of that was guesswork I was relieved to see that Jolly's expression had become downright worried.

'He didn't know about it until after Peters was charged,' he said, speaking more quickly now. 'It wasn't his idea at all, only he felt responsible because he'd told Peters the story in the first place, not believing it himself. He doesn't walk away from things.'

'So he paid Astley to defend Peters?'

'That's right.'

'Why Astley?'

'I don't know. I suppose he just picked him out.'

'Picked him out as a lawyer who might bend the evidence when necessary?'

'If you're thinking about that letter, it was Astley's idea. Mr Vickery had nothing to do with it.'

'But he felt responsible again when Astley was struck off?'

'I told you, he doesn't walk away. Look at him with George. No power on earth would make him give up that boy once he'd decided to take him on.'

Was it deliberate, I wondered, turning the conversation in that direction and away from the murder? I thought there were things about the fraud case that Jolly knew and wasn't saying. Still, he'd confirmed what I'd discovered – or guessed.

'Mr Legge and I aren't going to the police for now,' I said. 'But it's conditional. We'll go on trying to find out what happened the night she died and if we find anything the police should know, we'll tell them.' They nodded, Amos approvingly and Jolly reluctantly. 'I still think there's something you're not telling us,' I said to Jolly. 'It would be best all round if you'd only say it now instead of leaving us to find out.'

'*I am as true as truth's simplicity,*' Jolly announced. It took me a second to realize he was quoting Shakespeare. He grinned at me, some of his good spirits coming back. Even if we accepted the truth part – and I was by no means sure about that – I doubted the simplicity.

'You talked to George, didn't you?' I said. 'Back in London

you told him about those letters from Helena. Was that being loyal to Mr Vickery?'

He spread his hands out, palms up, and shrugged. 'A chatterbox, me. Besides, George finds out things. I don't always know how, but he does.'

I turned to Amos and asked if he had any questions for Jolly.

'I don't think it's particularly for him, but what I can't work out is where that carriage went most of Saturday. From what I heard at the stables it left London soon after midday and it wouldn't take more than a couple of hours to get here. If they wanted to use the horse to drive away fast later on they'd have to rest him somewhere.'

'A barn somewhere away from the road?' I suggested.

'But you'd have to know the country for that. More likely an inn or a public house.'

'And not so many of those out here.'

'No. I'm thinking they wouldn't use one in Muswell Hill, more likely out on the road going north.'

'Does it matter?' Jolly said.

'If we could find it, we might get an idea of whether she met the rest of the gang, if there ever was a gang,' Amos said.

'So was there ever a gang, outside Mr Vickery's head?' I asked Jolly. 'He seemed to make his mind up quite suddenly that something was going to happen on Saturday night and that break-in attempt wasn't much better than childish.'

'Mr Astley heard somebody outside,' Jolly said. It wasn't even half an answer.

'Yes, Mr Astley. Did it occur to you that he could even have done that damage to the back door lock himself then pretended to discover it?'

'Why would he do that?'

'I don't know. I just have the feeling that there was more than one thing going on that night.'

'I'll make some inquiries round the village tomorrow,' Amos said. He was following the hooves as usual. 'A carriage can't just disappear.'

'This isn't finding George, though, is it?' Jolly said. 'That's what Mr Vickery will want you to do. He's not concerned about the woman.'

'Have you any idea where George and McCloud might have gone?'

'I haven't, and that's the truth. Believe me, if I knew, I'd be there.'

I believed him on that, at any rate. Amos insisted on walking back up to the house with Jolly and me. I went in with Jolly by the back door, not wanting to draw attention to myself by knocking on the front. Amos said he'd bring the pony trap up after breakfast. I went up to my room, undressed to the skin and sponged myself all over with cold water, then my best rose water, but the smell was still in my mind and my dreams.

Mr Ridgeway was almost as early at the breakfast table as I was. He was hollow-eyed and said he'd slept badly. I asked him if George or McCloud had ever said anything to him that might give a clue as to where they'd go in London. He guessed possibly the area near the British Museum where he'd once had his own lodgings long ago, or not far from the theatres. But he admitted that he'd been so mistaken about McCloud, whom he'd regarded as a most reliable young man, that he didn't trust his judgement any more. The wheels of the pony cart sounded on the gravel before I'd finished my second cup of coffee and I went out. The cob was in the shafts. I'd have preferred to ride, but the only side saddle in the stables had proved a poor fit for the pony and was too small for the cob. We went first to the village and asked shop keepers and passers-by whether they'd seen anything of George and McCloud but found nothing to the purpose. The people at the inn knew nothing about a carriage driven by a pock-marked man with a lady inside it on the previous Saturday. No surprise, Amos said. They'd have chosen somewhere more out of the way. We turned northwards on the main road, meeting very little traffic except a coach and four driving fast towards London. The first inn we came to, a few miles on, was a fairly smart affair with a male servant who came out to meet us as we turned into the yard. Amos told him that the lady would take tea and bread and butter.

'Amos . . .' I'd brought no money with me. As the servant went inside he grinned and slid half a crown towards me. 'Gives me time to talk to them.' He nodded towards the two grooms, one sweeping the yard, the other grooming a hunter inside a box with the door open. I went inside, trying to ignore curious looks from the maid, and asked to be shown into a room to tidy up. A small mirror over the washstand told me that broken sleep had caused the predictable damage to my appearance and I repaired things as best I could. Two cups of tea helped the process. The bread was yesterday's but the butter good and thick. I lingered at the table, knowing that Amos would take his time. When I paid and went out to the yard he was standing at the cob's head. He caught my eye, gave a small shake of the head and looked up the road. When we were rolling again he confirmed he'd had no luck, beyond one of the grooms half-remembering a one-horse carriage driving past recently, but with no clear memory of the day.

About two miles up the road we came across another inn that had seen better days and was clearly sliding down the slope to a mere public house. The archway to the stable yard was big enough to take a coach and four, but bricks had fallen off it and buddleia bushes were growing out of it. The name was the Red Lion, in faded letters beside the front door, but the plaster beast above the door looked more like a bedraggled poodle. Amos drove us into the stable yard and nothing happened. After waiting for a while, with no living thing visible except pigeons, we got down and knocked on the door leading off the yard. Eventually it was opened by a young man with no front teeth, his skin yellowish and head as bald as an egg.

'We're not open.' It might have been the missing teeth that made his voice slurred, except that the smell of stale beer came off him like mist off a marsh. Amos wasted no time.

'We've come about the coach that was here last Saturday, the one with the lady.'

'Don't remember no lady.'

'I think you might.' Amos put his hand in his pocket and brought it out, holding a fistful of silver coins. The man's eyes went to it, then to Amos's face.

'Was it her who sent you?'

'After a fashion. Now this lady's waiting for you to ask her in to sit down.'

The man looked at me, then nodded and turned away, pushing

the door open for us. We followed him along a short corridor into the main room of the house. Wood ash was still faintly glowing in the fireplace from the night before, empty pewter mugs on two of the tables nearest to it. Trade hadn't been brisk. I sat down in a high-backed chair. Amos stayed standing and I let him get on with the questioning.

'What's your name?'

'Nat. Nathaniel.'

'Were you expecting them?'

'The owner was.'

'Where is he?'

'In his home, sick. He leaves everything to me.'

'So what did he say to you about her?'

'Only that she'd be arriving here sometime in the afternoon. I was to feed and water the horse and let her wait in the little parlour.'

'What about the coachman?'

'He waited in the bar. Five pints, he drank.'

'Was she on her own?'

'At first she was, until the gentleman came.'

'What gentleman?'

'The one she was waiting for, I suppose.'

'Was he a Scottish gentleman?' I asked. Nat blinked.

'Not that I know of. He didn't sound Scottish.'

'What did he sound like?'

'Just an ordinary gentleman. I never heard him speak more than two or three words to me, asking if the lady was here.'

'What did he look like? Young, old?'

'Not either particularly. Just ordinary.'

'How did he get here?'

'On a horse.'

'What sort of horse?' asked Amos.

'Ordinary brown horse.'

Amos and I looked at each other, exasperated. Here was an unknown gentleman coming to speak to Helena Shilling at a remote inn only a few hours before her death and our witness was hardly more observant than the plaster lion outside.

'Just tell us what happened from the time the gentleman arrived,' Amos said. 'Anything you can remember.'

'Why, what've they done? Anyhow, it's nothing to do with me.'

Amos took a step towards Nat. I knew that it would take a lot more provocation than the man's stubbornness to make Amos as much as raise a hand to him, but Nat didn't know that and Amos was a good foot taller. Nat backed away, raising ineffectual hands, and started talking fast but so low in tone that we had to bend forward to make out what he was saying.

'I told you, he said was the lady here so I showed him into the parlour. She was sitting there. She looked surprised when she saw him but she must have been expecting somebody. I went out and closed the door. They were in there some time before I heard him shouting at her.'

'Shouting? What was he saying?'

'Maybe not shouting exactly but loud enough to be heard through here. 'No more argument. You've been well paid to be there and you will be there.' Then the door slammed and he came through here, straight out to the yard where his horse was and rode off.'

'Rode off which direction?'

'I wasn't looking.'

'So what did the lady do?'

'Stayed in the parlour till after it got dark. Then she went out and got into her carriage and the driver harnessed up the horse and they drove off.'

'In the dark?'

'He had a candle lamp he asked me for a light for.'

'She paid the bill?'

'She didn't want to. She pretended she thought the gentleman had paid, only he hadn't. So I made her pay.'

'When they drove off, was anybody else with the lady?'

'Nobody that I saw.'

'And you didn't see them again, or the gentleman?'

'Not hide nor hair of them.'

Amos caught my eye and I nodded. He put a handful of silver on the table beside Nat. I thanked him, though all he'd done was add another puzzle to the ones we already had to deal with, and we went out to the yard.

'So was he telling the truth?' Amos said.

'I think he's too stupid to do otherwise. But who was the

gentleman? Not McCloud and certainly not Vickery. Even Nat wouldn't have thought he was ordinary looking.'

'She was waiting for somebody yet was surprised when she saw this gentleman. But either he was paying her himself or knew who was.'

'And was annoyed with her, even before they failed,' Amos said. 'Still, there's a long distance between being annoyed and shooting someone.'

He asked where now and I said I wanted to get back to London as soon as I could. I thought we'd found out all we could at Northlands, for the while at least, and it was time to look for George and McCloud there. Amos said there was an afternoon coach from the village he could drive me down to catch and he'd follow on by some means later, probably the next day. We went back to the house where I packed my bag and said goodbye to Ridgeway, promising to send him news if I heard anything of George and McCloud. As I was getting into the pony cart Jolly came up and asked me to give his regards to Mr Vickery and let him know that all was well at the house. It clearly wasn't, but I said I'd deliver the message.

'Don't go and see him before I'm back with you,' Amos said as he dropped me off at the inn where the London coach stopped.

'Why? He's not going to shoot me.'

But there were times when Amos was as immoveable as Stonehenge, so I promised. It was a slow journey back to London and late before I got to Abel Yard. Tabby was waiting at the bottom of the stairs.

'Where've you been?'

'Tomorrow,' I said. I was tired but I wasn't pleased with the situation Amos and I had got into and wasn't sure how much to tell to Tabby. She went to her cabin and I to my bed, but I didn't sleep well. Next day, Saturday, she and I spent some time in the area around the museum, looking for any trace of George and McCloud and, not greatly to my surprise, failed to find any. Amos arrived back in the middle of the afternoon in his travelling clothes and second best boots, downcast but determined.

'We're going to talk to Mr Vickery then?'

'Yes. I've been thinking that we must tell him this can't go on forever. Somebody will talk. If he really didn't kill her he should go to the police of his own accord and admit to burying her,' I said.

'That'd be enough to get him put in prison by himself, wouldn't it?'

'Yes. It's a serious offence, unlawfully disposing of a body.'

'He won't do it then, especially not with the boy missing. But it's in my mind she should be decently buried. Some people I know give even their dogs headstones.'

We walked, mostly in silence, across the park to Knightsbridge. The daylight was going and lamplight was coming on in the windows. A plain carriage was waiting outside Vickery's house. It would normally be unthinkable for a groom to march into a gentleman's home by the front door but this wasn't a normal situation. The maid who opened the door to us looked scared and stood there with her mouth open. When I asked her where Mr Vickery was she moved her chin towards the drawing room but didn't stand aside to let us in. I dodged past her and Amos followed me into the hall.

'You can't . . .' the maid started to say, then stopped and started crying. Male voices were coming from the drawing room – Mr Vickery's and somebody else's. The other voice sounded familiar to me but I couldn't place it at once. I crossed the hall and went through the half-open doorway into the drawing room, Amos close behind me, then stopped so abruptly that he cannoned into me. Vickery was there, standing by the fire, not looking especially worried. Two other men were with him. One was a uniformed police constable standing more or less to attention with his top hat under his arm. The other was a police sergeant, also in uniform. With a lurch to the stomach I recognized him as my former friend, Sergeant Bevan. He'd been saying something to Vickery but broke off when we came in.

'Miss Lane – I mean, Mrs Carmichael – and Mr Legge. How convenient. We shall want to have words with you.'

'I'm simply employing Mrs Carmichael to find George,' Vickery said. 'She has no knowledge of anything else whatsoever.'

'And have you found George?' Bevan sounded no more than politely interested. 'No? Well, we're taking Mr Vickery into

custody to ask him some questions about the death of an unidentified female near Muswell Hill last Saturday night.'

Vickery's face didn't change. 'And George?' he asked me.

'No sign so far.'

'I trust you to find him.' He spoke to me as if the police
officers weren't there. 'Whatever happens, see no harm comes
to George.'

Then he turned and walked out of the room so that they were
caught by surprise and had to hurry to catch up with him. I
heard Vickery out in the hall asking, with just an undertone of
sarcasm, if he were permitted to have his coat and hat and then
a pause, presumably while the crying maid brought them. Then
the front door opened and closed and the carriage rolled away,
leaving Amos and I staring at each other.

'Well, it looks as if they've done the job for us,' he said, but
he didn't sound happy about it.

FOURTEEN

I spent a lot of Sunday talking to Sergeant Bevan. He didn't arrest me, simply sent a constable to my door with a polite note, asking me to meet him at a certain police station at my earliest convenience. Sergeant Bevan and I had met on several cases of mine and I'd thought him honest, until something happened that made me revise my opinion to 'honest up to a point'. He'd let a ruthless murderer escape. I knew that the decision hadn't been his and had come from high up in the Home Office. I suspected that he'd disliked what he'd been ordered to do, but still, he'd done it. I hadn't spoken to him since. Now circumstances had pushed me back to him and if I doubted his honesty, at least I was sure of his intelligence. We talked in a room at the police station that was almost as bleak as a cell, with a police constable taking notes. The account I gave him was as bare as possible at first. I said I'd been staying with Vickery to help him guard George, that there'd been a kidnap attempt and I'd reason to believe that a woman calling herself Helena Shilling wanted to take George away from him. When I described finding Helena's body in the carriage he sat up straight and stared at me.

'That was how long ago?'

'Early last Sunday morning. Seven days.'

'And it never occurred to you to inform the authorities?'

'I believed that Mr Vickery was doing that.'

'You know it's an offence to conceal discovery of a body?'

'Yes.'

'And you're accusing Vickery of illegally disposing of one?'

'I'm not accusing him of anything, but I put it to him and he didn't deny it.'

'So you knew and you're only telling us now because we've arrested him?'

I tried a question of my own. 'Who told you about it?'

Naturally, he ignored it. 'He didn't deny to you that he killed this Shilling woman?'

'He denied killing her, not burying her.'

He groaned and glanced across at the constable, as if for sympathy. He'd have questioned Vickery by now and I didn't know what he'd found out, so I told him nearly everything, from the first meeting on Cephalonia. I left out our partial exhumation of the body, on the grounds that Amos and I were in enough trouble without rushing into more. When I told him about my visit to Helena's roommate, Elsa, in Dawson's Alley, he made sure that the constable took a note of the address. I was glad at least that I'd had a chance to tell her about the death before the police did, although that would be held against me too.

'And after all this, you doubt that he killed her?' he said.

'All I'm saying is that there's a doubt *about* it. I'm not sure that Mr Vickery could have killed her and got back to the house in time.'

'I'm sure his defence lawyer will be very grateful for your doubt. From your account, Mr Vickery had a motive to kill her. Men have hanged for less.'

'Yes, and some of them unjustly.'

It was sheer annoyance that made me come out with that and I knew it was a mistake when I saw the grin without humour on his face. He got down to practicalities, sending for blank paper and a pencil and getting me to draw a sketch map of the grounds of Northlands with the grave area marked. He said that he'd need to speak to Mr Legge and I said I'd ask Amos to see him as soon as he'd finished at the stables.

'It's an order, not a request,' Bevan said. 'He's in as much trouble as you are.'

Still, he let me go, into streets that were already dark. Rain was falling again, hazing the lamps on vehicles, glazing roads and pavements. I walked miserably to Amos's stables, going by road rather than across the park, dodging pedestrians under umbrellas. I knew I was part of a process that might all too probably put a noose round Vickery's neck. It would have been better by far for him if he'd never consulted me. And although I'd tried not to let Bevan see how worried I was, Amos and I

were in deep trouble. When I got to the stables he was super-
vising tack cleaning at the centre of a lamp-lit web of reins,
girths and harness straps as lads brushed, sponged and polished
all round him. When he saw my face he said something to the
head lad and came across to me.

'The police?'

'Yes. Bevan wants to see you.'

'Thought he would.'

He led the way across the yard to Rancie's box. She was
eating hay from the manger but turned and gave a snicker of
welcome when she saw me. I stroked her neck as we talked,
knowing that Amos had counted on her presence to calm me.
He nodded as I told him every detail of the interview with
Bevan and seemed unworried by the threat of arrest.

'Bevan's a reasonable enough man in his way. I'll see him
as soon as we've got the tack away. In his place, I'd be looking
for the man who had an argument with her at the Red Lion.'

'I don't think Bevan's looking for anybody else. He's
convinced it was Vickery.'

'I could go back to Perkins' Yard and try harder to find
Simmonds,' Amos said. 'He might have noticed more than the
lad in the public house did. He's got some questions to answer,
any road, going off like he did.'

'Yes, but be careful. The police might be there now. We don't
want to give Bevan any more reason for arresting us.'

'And we're still looking for the boy?'

'Yes. He seems to be all that Vickery cares about but Tabby
and I are getting nowhere.'

We closed the door on Rancie and Amos went in to
check the lads' work and dismiss them till six in the morning.
Then he put on his good tweed jacket and soft-topped hat,
locked up the tack room and came over to where I was standing.

'I'll see you home. Won't hurt Bevan to wait a bit longer.'

When we parted at the gate to Abel Yard he said he'd see
me for a ride in the morning as usual and I refrained from
saying I hoped he wouldn't be in a cell by then.

He was there in the morning, riding a grey hunter, leading
Rancie. I asked him how the interview with Sergeant Bevan
had gone. Fair enough, he said, once Bevan had said his piece.

'He'll be on the way to Northlands by now. I heard him before I left last night, organizing two constables with spades. He said he'll want to talk to both of us again.'

Predictable but a bad thought all the same. For once, the ride failed to lift my spirits and I spent the rest of the morning and some of the afternoon in my study thinking of the case for the defence. If Vickery hadn't killed Helena Shilling, the next most likely theory was the original one – a falling out among thieves. From that point of view, the evidence that Amos and I had collected of a meeting between Helena and the unknown man in the public house mattered very much. The man had been angry with her. The kidnap attempt – assuming for the sake of this argument that it was a real one – had failed. The unknown man killed Helena Shilling for her failure. It was possible, but the most serious flaw was that we had no idea who the man was and no prospect of finding out. He'd ridden in out of nowhere and disappeared into nowhere again, and even the most enthusiastic defence lawyer for Vickery couldn't make much out of him. I was still thinking about him and getting nowhere when somebody rapped smartly at the outside door to the staircase. I looked down and there was a cab driver.

'Gentleman says he won't get out of my cab unless a Mrs Carmichael lives here. Reckons I've brought him to the wrong place.'

'It's the right place. Who is he?'

But he went out of the gates without answering and soon afterwards a cab clattered away from the mews. I went downstairs and waited at the door. It was some time before a fat man in a black overcoat and top hat came in at the gateway, puffing like an old sea lion, placing his flipper-like feet disdainfully on the wet cobbles.

'Good afternoon, Mr Astley,' I said. 'What brings you here?'

'You know very well.'

I went down and opened the door. He treated the staircase like a mountain climb, placing both feet firmly on a stair before venturing on to the next one, groaning to himself. By the time he got into my office he was incapable of speaking and collapsed on a chair that was a tight fit for him, his chest pumping so that it threatened the buttons on his overcoat.

'So it was you who informed the police,' I said. 'Did you tell them you helped to bury her body?'

It had come to me suddenly as I saw him in the yard. His sudden decision to leave Northlands had been a desertion of Vickery. When he spoke at last his voice was surprisingly meek.

'I came to ask if the police have talked to you.'

'They have.'

'Then I don't think it unreasonable to ask if you said anything to them about me.'

He wheezed again and closed his eyes. As it happened, in my account to Bevan I'd only mentioned that he was present at Northlands and hadn't referred to the part he and Jolly had played in the burial. Still, I was in no hurry to let him know that.

'What sort of thing?'

'You might possibly have implied that I had something to do with the decision to bury the woman's body. In fact, if Mr Vickery had consulted me, I'd have advised him very strongly against it.'

I had to work hard to stop my jaw dropping at that. 'You of all people must have known there should be an inquest.'

'If you're implying that I should have questioned him more closely at the time, then perhaps you're right. As it was, I trusted that he'd been in touch with the authorities and that matters were proceeding.'

He was still very much the solicitor in his manner, even now that he was making an appeal to me.

'As it happens, I said nothing about your part in it to the police – so far,' I said.

He couldn't hide the relief in his eyes, though it faded as the last two words hit him.

'I can't see that it would be necessary to do it. I was no more than a bystander to what happened, hardly even that.'

'And that's what you'll say if you have to give evidence in court at Mr Vickery's trial?'

He winced at that. 'He has not yet been charged. Let's hope it won't come to that.'

'But he will be charged, at least with improperly disposing of her body and quite probably with murder. You know that.'

'I believe that Mr Vickery would be a friend enough not to mention my name in this. It seems to me reasonable to ask that you should do the same.'

'So you'll stand by and see him hanged, if necessary?'

He said again that he hoped it wouldn't come to that but didn't deny it. I tried not to show how angry I was at his treachery.

'So you've come to me to make sure I don't reveal your complicity in a crime. I'll make one concession to you. I shan't tell the police you were there when they buried her body unless it's helpful in defending Mr Vickery.'

It was a lot less than he wanted but he could see it was all he was going to get. He started to paw at the edge of the chair, getting ready to push himself up to go.

'You and Mr Vickery have been friends for some time, haven't you?' I said.

He looked at me suspiciously. 'It was mainly a professional relationship.'

'More than that, I think. At the time of the Lord Byron fraud, you two might have been described as conspirators.'

He fairly yelped, 'Who told you about that? I wasn't charged.'

'But should you and he have been charged, along with Peters? Was Mr Vickery part of the fraud?'

'No blame was attached to Mr Vickery.'

'But some blame was attached to you. That letter.'

'The letter was a clerical error. It has nothing to do with any of this. It was all over long ago.'

In his indignation he'd even stopped wheezing, though he was having to fire out what he said a few words at a time. His eyes were furious. I changed tack.

'Do you know anything about George's disappearance?'

'Oh, the wretched, wretched boy.' It burst out of him with more force than anything so far. 'Wherever he's gone, good riddance. Vickery's got other things to bother about now.'

'Mr Vickery doesn't feel like that. He begged me to find George whatever happened.'

'Vickery was hardly sane on the subject. They should have left him where he was. He was no use to them.'

'Them? And use for what?'

He looked away from me and didn't answer.

'Mr Vickery and Father Demetrios? Who?'

'No use to Vickery, I meant. The boy wanted his money and that was all.'

'Did George leave because he knew about the woman being killed?'

'I don't know why he left. I hardly spoke to him.'

'The signs are that he left with McCloud. As far as you saw, were the two of them particularly close?'

The change in the direction of questioning seemed to come as a relief to him. He looked at me and held the first two fingers of his right hand close together. 'The boy and McCloud were like that. Anybody could see it but Vickery didn't want to and Ridgeway hasn't got a thought in his head beyond Latin and Shakespeare. They were together for hours every day, walking, McCloud reading to him, heaven knows what. If the lad is Byron's then by-blow, he's got bad blood in him and will go to the devil like his father, wherever he is.'

'Did McCloud talk about having friends in London or elsewhere?'

'I hardly exchanged a word with him. I wasn't interested in him then and I'm not now.'

He began to rock himself forward in the chair, pushing so hard against the arms that I thought he'd break them. After some time, he levered himself to his feet.

'So we have an agreement?'

'A limited one. For the present, I shan't mention your name to the police unless they mention it to me first. Provided you tell me about anything that comes to mind about where George might be.'

'I've told you all I know. I hope it won't be necessary for us to meet again.'

After that, I didn't bother to see him out but watched from the window as he flippered his way across the yard and out of the gates. He'd have to walk all the way along the mews before he found a cab and might have his pocket picked on the way by one of the more unruly members of Tabby's gang. As far as I was concerned, that was acceptable.

*　*　*

'So why didn't you tell me about Mr Astley?' Sergeant Bevan said, smiling at me from the other side of the police station table. The constable with the notebook sat at Bevan's side. It was early on Monday evening, just getting dark and only four hours since I'd watched Astley leaving. I was at the police station because a uniformed constable had arrived at my door and informed me that I was wanted, here and now. When I'd gone to the parlour to collect my cloak and bonnet Mrs Martley had wanted to know if I was being arrested. Not as far as I knew, I'd said, just helping the police. At least when we got to the police station Sergeant Bevan was waiting by the desk and thanked me for coming in again, apparently without irony. He hoped I'd be kind enough to help them with a few more questions and we'd gone back to the cell-like room. As soon as we'd sat down I asked him if they'd found the body. He nodded.

'Your map was surprisingly accurate. The woman has been identified as Helena Claremont, who sometimes went by the name of Helena Shilling. Is this the woman you knew?'

I'd been afraid I'd have to look at the body again and was relieved when he passed over a good pencil sketch, her eyes closed as if sleeping.

'Yes, that's the woman I knew as Helena Shilling.'

I hoped they'd been as merciful to her roommate. Then he'd come out with the question about Astley.

'You didn't mention that he was present when Vickery buried her,' he said.

How had he found out? Jolly? The boot boy?

'I didn't know for certain,' I said. 'I don't know for certain now.'

It was as near as I could get to keeping my promise to Astley.

'But you have reason to think he was?'

'I've told you, I don't know for certain who was there.'

'We know something about Mr Astley,' Bevan said. 'There was a fraud case. I've been speaking to a colleague who was involved in it. It still rankles with him that he didn't get Astley and Vickery in dock as well as the man they deported. Of course, Vickery's a rich man though nobody knows where his money comes from. He seems to have spent a lot of time abroad.'

I asked about George. Sergeant Bevan knew from Vickery that he was missing but I had the impression that the police were not very interested in looking for him. Seventeen- or eighteen-year-old lads walking out on their guardians were not unusual, even if this one had experienced some passing fame. McCloud, who was of age and had done nothing wrong, was of even less interest. After that, he let me go with a warning to come to him at once if I learned anything, and that went for Amos Legge too. Unlike George, we were still of interest to the police. As we parted, I asked him about the inquest.

'Opened at Muswell Hill this morning and adjourned for further inquiries. At least we have her identified now.'

He didn't say thanks to me and I didn't expect him to. I went before he could think of anything else to ask.

FIFTEEN

Most of Tuesday I wasted in the wearisome business of looking for George and McCloud, with Tabby's help. They probably wouldn't have much money between them, a few pounds in George's case and probably less in McCloud's, so would avoid the more usual hotels and inns. But London was so full of cheap sleeping places, from shared beds full of lice in slum lodging houses to rooms where there were no beds at all and men slept slumped over ropes all night, that it was hopeless. One of the few things I knew about McCloud was that he was interested in theatre and more for desperation than anything else we walked outside the theatres, watching for them in the gallery queues. Nothing. I gave Tabby some money to get a pie for her supper, then walked on my own to Vickery's house. It was dark and drizzling and I was feeling closed in by several blank walls. I didn't know where George was. I didn't know whether Vickery was a murderer. I didn't know whether Bevan was really thinking of arresting Amos and me. The front of the house was dark and I waited for a long time before anybody came to the front door. It was opened at last by Jolly, carrying a candlestick that deepened shadows and made his round face look skull-like.

'You found him?'

'No.' I was through the door before he had a chance to shut it.

'I thought you might be him,' Jolly said.

He was sweating and the wine fumes on his breath were detectable from yards away.

He looked older and wilder than at Northlands and I supposed the news of Mr Vickery's arrest had hit him badly because he was so accustomed to the man getting his own way.

'I don't think George would come here. What's the news of Mr Vickery?'

'Charged,' Jolly said bitterly. 'Charged with killing her. I went to see him in Newgate today, as soon as I got here. Of course, he's trying to be cheerful about it as usual. He says he's all right there for the present. He's only three others to share with and he's allowed his own clothes on account of only being charged and not convicted. But he's worrying about the boy. He's relying on you even more now he can't do anything.'

'Can we talk?' I said.

He looked round the dark hall and the unlit doorways leading off it. 'We're all out the back, the ones who've stayed. Three have gone already, so there's only five of us left.'

'Then let's go out to the back.'

He looked doubtful for a moment, then nodded and led the way across the hall and through the servants' door. It was brighter there, with lamps lit on the walls and subdued conversation coming from behind a half-open door. I followed him through the door into something like a banquet. A young maid and an older one, a cook and a male servant were sitting at a plain table loaded with luxuries: a ham, the remains of two roast fowls, brawn, half a pineapple, several bottles of wine and one of port. A candelabra with good wax candles lit the table and from the empty plates and full glasses the feast had been going on for some time.

'Can't let it go to waste,' Jolly said. 'May we offer you something?'

I said no, though I felt a twitch of hunger at the sight of it. The others were looking at me curiously. Jolly picked up a bottle of wine and, with that in one hand and the candle-holder in the other, he led the way to a room off the servants' hall. It was probably the pantry of the absent butler, small but equipped with a comfortable chair and an upright one. Jolly indicated politely that I should sit in the comfortable chair, put the candle-holder on the table, took two glasses off a shelf and poured wine. He waited for my nod before taking the upright chair.

'So what are we going to do to get him out?' The tone was comradely.

'Did you tell the police that he was on guard in the hall that night?'

'I did, but I don't know if they believed me. He says it doesn't matter, I can say it again at the trial. He's been in tight places before this.'

He drank and I followed his example. It was good Beaujolais.

'Goodness knows what will be left of Mr Vickery's cellars by the time he's released,' I said. 'Or hanged.' Something about Jolly made me want to provoke him.

'They won't hang him.' But his round face looked unexpectedly grim, like a clown who'd wandered into a tragedy. He drained half his glass in one gulp. 'I'm bothered, though. He should want to get out of Newgate more than he does. It's as if he's just sitting there and taking it.'

'Who do you think told the police?' I asked.

'Astley. If I see the man I'll kick all of the lard off his arse.'

'And yet he was Mr Vickery's friend,' I said.

He swallowed what was left in his glass and refilled it. 'Incubus, more like. Astley wasn't the only one battening on him for a living.'

'Mr Vickery did owe him something,' I said. 'There was that letter he forged.'

Jolly held the wine glass to his face and squinted at me through it. 'Oh, that. That's all in the past.'

'I don't think it is. I think Mr Vickery must have told him to do it.'

He looked at me straight on this time. 'Not quite. As I understood it, Mr Vickery mentioned it was a pity there wasn't a letter and Astley took it as instructions. Mr Vickery looked after him all right, and the other one even though there was no need.'

'The other one being Peters, who was deported?' A nod. 'So how did Mr Vickery look after him?'

'He was seeing him, all right, after he came back from being deported. And he was taken advantage of, as usual. No gratitude, either of them.'

'So Peters is back already?'

'Oh, he came back. Made straight for Mr Vickery, bags and baggage.'

The sheer unlikelihood of a man coming back from transportation with a lot of luggage threw me for a moment, then something started to take shape in my mind. I stared at Jolly as the wavering candle made hollows in his face and when he grinned and nodded I knew I was on the right track.

'Geoffrey Panter. He was Peters, come back from deportation?'
Another nod.

'And his wife, Emilia. Were they married before he was deported?'

'Wife?' Jolly spluttered with laughter. 'Not unless they do weddings on the convict ships. She was never his wife. Emilia was deported as well for bedrolling. You know what that is? Getting men into bed, drunk usually, then robbing them. She was only just nineteen before she was sent away and they said nobody in London was as good at it as she was – as beautiful and innocent looking as a statue on an altar. She and Panter met in Van Diemen's Land, when they were out breaking stones together, for all I know. Did you ever feel her hands? Hard as a navvy's.'

'But she and George . . .?'

Jolly scowled. 'You saw that, did you? Yes, she did it with the boy. Probably she was the first woman he ever had. I don't know what she expected to get from it or perhaps it was just habit with her – any man she came across.'

'Did Mr Vickery know?'

'I don't know whether he did or didn't, that's the truth. He might have thought that the boy was of an age, she was there and good luck to them. He's never been prudish in that way.'

'Didn't her husband . . . didn't Panter mind?'

'Not a lot he could do about it if he did. He was as dependent on Vickery as a five-year-old for its Saturday penny and she'd sniff the richest man out of a hundred. As far as she was concerned, Panter had served his purpose. Convenient, really, him drowning.'

The look on his face suggested he might be prepared to say more.

'You're suggesting Emilia drowned him?'

'I wouldn't put anything past her.'

'But George was there in the sea. He'd have sensed Emilia.'

'More ways than one of bribing a boy to keep quiet.'

'But George . . . he's only seventeen and . . .'

'His father's son, or so they say.'

I stared at him, not wanting to believe it. 'Do you think Mr Vickery suspected that?'

'No telling what he suspects or what he doesn't. One thing I do know – after Panter drowned he could hardly wait to get back to London and pay her off, which I'm sure he did handsomely as usual. It was a mistake he made, taking up with either of them. Peters had changed more than in name. I suppose transportation would do that to anybody. Mr Vickery thought he was still the ambitious little clerk he'd known eight years before. When he heard Peters, or Panter, was back in England he sent him the money to come and join him on Cephalonia, not knowing he'd bring the so-called wife along as well. But by the time they arrived, Mr Vickery had adopted George and he could see Panter was no fit company for His Lordship's son and he'd done wrong in putting them together. If he hadn't happened to drown when he did, I reckon Mr Vickery would have sent him away in any case. Convenient, really.'

'Why was it so wrong, bringing George and Panter together?'

'Don't you see?' Jolly took another great swallow of wine. 'Panter really believed the story about Lord Byron's treasure. Mr Vickery knew it for what it was, but it appealed to Panter. That's what made his fraud so successful – until he got over-ambitious. What was more, he'd managed to convince himself that George knew where it was.'

'But that's ridiculous. George wasn't born when Lord Byron died.'

'I suppose Panter had been brooding on it all that time and convinced himself more and more. So when he was introduced to George as Lord Byron's son, he was sure the boy knew where it's buried.'

'How?'

'Lord Byron tells the boy's mother . . .'

'Who died soon after he was born.'

'. . . and she tells her grandmother on her deathbed, and her grandmother passes it on to the great-grandson, who's just waiting till he gets the chance to go and dig it up.'

'That's madness.'

'Yes. I suppose Peters had been turning it over in his mind all the time he was sent away. So he comes back and tries again.

He kept trying to get the boy on his own and talk to him, then
one day I caught him trying to do him harm, twisting his arm
behind his back. George wrenched away from him and hit him
in the neck, aiming for the jaw, I suppose, but pretty accurate
for a lad who couldn't see. When Panter saw me, he pretended
they'd just been fighting in play. I told Mr Vickery and after
that Panter was never left alone with George. Of course, George
didn't care for Panter one little bit.'

'Because of the arm twisting or because of Emilia?'

'Probably both, or he just plain didn't like him.'

'All in all, it's a pity Mr Vickery ever mentioned the Byron
treasure story to Peters or Panter,' I said. 'How did Mr Vickery
hear of it in any case?'

'Because we were there at the time.'

'Where?'

'Cephalonia, same time as Lord Byron.'

I stared at him. 'You and Mr Vickery were in Lord Byron's
party?'

'Not actually with him, no, though there's plenty who will
claim they were with him when they weren't. What happens
when there's fighting going on is there's the heroes who fight
for whatever they're supposed to be fighting for, then the ones
who just want to be fighting each other for some other reason,
then the third lot who don't particularly want to fight at all but
are in there for whatever can be picked up while the others
are stirring up the dust. Mr Vickery was one of the third sort.
He was out there, with a little bit of a boat he had and a crew
of Italians who'd cut your throat if you didn't sleep with one
eye open, collecting things that would sell for a lot of money
elsewhere – statues that had been picked up, looted gold and
jewellery from the Turks, old coins, anything. That's when I
joined him. I'd been on a merchant ship and got thrown off in
Cephalonia for reasons we won't go into, and he took me on.
We were out there for a year nearly and he made enough out
of it to start investing and made a fortune, fair and square. He
did all right by me, but money runs through my hands like
water. In the time we were out there, after Lord Byron had
died, Mr Vickery heard this story about the buried treasure he'd
left on Cephalonia. Everybody out there believed it. To this day

there are still people digging holes up there in the hills, trying to find it.'

I thought of the pits Robert and I had seen on Cephalonia. 'I saw them but I didn't realize what they were.'

He nodded. 'Early on, we did some of the digging ourselves. But Mr Vickery came to the conclusion that it was fool's gold. Everything Lord Byron took out with him was spent. There was no hidden treasure. So when, later on in London, he told Peters about it, he told it as a joke. Only Peters believed it.'

Under it all, something else was in my mind – the morning on Cephalonia when Panter drowned. Everything Jolly said made the death look less and less like an accident. Emilia may have wanted Panter dead but Mr Vickery was quite capable of killing anybody who wished harm to George. And George himself? His feeling that he was responsible for Panter's death might, after all, have been something more than superstition.

'But it's not relevant,' I said, as much to myself as Jolly. 'It's Helena Shilling he's accused of killing, not Panter.'

'So why did you lead me on about it?' Jolly said. 'And how will it help him?'

They were fair questions. 'The only thing that will help him is finding out that somebody else killed her.'

He shrugged. 'In any case, that's not what he wants you to do. He said to me several times that he's relying on you to find the boy and so far it looks as if you haven't done anything.'

No sense in telling him about our weary trudge round the coach yards and theatre queues. It was true: I'd done nothing. I thanked him and promised to let him know if I had any news. He stood up, quite steady on his feet though he'd drunk the best part of the bottle of Beaujolais and goodness knew how much before, escorted me to the front door and let me out.

It was late and I was so tired that for once I took a cab home, though I regretted it because the horse was tired and I could have walked faster on my own two feet. Mrs Martley had gone to bed so I poked the fire into life and heated up some of her good beef broth. There was a letter on the table, addressed to me in Celia's neat handwriting.

You really must come and see me. We're going to the country next week and I'm sitting here dying of boredom. They say he's written a book of poetry. Do you know anything about it? Come and tell me tomorrow, or if you don't know come in any case. Yours most affectionately, Celia.

SIXTEEN

'I heard it from Philip,' Celia said, sipping her chocolate. 'Of course, he's not interested in poetry at all and he'd only gone to the bookseller's to ask him to send down some books on crop rotation. A salesman was clearing some space in the window and when Philip asked about it he said they were expecting delivery of a poem by Lord Byron's son. I thought there must be some mistake, the boy being so young and blind. I know Homer was supposed to be blind but then he was old, wasn't he? But Philip was quite definite he'd said Byron's son so I thought you might know about it. Do you suppose it will be as good as *Childe Harold*?'

It was out of the question to tell her about George being missing or I'd have been there all morning. I established that the bookseller in question was in Fleet Street, finished my chocolate, promised to come down and see her in her country exile and walked to the place as quickly as I could. It was easy enough to find it because a queue had built up, extending on to the pavement. I joined the queue and as it shuffled along looked in the shop's small and crowded window. In the middle was a pile of books, a dozen or so, thin and cheaply bound in blue cloth, one opened on a bookrest at the title page. It showed two pictures side by side in oval frames. One had a laurel wreath around it and was the idealized portrait of the late Lord Byron I knew from my youthful hero worship. It was over-inked and looked as if the sharpness of the engraving had faded through much use. The other was more roughly done but newer, from a woodcut rather than a metal plate. It showed a young man with dark, curly hair, his eyes upraised to the heavens. Blank, blind eyes. Above the pictures, on a scroll, the title *Retorts and Reflection, by a son*. Below it, *By George Byron, son of the late Lord Byron. Five shillings.* Inside the shop two assistants were taking the money faster than cooks gutting fish and handing over copies of the book. The queue shuffled forward and

delivered me inside the shop, where I paid my five shillings
and received my copy. I'd have liked to ask questions but there
were people behind me. Luckily I'd long ago perfected the skill
of reading standing up so I planted myself in the doorway of
an empty office and read. It didn't take long to see that the
book wasn't very good. It would have been a miracle if it had
been. On the other hand, it wasn't so very bad either, written
in the metre of Lord Byron's *Don Juan*, a satirical tour of
modern politicians, writers and reviewers with a Candide-like
hero looking wide-eyed at them all. Very much a young man's
book. But not George's. Vickery's education programme had
been thorough but not thorough enough to give him the grasp
of poetical metre, politics, modern literature and classical
learning paraded in *Retorts and Reflections.* I thought I could
guess whose work it was. Back at the bookshop, the pile of
books had gone from the window and been replaced by a 'Sold
Out' sign. I went in. A middle-aged man at the desk, bald
headed and freckled of face, was counting money. I waited until
he'd got several pounds' worth of shillings stowed away in the
drawer and held up my copy of the book.

'This interests me very much. I wonder – did you meet the
author?'

He nodded. With Byron mania a force to be reckoned with,
I probably wasn't the first to ask the question. 'Last Tuesday.
He and his friend walked in, out of the blue. I hadn't met him
before but I saw the resemblance at once.'

'What did the friend look like?'

'Young, dark-haired, a Scottish gentleman. He seemed to be
in charge of the business side of things and did most of the
talking. The poem was with the printer and would be out this
week. He wanted to know how many copies we'd take. I took
a risk and said five dozen. I wish now I'd asked for more.'

'Who delivered them?'

'The Scottish gentleman, on his own, soon after we opened
this morning. He had a sort of cart like the street-sellers use,
full of them. He seemed surprised that I didn't pay him at once
but I explained it was sale or return, split between the writer
and the seller. He said he'd come back for the money this
evening.'

It struck me that the bookseller had used the Scottish gentleman's inexperience to negotiate a more than usually good deal
for himself. Still, his share on sixty copies would come to seven
pounds and ten shillings, well worth collecting. The name of
the printer was on the title page and the man said it was a small
place at the St Paul's end of the street. It mainly produced
sketches of a certain kind and quantities of political leaflets but
didn't usually go in for poetry. He seemed to have a low opinion
of it but said it had a reputation for producing things quickly.
I thanked the man and went off to find it. The walk along Fleet
Street showed one other bookseller with a 'Sold Out' sign in
the window and another with a few copies left. Like the
first shop, they were the smaller operators. Either the larger
establishments had been more wary or possibly McCloud's
self-confidence had failed in the face of them. Either way, those
shops must be regretting it because the book was clearly the
sensation of the week. A long and not notably good poem that
many of the buyers wouldn't understand in any case was desir-
able because it came from Byron's son. (The irony that it did
not might come to public notice sooner or later, but booksellers
wouldn't take the books back.) The two of them must have
done the rounds of the bookshops almost as soon as they arrived
in London. As for the poem, it was too long to have been written
in the short time McCloud had been in England so he would
have brought it with him in his luggage from Edinburgh, with
a hope of publication that had been small to vanishing point
until the acquaintance with George and a shrewd appreciation
of the importance of the Byron connection showed him a way
of bringing it to market. Would he claim it for his own at some
point? I doubted if he'd thought that far ahead. The main question was whether George had gone along willingly with the
deception or McCloud had tricked or bullied him. McCloud
would have known that he'd have to show George to the
booksellers at some point to give any credibility to the author-
ship. I wished I'd asked the bookseller more about the manner
of the young Byron when they were in his shop. In any case,
it suggested a motive for George's and McCloud's flight that
had nothing to do with the other events at Northlands. But we
had them now because it was unthinkable that McCloud

wouldn't be back that evening to collect his money. For one thing, they'd need it. Neither he nor George would have had much to bring from Northlands and most of that would have gone towards printing the book. I assumed some of the negotiations about that had gone on in letters that McCloud had sent by way of the village girl and probably the thing I'd seen him hand to her had been part of the poem for posting. I knew my way round the printers at the St Paul's end of the street and found this one without much trouble. The place was only a narrow slice of a terrace of buildings, canted so far to one side that the windows of the top floor overhung the doorway of its neighbour. On the ground floor, a larger window showed lines of prints inside, hung up to dry. The ones visible from the window were characters from Greek and Roman mythology engaged in activities that should have made a respectable woman look aside and walk on hastily. Since I'd decided long since that respectability and inquiry seldom went together, I opened the door and stepped inside. An elderly man in a green baize apron and a paper cap on his bald head looked alarmed and made go away gestures.

'You printed the Byron book,' I said.

He promptly disappeared through a curtain into a back room. Soon afterwards, a younger man came out. He was short and square in build, also bald, perhaps the son of the first man. A smear of printer's ink was on his cheek and his hands were at his side, fists clenched.

'What's the trouble?'

'No trouble at all,' I said. 'Only I'm acquainted with the author and I'd like to know where to find him.'

'Because if there's trouble, we only printed it. We've got nothing to do with the writing.'

'I told you, there's no trouble. I just want to find him.'

The fists unclenched but he was still tense. 'I want to find him and all. We've had the bookshops bothering us, wanting more. Five hundred more copies we can print, only he has to pay for them.'

'He paid for the first lot?'

'His friend did, or we wouldn't have printed them.'

'Was the friend a Scotsman?'

'He was.'

'How long ago did he pay for them?'

'Why do you want to know?'

It cost me a sovereign to get some answers out of him, four times what I'd normally expect to pay. Clearly the trade in mythology set high financial standards. McCloud had first come into the shop to inquire about printing times and costs about three weeks ago, presumably just before Mr Vickery moved his household to the country. The first half of the fee had been paid two weeks before by a draft on an Edinburgh bank, signed by McCloud, and three separate packets had arrived with the text of the poem. It had been agreed that the balance would be paid in cash when McCloud collected the books. He'd done that this very morning in a rickety handcart, presumably to try them on the booksellers. The printer had not personally set eyes on Byron's son and in his own words didn't care a hang about him once printing costs were paid. As for where McCloud was, the printer simply didn't know. He hadn't expected to see the man again once he took the books away and he'd been caught by surprise at the thing's commercial success. In spite of the requests from the bookshops, he wasn't going to bear the risk of printing them until he had some more money in his hand.

I went straight back to Abel Yard and found Tabby. She'd recognize McCloud from her time at Northlands and could describe him to Plush. We walked back to Fleet Street, mostly by back roads, in a hurry. McCloud had told the bookseller he'd be back for his money in the evening, but if he knew that shops had sold out already it might be earlier. For all I knew, he might have been lurking around Fleet Street watching the book sell. I only hoped he hadn't seen me. When I thought about this I walked faster. We were so near to them now that it was unthinkable that he might slip away. What we'd do when we found him was another question. McCloud was of age and could do as he liked. Publishing your poem under another's name was no crime if the other man agreed to it. It made sense financially. A learned satire by an unknown Scottish graduate might have sat on the bookshelves for a long time before attracting a single buyer. George's safety was another matter. Although Mr Vickery had intended to adopt him, there'd been no time for him to go through the legal process. He was not of age but nobody had a guardian's authority over him. I'd have to tread carefully with both of them. When we got to Fleet Street we split up, with Plush watching the first bookshop I'd been to because McCloud wouldn't recognize him. It was within sight of the second bookshop, where Tabby was on guard and Plush would signal to her if McCloud went inside his shop. I took the third shop and stationed myself on the pavement opposite, though I walked up the street now and then to have sight of Tabby. She was inside the doorway opposite her shop, practically invisible if you didn't know she was there. We waited for nearly three hours, until lamps were coming on in the doorways of the public houses, carts with the early editions of the newspapers were grinding along the street and people were beginning to be reduced to silhouettes in the light from occasional windows. That was how I saw him. I'd just got back to my position from a walk towards Tabby and there he was, a figure in a topcoat and soft hat, looking into the bookshop window at the 'Sold Out' sign. He half turned to open the door and go into the shop and there wasn't a doubt about it: Hamish McCloud. I walked far enough towards Tabby to signal to her, knowing her sight was as good as a cat's, even in failing light. We had choices now. If he turned eastwards as he came out of the shop I'd have to stop him on my own and hope Tabby and Plush would run up in time to help. If he turned westwards, he'd be walking towards Tabby's shop, I could follow and we'd tackle him together. I hoped and believed he'd go westwards. If he'd come from that direction surely Tabby or I would have seen him. He seemed to be inside my bookshop for a long time, possibly checking his money. Then, after ten minutes or more, he was outside with his hand in his pocket. He hesitated a moment then turned westwards, towards Tabby. I followed. He was a fast walker and by the time I got to her he was inside the second bookshop. She nodded at me and pointed with her chin.

'We won't try to stop him here,' I said. 'We'll follow him and see where he goes.'

I'd decided that as I walked. With so many people around he might play the outraged citizen and shake us off. On my own, I might have hesitated about following a man in the dusk without losing him but nobody in London was better at following than Tabby. Again, he was in the bookshop for some time. We could see his back through the window then a side view, lamp-lit, as he and the shop-owner shook hands. I couldn't see his expression but I guessed there'd be satisfaction in it in spite of the large cut the bookseller was taking. The man who'd arrived with books in a handcart was now a success. It seemed a pity that we were going to spoil it. Tabby and I followed on the opposite side of the street as he walked, more slowly now, to the third bookshop where Plush was on guard in a doorway on the same side of the street. He wasn't quite as good as Tabby at merging into the background but McCloud had no reason to notice him and passed within a few yards as he went into the shop. We crossed to join Plush and Tabby told him the job was done and he could go. I added thanks and a few coins and he disappeared, slick as a lizard into a sand dune. Again, it was some time before McCloud came out, this time with his hand in the other pocket, nicely balanced. He was looking thoughtful and I doubted if he'd have noticed if the queen with ladies-in-waiting were standing at the bookshop window. He set off at a good pace westwards, towards the Strand, and we followed.

It wasn't difficult at first. Just before we reached the Strand he turned up Chancery Lane and across Holborn and into the maze of small streets and courtyards, near enough Smithfield Market to catch the smells of dung and animal blood on the air. At this time of day there were plenty of people and carts around and McCloud seemed to have no idea that he was being followed. Then he began to walk more slowly, like a man not quite certain of his way, and once took a wrong turning and doubled back, so that Tabby and I had to stand in the mouth of a dark courtyard as he walked past within a few feet of us. Soon afterwards he walked past a shoddy little bakery, the shelves in its window empty and only the dim glow of an oven inside. He hesitated, then suddenly doubled back again and went in. We waited a few doorways back and he came out carrying a small parcel. The smell of cheap meat and warm pastry spread over the street as he raised the parcel to his face and took a long and loving sniff of it before going on his way. I thought he wasn't far now from home and supper, and soon afterwards he came to a narrow opening opposite a public house and disappeared into it. We followed, closing in on him. The place was a short cul-de-sac with a few sagging two-storey buildings in it, ending in a blank brick wall. McCloud was on the step of one of the tumbledown buildings, taking a key out of his pocket with difficulty since one hand was still balancing the pies. Tabby looked at me. I nodded and we moved in behind him.

'Good evening, Mr McCloud,' I said.

He turned, the key in his hand, and almost dropped the pies. After a moment of incomprehension, he recognized us.

'What are you doing here?' It was a simple bewildered inquiry. We might have dropped from the sky.

'Looking for George,' I said.

'To take him back to Vickery? You can't. He won't go.'

'I think we'd better come in,' I said.

'It's not convenient.'

I looked at his face, then at the key in his hand. He held my look for a moment then gave a shake of the shoulders, as if saying that none of this was his fault, and unlocked the door. It grated on the stone floor inside and juddered as if about to fall off its hinges. We followed him directly into a nearly bare room and he made a long business of lighting the lamp. The room took up the whole ground floor, with a door at the back, a tattered curtain drawn over a window and a disintegrating market cart and several battered porter's baskets on the floor. An armchair with the stuffing coming out, one leg propped up on wooden blocks, stood by a narrow fireplace that couldn't have held more than a few coals at best and now had nothing but ashes. A rough ladder was fixed to the wall in the corner. McCloud looked at it then at us.

'He's up there?'

He nodded. 'He sleeps a lot.'

'Are you going to wake him and tell him he's a runaway literary success?'

He put the pies down on the remains of the cart. 'The money's all for him, if you're wondering. We'll get a better place.'

I sat down on the armchair, balancing it carefully on the blocks. 'He agreed to put his name to your poem?'

'Why not? The name's all he has. Why not make use of it?'

'You sent the poem off from Northlands?'

'Yes. I've been working on it for two years. Nobody would publish it – a political poem from a Scottish nobody. Even with George's name on it we had to pay for the printing and it took every bit of money I had. Now it's succeeded we don't have to go back to Vickery. He has no claim on George. You can go back and tell him that.'

'I can't. He's been arrested for murder.'

He stared. 'That woman? The one who said she was George's mother?'

'You knew about that?'

'We knew about her, George and I. You say he killed her?'

'I said he'd been arrested.'

He took a deep breath, still staring at me. He looked surprised and, I thought, relieved.

'Was she?' he said.

'Was she what?'

'His mother?'

'No. She was a hired actress.'

He glanced up the ladder, as if wondering if George had heard. 'So what do you want from us?' he said.

SEVENTEEN

He was standing by the market cart and, unconsciously, his hand had gone to one of the pies, breaking it up and putting a fragment into his mouth. From the way he chewed the meat was mostly gristle and I wondered how long it was since he'd last eaten.

'How did you know there was a woman claiming to be his mother?' I said.

He swallowed and thought before answering. 'One of the servants.'

'Jolly?'

A nod.

'When did he tell you?'

'Back in London. He told George about the letters from her. Jolly talks. He wants to know everything that's happening then he wants people to know he knows.'

'And George told you?'

'Yes. He'd have gone to meet the woman if he could, only Jolly didn't tell him until it was too late.'

'But surely he knew she couldn't be his mother. He'd had a mother on Cephalonia.'

McCloud frowned, angry and suddenly surer of himself. 'Don't you understand how you can know and not know something at the same time? Just suppose she hadn't died as he'd been told. Just suppose she was in London and looking for him. In one way he'd know it couldn't be true, in another he'd hope so much it might be that it almost made it true. I can understand that, even if you can't.'

'I can understand, yes.' And I could. I wondered what loss in McCloud's own life had given him such an understanding of George's. 'You're very close to George.'

'From the start. He'd had nobody he could talk to. You can't count Ridgeway. It was like finding you had a brother. George is clever, cleverer than anyone realizes. But he's a boy and a scared one. All that time together – some of it we really were reading Shakespeare and Virgil but he talked to me the way he's never talked to anybody, certainly not to Vickery.'

'And yet Mr Vickery was kind to him.'

'He didn't understand anything about him. He was trying to make George into his idea of a gentleman. He never knew how lost George felt.'

'Lost?'

'How could he not be?' His eyes were bright, voice low but urgent. 'He's Lord Byron's son but a year ago he was a peasant boy on a mountain. A person can't live like that all his life and change in a matter of months.'

'So who decided to run away to London, you or George?'

'We decided it together. George couldn't stay at Northlands. He was having waking nightmares about her getting up from her grave and trying to pull him back in with her.'

'Who told you they'd buried her? Jolly again?'

A hesitation. 'I watched them from upstairs – Vickery, Jolly and the fat lawyer. I saw them take her out of the old game larder. I didn't know where they'd taken her until later.'

'And you told George?'

'I thought he had a right to know.' He glanced towards the ladder, probably wondering as I was if George were awake and listening. There was no sound from upstairs. 'But perhaps I was wrong to do it. In some ways he's as superstitious as any Greek peasant. You know he thinks he's haunted by people, says he sees them when he's asleep? He wakes up at night, calling out to them in Greek. Modern Greek, that is. I only partially understand it. That's why I'm letting him sleep now, because he doesn't sleep much at nights. He blames himself for killing her. There's another one too, a man he says he drowned back on Cephalonia. He says everybody he has anything to do with dies. He's scared for me too. I tell him it's nonsense but he doesn't believe me.'

'How did you get to London?' I said.

'Walked a mile or two then a carriage driver gave us a ride. Not talkative and on the make, probably.'

'He wanted money?'

'Not directly, no. But he found out we had nowhere to stay

in London and offered to find us a room. It seemed to me altogether too helpful, so when he got down and went in a house, George and I walked away. I found this place by asking a man in a public house. We can move somewhere better now.'

'And when you'd found a room, you went straight to a printer?'

'I'd met the printer before, almost as soon as I came to London. That's why I took the situation with Vickery. I'd saved up some money and was going to print it under my own name until George and I came up with a better idea and it's working very well. So you couldn't have made us go back to Vickery, even if he hadn't been in prison.'

'I can't make you do anything, but at least Mr Vickery should know that George is safe and with you of his own free will.'

'He is that.'

'I think I should hear that from George himself.'

'Then what will you do?'

The answer should be that I'd get word to Vickery in prison. Certainly George would be more comfortable in the Knightsbridge house than in this squalor. But in spite of his youth and that mediocre poem, there was something that impressed me more than I expected about McCloud.

'At least give him the chance to say that he wants to stay here with you, and I'll think about it and not tell Mr Vickery at once.'

He thought about it, frowning, then nodded. 'Very well. But I want to be there when you speak to him.'

With George's quick hearing, he must know that we were there.

'You can go first and wake him up,' I said.

Reluctantly McCloud nodded and went over to the foot of the ladder. 'George, we have visitors.'

No answer. McCloud stood on the bottom rung with his head through the open hatchway. 'You might . . .' Then a gasp and he was up the ladder and into the loft. Tabby got to the ladder before I did and followed him up.

'He's not here.'

My feet were on the ladder as she said it and I squeezed down my petticoats to get through the hatch and joined them.

There was only just room for the three of us and McCloud and I had to stand with heads bent because of the steep slope of the ceiling. The room was no more than a cabin. A bed with scrunched-up blankets, a stained bolster and no sheets was pushed up against the wall. Another disordered blanket and a knapsack of the kind soldiers carry formed what might have been a second sleeping place by the opposite wall. A jacket and low-crowned hat hung from nails. An uncurtained triangular window looked down on a dark courtyard. There was nowhere to hide a dishcloth, let alone a person. The expression on McCloud's face showed the absence of George was a total shock to him. He said, several times, 'Where's he gone?' looking at me as if I had the answer. Then: 'Where would he go? He knew I'd be coming back with money.'

For the sake of doing something we turned back the blankets. They'd been left anyhow, not folded, but that looked like ordinary untidiness rather than the result of a struggle. Squeezing down through the hatchway and on to the ladder was more difficult than going up.

'I'd locked it,' McCloud said when we were down. 'There's only one key and I had it. And the back door latches from the inside. I made sure it was closed.'

I went and looked. The latch was no more than a piece of wood that rotated on a screw and, when horizontal, dropped on to a nail hammered at an angle into the door frame. It was vertical, open. A child with a blunt knife could have operated it from outside. I showed McCloud, without saying anything, and he put his head in his hands. The courtyard was shared with the house next door, a foul-smelling privy in the corner. Nobody there. There was no gate in the yard but the fence was so broken down that anybody could have stepped across it to a scrubby piece of grass on the far side then out to a street more or less parallel to this one.

'They could have coshed him and carried him out,' Tabby said.

'Somebody would have noticed.'

'Places like this, nobody notices nothing. Still, I'll ask around if you want.'

I nodded. We went back inside and she left by the front door.

McCloud was standing in the middle of the room, still looking stunned.

'Who knew you were here?' I said.

'Nobody. Just nobody.'

'Then you must have been followed. We followed you today. Somebody else must have done it earlier, if you're sure George didn't leave of his own accord.'

'I'm sure of it.'

'So either he was taken away by force or somebody persuaded him. Suppose somebody brought a message from you, asking him to go and meet you. He'd have gone?'

'Yes.'

'Could somebody have followed you all the way from Northlands?'

'No, we'd have noticed.'

'So somebody must have followed you, either from the printers or from one of the bookshops yesterday. The question is how they knew you'd be there.'

'Suppose the printer talked?' His mind was beginning to move again. 'A poem by Byron's son – that would be an event after all. If gossip got round . . .'

'Possibly.' I didn't tell him so but I was doubtful about that. His particular jobbing printer didn't seem to me to have any great interest in the work and would hardly be putting gossip round the salons.

'But why, that's what I don't understand.' It came almost as a howl. 'It's Vickery who wants George so much and you tell me he's in prison. Unless you're lying about that.'

'I'm not lying. Whoever took George away, it can't be Mr Vickery.'

He became restless, wanted to go out to the streets and question people until we'd found somebody who'd seen George go. I said that as far as this area was concerned we should leave it to Tabby. She understood places where people saw most things and said nothing. We waited for half an hour or so before the door opened and she walked in looking discontented with herself.

'Left it too late. Dipped and scarpered.'

'Dipped?'

'Pocket picked, only anything that might have helped they got rid of soon as it was in their hands.' Then, seeing from my face that it needed more explanation, she gave details. 'Couldn't find many people to speak to round here and of course the ones I did find wouldn't have told me if they'd seen a parade of elephants with drums and bugles. Then I found a couple of boys. I had to play the thimble trick with them and let them win tuppence before they'd even start talking – that's what took me so long. Then they let on that the blind one left with a man and a woman two hours or more ago when it was still just daylight, out of the back door and through the fence. From what they said, he was going willingly, not dragged or carried. Nothing special about the man, they said, he was just ordinary, and the woman had the hood of her cloak up. So of course they decided to see what they had. Normal for them – any stranger round here would do the same thing. So one of them distracts them, getting in front and shouting things at the blind one while the other moves in from behind and slips his hand in the pocket of the man because they suppose he's more likely to have something. He gets a leather wallet. The man and woman don't notice because they're too busy with the other boy. The boys don't see which way they went because by then they're occupied with the wallet. They say all there is inside it is a sixpence halfpenny and it's so battered it's hardly worth passing on to the man they know who takes wallets, but they do and he says it's not even a farthing-worth but he'll put it on their account for next time.'

McCloud was looking dazed.

'You understood that?' I asked him.

'George went willingly.' He'd grasped that much, at any rate. 'He'd only have done that if he thought he was being taken to meet me.'

'Yes, so the man and woman must have known something about the two of you to convince him. The question is where've they taken him? I don't suppose we could get the wallet back in case it tells us anything.'

Tabby shook her head. 'It'll have changed hands three times over by now. But there was nothing in it except the coins – and this.'

She stretched out her hand and unfolded it to show a small, scrumpled piece of paper. Tabby can't read and refuses to learn so anything in the nature of written evidence annoys her. I took it from her. It was no more than a strip torn from what looked like a blank sheet of business writing paper with a few figures written in blunt pencil, small sums in shillings and pence with a total of nine shillings and threepence. Hardly the takings of a successful criminal. The other side was blank except for four embossed and printed letters at the top right hand – *TLEY* and beneath them *gh Holborn*. They only meant something to me because he'd so recently been in my mind.

'Astley,' I said. 'It was Astley who sent them.'

'Where is he?' McCloud said. His fists were clenched, his voice almost a growl.

'High Holborn, judging by this.'

'Let's go there.'

I pointed out that we had no number and it was so late in the evening that people would be going to their beds. We'd have to wait till morning. McCloud was so full of energy and frustration that he was practically giving off electric sparks. There was no telling what he'd do if we simply left him in the lodgings, so I suggested he should come home with us. My study and the separate staircase to it would provide sleeping place for him that was just on the right side of respectable. It was partly in my mind that I wanted him under my eye, just in case he were playing a deeper game than I thought. In the end he agreed and came with us on the long walk to Abel Yard. Tabby disappeared into her cabin and Mrs Martley, in her dressing gown with her hair in curling rags, retreated protesting to her bedroom while I made up a bed on my chaise longue for McCloud. I didn't suppose he'd sleep much and I didn't expect to either, but by the time I got to my own bed I was surprisingly sleepy. My last conscious thought was that McCloud had been surprised when I told him that Vickery was charged with murder, and I wondered why.

EIGHTEEN

I made Hamish McCloud wait in the morning. He was down in the yard, fully dressed and ready to go, when Amos arrived with Rancie. McCloud was furious to find me doing anything so frivolous as going riding but a lot of things had happened since I last spoke to Amos and he needed to know about them.

'You're sure it was Astley who took him away?' he said when I'd told him.

'Far from sure, no. But that torn piece of paper is all we have to go by. That and the certainty that somebody must have known George and McCloud well enough to follow them when they'd got to London.'

'The McCloud fellow would have left a pretty wide trail from the printers.'

'But somebody would have had to follow him to the printers in the first place. I think Astley was spying on them back at Northlands. He pretended to me that he wasn't interested in George at all; he really went out of his way to make me believe that.'

'There's another thing,' Amos said. 'That carriage that picked them up. We asked all over the shop and couldn't find a carriage that stopped in the village. Does it strike you that there was one carriage on the road that morning that didn't want to stop and be recognized?'

'Ye gods.' In my surprise I moved my hands and Rancie threw up her head. 'Simmonds. You said he collected his carriage from the stables early on Monday morning. He's driving back to London then sees the boy all the fuss is about just walking along the road.'

'Possible, isn't it? The McCloud fellow's never seen Simmonds so has no reason to be suspicious. The trouble is I can't think why Simmonds would let George go once he's got his hands on him.'

'Because he's not the most intelligent of men and almost

certainly only on the fringes of whatever's going on. So the best he can do is promise them a room then ask his employer what to do with them. While he's doing that, McCloud takes George away. So whoever tries to get him knows he's in London but not where. That's why somebody must have known about the book to track them.'

'One thing,' Amos said, 'it's not an ordinary kidnap. The only man who'd pay a ransom for him was in prison when he was taken and looks like staying there.'

My heart sank because I'd been thinking it too. 'So we're back with people believing he knows about Lord Byron's mythical treasure.'

'Did Astley?'

'I suppose he must do if he had anything to do with taking George. The boy went without a struggle. I don't think he liked the man very much but at least he'd have been familiar to him.'

Amos offered to go with us in the search of High Holborn but I said it would be a waste of his time and probably ours as well. So instead he volunteered to go back to Perkins' Yard in the evening and have another drink with the jockey in case he'd heard or seen anything of Simmonds.

We agreed to meet again the next morning. When he'd gone I changed out of my riding habit and ignored Mrs Martley's disapproval to organize breakfast in the parlour for McCloud, Tabby and myself. I guessed it was going to be a long morning and none of us had eaten properly the night before. We set off together for High Holborn and by then it was busy, crowded with carts and carriages, pavements full of clerks carrying bundles of legal documents, legal-looking gentlemen, the occasional nursemaid with toddlers or servants walking dogs, heading for Lincoln's Inn Fields. When we got there we split up and worked our way along the road, McCloud trying one door, Tabby and I the next. All down one side we found nothing. Tabby and I were used to the work but McCloud was discouraged and discontented, only just managing to be polite to the various servants, householders or craftsmen who opened doors to us and variously regretted that they'd never heard of anybody called Astley. Quite a few doors didn't open to our knocking. He could have been behind any of them and all the weariness

and frequent uselessness of searches like this was coming back
to me. Then it happened, halfway down the second side of the
street towards the end of the afternoon. McCloud, on the step
of the house next door, was trying without success to question
a deaf old man who'd mistaken him for the fish salesman. Tabby
and I walked up to a door that looked much like any other,
black painted with a horseshoe-shaped knocker. It was some
time before it was answered by a plump and respectable woman
with her hair tied up in a scarf as if she'd been doing some
serious cleaning. Her hands were red and rough and the flesh
of her finger bulged on either side of her wedding ring so that
she wouldn't have been able to take it off even if she'd wanted
to. I asked if a gentleman named Astley lived there and was so
used by now to the answer no that I could hardly believe it
when she nodded.

'He has the rooms at the top. I don't know if he's in, though.
I haven't seen him since yesterday and that was only to say
good afternoon to. I clean for the others, only I don't clean for
him. He said he didn't want it.'

'Might he have come in without your knowing?'

'I suppose so. He's got his own key and I was out most of
the day.'

I asked if Tabby and I could go up and knock on his door
and she said to please ourselves if we didn't mind the climb.
She was anxious to get back to whatever work she'd been doing
and, I thought, not notably fond of Astley. The two flights of
stairs were steep enough to give a picture of Astley puffing and
perspiring as he walked up them. On the top landing we were
faced with another black door with no knocker. I tapped on it
and called, 'Mr Astley?' Silence. Tabby, whose hearing was
very acute, shook her head. Still, I tried again with the same
result. I was about to go downstairs and beg writing material
to leave a note for him when Tabby simply walked up to the
door and gave it a good push. It opened. That surprised me
because I'd have thought he was the kind of man who locked
everything.

'Well, aren't we going in?' she said.

I went in ahead of her, calling out his name again, just
in case. The door gave directly into a sitting room, a plain,

bachelor sort of place with a couple of good leather chairs at a cold fire grate, shelves of books, mostly law, and a tantalus on the table about a quarter full of brandy. A roll-top desk stood in the corner. I rolled the top back and investigated a dozen or so shelves and pigeonholes, all of them as empty as a blown egg. Nobody, especially not a man who still claimed to be a lawyer, would keep a desk so empty. It had been deliberately cleared out.

'Moved out,' Tabby said, watching me. Another door led into what was probably the bedroom. I opened it, intending to check if the clothes had gone from his wardrobe, and stopped a few feet inside the room. Tabby cannoned into my back.

'He's in here,' I said, surprised to find my voice sounding normal though my heart was hammering. The room was almost dark with only a small window, heavily curtained. I moved across the room, avoiding the bed and, hearing something scrunching under my feet, drew back the curtains. There'd been a struggle. Blankets and sheets had been partly dragged off the bed. What had scrunched were fragments of the glass funnel of a lamp that lay on its side on a rug beside the bed. It must have been lit when it fell because there was a burn on the rug, a circle of lamp oil and sooty marks as if somebody had stamped the fire out. I looked at the lamp first because I didn't want to look at what was on the bed, but the legs weren't far away. The toe of one well-worn shoe was touching the carpet but not taking any weight. The trouser leg was rucked up showing a sock suspender and black woollen socks. The other foot was just off the carpet. My eyes followed it up a black-trousered leg to a stomach that looked even more prominent than it had in life. He was lying on his back across the disordered bed, his eyes open. It had not been done tidily. His chest had several gashes in it. One had torn raggedly across the fabric of his waistcoat so that an expanse of shirt showed, stained red. At least one other stroke must have gone deeper and found his heart because it had pumped out great volumes of blood, now congealed on his chest and neck and around him on the bedclothes. Some of it must have gone on the floor because I could feel it tacky under my feet as I moved.

'Done last night,' Tabby said. She was probably going by the lamp and the congealed blood.

'Or in the early hours of the morning. There's no sign of a break-in so it was probably somebody he knew.'

Tabby's head came up. She'd caught footsteps on the stairs. Then McCloud's voice.

'What's happening? Have you found him?'

I went out to the landing. 'We've found him. He's been stabbed.'

I let him come back into the bedroom with me. It was a mistake because when he saw Astley he buckled at the knees. We managed to get him through the door and into one of the armchairs.

'I'm sorry. I've never seen a dead body close to before and . . .'

'Get your breath back,' I said. 'Then go downstairs and find a police constable. There should be one not far away. Don't say anything to the woman downstairs.'

He went after a few minutes. Tabby was giving me reproachful looks.

'No help for it,' I said. 'The woman will have our descriptions and quite a few of the police know who I am. You can go if you like.'

'Found this in the bedclothes.' She was holding something long and white, blood-soaked at one end, clotted and still damp. I took it from her carefully and gasped as the room rocked round me.

'Looks like somebody's shawl,' Tabby said.

The finest white wool, embroidered in white silk with patterns of dolphins and waves. When we'd bought it at the market in Athens it had seemed so light that I'd half expected it to float away out of my hands. Now it felt pulled down to the earth by the weight of blood.

'It is,' I said. 'It's mine.'

Last seen in the villa on Cephalonia. There'd hardly be another one like it in London and, if there were, arriving here would be an impossible coincidence.

'You weren't wearing it when we came in.'

My first panicked thought was that somebody wanted to

incriminate me in Astley's death, but if that had been the case they'd surely have chosen something more obvious than this. I made myself look at it more closely and saw blobs of blood along it that might have been finger marks. Had Astley clutched at it and dragged it away from somebody, or somebody tried to drag it away from Astley? I could see Tabby staring at me as I tried to make my mind move. As far as I knew there were three people in London who'd been at the villa on Cephalonia and might have taken my shawl: Vickery, who was in prison, George and Jolly. Could George have taken it from sentiment? He was of an age when a boy might do such a thing. But then he'd have to take it with him on the escape to London. Not impossible, in which case George had been in this room. I imagined him, blind and panicked, somehow possessed of a knife and hacking at Astley. There'd been several cuts, as if the killer had experimented before finding the fatal one. The picture was all too vivid, so I thought instead of Jolly's round, smiling face. Friendly, talkative Jolly, who knew everything that was going on. He could easily have picked up the shawl on Cephalonia. But what motive would he have to kill Astley, and why bring the shawl with him? Tabby knew when not to ask questions. She waited until I'd dragged my mind back to the immediate problem and chose to stay in the sitting room while I went downstairs and broke the news to the woman. I folded up the shawl as best I could, keeping most of the blood on the inside, and stuffed it into the pocket in my skirt. Even through petticoats, it felt heavy against my thigh. I knew I should have put it back with the bedclothes where Tabby found it but couldn't see how it would help the police. Twenty minutes or so later, McCloud arrived back with two constables. By then Tabby had disappeared.

The room in the police station was quiet except for the plopping of the lamp and the murmuring voice of a constable in the hall outside talking to a member of the public. From the sound, it was the same member of the public who'd been there when I'd arrived, talking about a stolen parrot. Apart from that, most of the bustle of the day was over and the disturbances of the night still some way off. The police at Astley's lodgings had taken down the story from McCloud and me, then allowed us to go back to Abel Yard. But I'd hardly had time to take off my cloak before a constable arrived with the usual message from Sergeant Bevan. He wanted to see me immediately. I'd be at the police station within the hour, I told the police officer. Abel Yard's standing wasn't high but I didn't want to lower it further by being escorted out by the police. The constable didn't like it but since he had no warrant for my arrest he had to accept it. Now, sitting opposite Sergeant Bevan at a scratched and pitted table with a police constable standing at the door, I was getting the full weight of official disapproval. He started by saying sarcastically that he supposed it wasn't coincidence that had brought us on the scene of Astley's murder. I'd thought about it on my way and decided to tell him most of the story, from the arrival in London of George and McCloud to the scrap of paper in the stolen wallet. He made notes then looked up, his eyebrows raised. It struck me that he was less respectful these days than when we'd first met on a case, but then a lot of things had happened since then, his promotion among them.

'So this young man McCloud decoyed George to London then lost him.'

'I don't think it was a case of decoying. From what McCloud says, George was eager to get away from Northlands.'

'Judging by what was going on there I'm not entirely surprised. Vickery said nothing to us about the boy being missing.'

'But then, you wouldn't have looked for him in any case.'

'Even if we had considered it a case of kidnap, I doubt if Vickery would have had any standing in the matter.'

'But he has been kidnapped now.'

'Not by your own account. The people your girl spoke to said he went voluntarily.'

'He was tricked and Astley knew something about it.'

'You can't prove that.'

'Somebody killed Astley,' I said. 'There must have been a reason for that.'

'Not necessarily a reason connected with George and Vickery. We know about Astley. That man had his fingers in a lot of pies.'

A new drunk voice came from the hall outside, a man shouting about being robbed then sounds of a scuffle. The constable by the door caught Bevan's eye and went out. More scuffling, then a door slamming.

'If we hadn't got Vickery safely shut up – I'd have suspected him,' Bevan said.

'Astley was his friend.'

'A man like Astley doesn't have friends. If you're right and Astley had something to do with taking the boy away, Vickery would want to kill him.'

'Only, as you've pointed out, he didn't. So you accept that Astley's death had something to do with George?'

'On the record and in logic, no. In my instincts, yes,' Bevan said.

The constable came back, dusting off his uniform.

'So we accept that Vickery can't have killed Astley,' I said. 'Isn't there a possibility that whoever killed Astley killed Helena Shilling as well?'

Bevan looked genuinely astonished. 'The man buried her.'

'Yes, but he denies killing her. Unless he's changed his story.'

Bevan shook his head.

'Somebody's been going to great trouble and expense to get his hands on George,' I said. 'Down in the country, Helena Shilling met a man at a public house a few hours before she was killed. He was angry with her. Nobody's found out who that man was, but the strong likelihood is that he was part of a kidnap attempt. Then McCloud and George play into the kidnappers' hands by going up to London and drawing attention to themselves by publishing a book. Somebody must have been close enough to the household at Northlands to know what they were going to do. Perhaps Astley had been on the kidnappers' side from the start, or perhaps they paid him enough to change sides. By your own account, he was quite capable of doing that.'

'So why was he killed?'

'Because he'd served their purpose. He'd found the boy for them.'

'So where is the boy now?'

Bevan said it as if humouring me, not accepting the theory. The answer as it took shape in my head chilled me because it was probably the truth.

'In the hands of people who've killed twice already, people who think he has the secret of Lord Byron's treasure.'

Bevan sighed, unconvinced. 'And if you're right?'

'Then you should have every man in London out looking for him.'

I knew it was unreasonable even as I said it, and wasn't surprised when Bevan shook his head. 'I can't do that. I'm investigating Astley's murder, that's all. There's no official complaint about the boy.' He tried another tack. 'To the best of your knowledge, did Mr Astley have a lady friend?'

In spite of the circumstances, I couldn't help smiling at the thought of it. 'He was very far from being an attractive man. To the best of my knowledge, no.'

'I ask because the woman who owns the house thinks he might have gone up to his rooms with a female last night.'

'She didn't say anything to me about that.'

'Delicacy, perhaps. The constable who was questioning her had the impression that she thought the woman might have been a temporary friend, so to speak. Apparently that has happened occasionally in the past. She said she half remembered two lots of footsteps on the stairs sometime in the middle of the night and one of them was lighter than a man's.'

Or a light-footed boy? I wondered that but didn't say it. He asked me a few more things about my acquaintance with Astley, none of them to the point, then let me go. The man of the lost parrot had been replaced by a woman talking about dogs. The constable at the desk looked almost as weary as I felt.

Back at Abel Yard, Mrs Martley had a note for me from McCloud: he couldn't rest so he'd gone out with Tabby to look for George. He said I shouldn't expect him back before morning. Unless he had some information that he hadn't confided to me I couldn't see that his search would amount to anything except walking the streets, but I wasn't sorry to have him off the premises. I drank soup, slept fitfully and was down at the yard in the morning when Amos arrived on a horse that looked like an ex-cavalry charger, leading Rancie. When we were across in the park I told him what had happened, including finding the shawl. As usual, his shock at the news became anger at himself for not being there. He said he'd known he should have come to High Holborn with us and he shouldn't have let me out of his sight. On the shawl, he thought it most likely that George had taken it. After some miles he calmed down and reported on what he'd found out from the jockey the evening before.

'He says a solicitor kind of a fellow turned up there early yesterday morning with a letter signed by the owner telling him to sell the rest of the horses and take his wages out of the money he gets for them.'

'And the jockey accepted it?'

'Like a seal taking a fish. He's sold them already at a knock-down price. He reckons what he got for them just about paid what he was due and, as far as he's concerned, that's it.'

'So he's not going back to the stables?'

'No reason to.'

We rode on in silence for a while, then I asked him something that had just come into my mind.

'You mentioned something about the coachman's niece and the stables. The jockey said they didn't see much of her because she wasn't that type of horsewoman. I suppose we know what he meant by that.'

Amos could blush sometimes and he did now. He's never quite accepted that my work isn't ladylike. 'I suppose we do.'

I asked if he'd happened to get a description of the niece, and there'd been no occasion for it. It was a disappointment but not a surprise. We rode in silence for a while. Something was clearly bothering him. After a while, I asked him what it was. He looked straight ahead, over the charger's ears, and for once I had to lean in to hear him.

'So if it was George that took your shawl . . .' He let his voice die away, then: 'If they'd got him and taken him to Astley, he'd have to do what he could to get away. I'm not saying that's what happened, but if it was you couldn't blame him, could you?'

I shook my head and we rode back in silence. Amos looked sorrier than if he'd killed the man himself.

Tabby was back in the yard, having given up McCloud as a bad job. It was all walking, walking with no idea what he was doing, she said. She clearly hoped I'd do better and was disappointed at first when I asked her for something quite different and, to her mind, irrelevant. Yes, of course she knew the women who worked Covent Garden. Some of them had been all right to her when she was growing up, let her look out for them and paid her a penny or two sometimes. Her mother had worked there for a while, she thought. Anyhow, she could pick up what gossip there was about anybody who'd been away and come back. She left and I went back to my office and the shawl I'd put on the table. The blood had dried by now, gluing the folds at one end of it together. The ferric smell seemed to fill the little room but there was something else as well, more delicate and almost overcome by it but not quite. I bent my head to it and sniffed. A tuberose smell, a woman's perfume but not one I'd ever used. I'd smelled it three months ago, in a villa by the sea with a storm brewing. I waited till Tabby came back, almost sure what she'd say.

'She got deported for seven years and came back again. Fair hair, natural. Some of the women have seen her since she came back, but she's not working now, at least not at the Garden. Any use?'

'A lot of use,' I said.

She looked at the shawl on the table. 'It really was yours?'

'Once.'

NINETEEN

McCloud came back halfway through the morning, tired, hungry and angry. I brewed coffee for him, sat at the parlour table and asked him where he'd been. He bit into a slice of bread and butter like a mastiff savaging a steak and swallowed.

'Everywhere.'

I didn't have to ask if he'd found anything to the purpose. The anger burning off him was against himself. When he'd gulped down his second cup of coffee he sighed, planted his elbows on the table and sank his head into his hands.

'Was it George who killed him?' His voice was muffled, as if he didn't want the idea to escape into the air.

'I don't know. I hope not.'

'So where is he?'

I said if I'd known the answer to that I'd have told him as soon as he came in. He stayed as he was for some minutes and I wondered if he'd gone to sleep, then he raised his head.

'Of all the evil luck, to have got him safely to London, money to spend and now this.'

'It wasn't luck,' I said. 'Astley had been spying on you. He probably read the letters between you and the printer. I don't suppose you kept your door locked at Northlands.'

He shook his head. 'He never seemed remotely interested in what George was doing.'

'He read your letters and knew the printers would be the first place you made for in London, so he had somebody watching the place and trailing you home after that first visit. Then he organized for a man and a woman to go and collect George when you were away.'

'With a false message from me.'

'Probably, yes.' I decided not to mention to him another possibility. Emilia had been close to George for some of the time on Cephalonia. Her voice might have been enough to draw him away again. 'They deliver him to Astley at his lodgings then the murder happens.'

'And George goes where? He'd be scared, bloodstained. He can't see. He doesn't know anybody in London.'

He was staring at me as if he thought I could still produce George if I tried. His confidence had drained away and he looked younger and defeated. There wasn't much I could have said to comfort him but I wasn't intending to in any case. I thought there were still things he hadn't told me. I let the silence draw out, listening to the clanging of metal from Mr Grindley's forge.

After a long time, he sighed. 'I have not been entirely frank with you.'

'No, I didn't think you had.'

'I haven't told you anything that's untrue, but there's something I left out. I told you we knew about the letters in London from the woman who said she was his mother. What I didn't tell you was that I saw her down at Northlands.'

'What! When?'

'The Saturday afternoon, before the night when she was killed. George was with Ridgeway so I was out walking on my own. There's an old summerhouse on the edge of the garden I went to sometimes when I wanted to be undisturbed. I was sitting there thinking and suddenly there was this woman in front of me. She must have moved quietly. I don't even know what direction she came from. She just sat down beside me and said, "You're George's tutor. I'm his mother". Quite quietly, like a statement of fact, no drama at all. I suppose I just stared at first and she smiled – a stiff sort of smile. I said was she the one who wrote the letters and she said yes. I asked what she wanted and she said, "I want to see my son". I could hardly believe what I was hearing. George and I had talked so much about her and here she was. When I got my wits back I said that would be difficult because of Vickery and she said she'd wait at night, in the lane by the old cottage. She wasn't quite sure when she'd be there but it would be late, sometime after midnight. She knew George would want to see her and she believed that I was his friend. She was sure I could manage it for him. She . . . seemed so certain I could do it. I wanted to help her. I made no promises but I said I'd tell George and see what he wanted to do. I knew, though, that he'd be desperate to see her. So she stood up, wished me goodbye and went. She went in the direction of the back lane but the path goes round a corner and I soon lost sight of her. So I walked back and told George and of course nothing would content him except seeing her, only it was difficult because Vickery had practically put the place into a state of siege.'

'With you and Mr Ridgeway guarding George.'

McCloud laughed. 'Oh, Ridgeway was never a problem to us. He's no great drinker but he always had a little glass of port to take up to bed with him to settle his stomach. I keep some laudanum for when I can't sleep. A few drops of laudanum in that and he was dead to the world. I used it several times when George and I wanted to stay up and talk.'

'But the house was guarded back and front and . . . You two got out, didn't you? How?'

'Vickery was putting his guards on from midnight so we knew we had to get out before that. He thought George was safely penned up with Ridgeway sleeping on one side and me on the other. We waited until Ridgeway was snoring – sometime after eleven, that would have been – and went out by the back door. Nobody saw us. I knew we might have to wait some time so I bundled up blankets and some food. We went over the fields in case Legge was listening out at the stables. I know those fields from walking over them, and for George night is as good as day. I had a lantern but didn't use it until we were well clear of the house. We must have got to the cottage sometime around midnight. There was nobody waiting in the lane so I persuaded George to come inside the cottage and we made ourselves as comfortable as we could. George was on edge, worrying that we'd already missed her but I said she'd be there. We kept looking out of the window. I suppose I just expected her to appear on foot, the way she had at the summerhouse. It never occurred to me she'd drive up in a carriage.'

'But that's what happened?'

'Yes. I think I might have dozed, then George dug me in the ribs. He was quivering like a pointer. He'd heard something. My hearing isn't as good as his but after a while I heard it too.

Wheels coming up the lane from the road, quite slowly, then hooves and harness creaking. I'd let the lamp go out by then, but I lit it and got out my watch. Quarter past two. I'll be honest with you – this was the point when I knew we shouldn't be there. Up to then I'd thought there could be no harm, the two of us and one woman meeting in the lane. Even if she had tried to get George away, there'd have been no chance against me, no danger. But a vehicle meant more than one person, her and a driver, at least, and what was more important, the possibility of hustling George away. I could imagine it – he goes trustingly out there in the dark, they bundle him into the carriage or whatever it is, and that's it. Vickery's worry about kidnapping didn't look so ridiculous any more and here I was, practically handing George over to them. Of course, he wasn't thinking any of that. He was making for the door, going out. I had to wrestle with him to stop him. He was kicking, biting, everything. In the end I got him on the floor and told him to wait a bit, at least until I'd looked out and seen what was there. I did and the carriage had come to a stop outside. There was a driver on the box. It had a candle lamp on the front and there must have been a lamp of some kind inside because the door was open and I could see the silhouette of a man standing by it. He wore a tall hat and, I think, a cloak. I couldn't see if there was anybody inside. Then he went inside the carriage and the door closed and I'd started to say to George that we should go back, then it happened. A shot.'

He ran his hands through his hair and took in a deep breath.

'So what did you do then?'

'Went back. George was all for going on down there in spite of it. I didn't know what had happened, whether she'd shot the man or the other way around. I had to get hold of his arm and practically march him back across the fields, and at some point I lost my way. I suppose I was rattled at what had happened. It must have been after four when we came to the house and my first thought was to get George safe and inside. Then I saw somebody pacing up and down outside and knew it was Vickery. I came to my senses and thought what would happen if he saw us. The whole story would come out, I'd be dismissed on the spot for putting George in danger and it would all be over. So we went round to the back and my mind started moving again. I remembered hearing Vickery's great plan and thinking Astley on the back door wouldn't be much use so I told George to wait, picked up a chisel that was lying there and started scraping away at the back-door lock. Just as I hoped, Astley didn't come to the door and just started ringing his alarm bell. So of course Vickery and everybody else rushed to the back door and we went round and in at the front. By the time Vickery called up to tell George to stay where he was, we were back in our bedrooms. Then, of course, we heard later that she was dead and you'd found her.'

Silence. Even the metal hammering had stopped. A late fly was jittering around the window. Did I believe him?

'You do realize this means Mr Vickery has a defence against killing her?' I said.

He nodded. 'I didn't at the time, especially when he buried her. I thought he could have left the house and been the man I saw. But I've been less and less sure about that.'

'He was in the house until four, long after you heard the shot.'

'He could have paid somebody else, I suppose.'

'Possibly. But he's a man who likes to keep things in his own hands.' Another question was stirring in my mind but I wasn't sure why I asked it. 'The woman who claimed to be his mother – what did she look like?'

He considered. 'Small, pretty, almost beautiful, and not as old as I expected. When I saw her, I thought that if she was George's mother she must have had him when she was very young. Ladylike, but somehow not entirely a lady.'

I tried to keep my voice casual for the next question. 'Dark hair?'

He shook his head. 'No, very fair. There were quite a lot of curls outside her bonnet.'

'At Astley's rooms yesterday, you said you'd never seen a dead body close to before. So you didn't see the woman from the coach properly before they buried her?'

He shook his head vigorously. 'Not close to, no. Just the shape.'

I wondered whether to tell him that it was Emilia and not Helena Shilling who'd come to him in the garden and decided it would be too complicated. So it was a certainty that she'd been at Northlands on the night that Helena Shilling died, a near certainty that she'd been the woman who took George away.

'You do realize that if you told your story to the police, they might release Mr Vickery?' I said.

'No.' A protest against having anything to do with the police, then a more considered reaction. 'It doesn't prove he didn't know about it. In any case, it's finding George that matters now. If they've kidnapped him, they'll have to send some sort of ransom demand, won't they? But who to?'

I knew it wasn't an ordinary kidnapping that was in question. Emilia must have been as convinced of the treasure as her late almost-husband and found her way to Astley, a fellow believer. If it seemed unlikely that they could be so credulous, I only had to think of the list of people who'd been cheated of their money in Geoffrey Panter's fraud to remember that where money's concerned, greed unbalances judgement. I tried to think myself into Emilia's place. She'd delivered George to Astley and Astley was dead. The landlady thought she'd heard the footsteps of Astley and a woman on the stairs but suppose Astley was in his rooms already and what she'd heard was Emilia taking George up to him, unprotestingly because he knew Emilia. So three of them in the room, Astley, Emilia and George and Astley dies. Emilia hustles George away.

McCloud was looking at me, waiting for an answer to his question but I gave him another question instead.

'When you were walking round, did you go back to High Holborn?'

He nodded. 'I walked up and down for a while on the pavement opposite, then a constable came past and I thought he looked at me suspiciously so I walked on.'

'Did you talk to anybody?'

He hadn't. He was a young man in a strange city, scared and out of his depth.

'We're going back there now,' I said. 'It's a busy street. They can't have got away without somebody seeing them.'

It took us nearly four hours and in that time we – meaning mostly I – must have spoken to a hundred or more people, crossing sweepers, shopkeepers, pie- and fish-sellers, legal clerks, nursemaids, beggars, loitering lads and a man with a barrel organ and a monkey. I paid out a pocketful of loose change, met with more friendliness than otherwise, but for three and a half hours found nobody with any recollection of a good-looking woman and a blind boy. By the time McCloud and I were back almost opposite the house where Astley had died I was discouraged and he looked entirely hopeless.

'So what do we do now?'

Next to us was a house that looked as if it had been empty for some time. Tufts of grass were growing in the earth, manure had been blown on to the front doorstep and the windows were tightly shuttered. We'd ignored it on our search for Astley because it was so clearly uninhabited. A flight of weed-grown steps led down from the pavement to a semicircular paved area outside the windows of the basement. I pointed to some crushed weeds on the steps. Somebody had been up or down recently. McCloud was halfway down the steps before me but came to a sudden stop. Looking over his shoulder, I saw that a pile of rags against the basement wall was pulling itself slowly upright. A face looked out of them, pale and bearded with vague eyes trying to focus on us. When he was sitting up the pile became an approximately triangular shape of many shawls and blankets swathed on top of each other, brown, off-white and tartan. He wore two dark-coloured caps, one on top of the other.

'This place is taken. It's let. I am the caretaker.' The voice was weak and surprisingly gentle. A man from out in the country, by the sound of it. McCloud turned to look at me questioningly then stepped down into the basement. It was surprisingly orderly, with a range of bags lined up on either side of the man and a makeshift canvas canopy above, now folded, that might be pulled down in case of rain. 'I don't go inside, you see. It's illegal if you break the lock and go inside.'

By the look of it, the rusty lock on the basement door could have been broken by breathing on it hard. The man had his own morality.

'We don't want to disturb you,' I said. 'We're trying to find somebody who might have gone past the night before last.'

'A great many people go past. I see their feet all the time.'
He looked up towards the pavement. We followed his look
and saw what he meant. A pair of man's shoes went past,
neat and polished. Then a woman's boots just visible under
an old brown skirt, scuffed, and beside them a pair of child's
shoes, too big for the feet inside them, dragging as the child
was hurried along.

'They're late today,' the man commented. 'That's why she's
hurrying.'

I stared at him. Surely there was no watch under that heap
of blankets. 'How do you know?'

'I have my regulars.'

'The night before yesterday,' I said, 'a woman and a young
blind man.' It seemed hopeless.

'Blind?' He looked at me, something alive in his eyes. 'Could
have been. Out with a woman he wasn't used to.'

'What? You remember?'

'In the dark. I don't know what time it was. They stopped,
just by the railings here, and woke me up. I think he must have
stumbled and perhaps nearly pulled her over because his voice
came from near the pavement at first and he said she didn't
need to keep hold of his arm, just walk close to him. He seemed
to think she'd be angry with him because then he said he didn't
mean to, several times over, then he said it was his fault, almost
crying. She said to stop talking about it and come on.'

'Which direction?'

He gestured westwards. That might mean towards Covent
Garden among other places.

'You can't remember any more about them?'

'I wouldn't have remembered that, except when you said he
was blind I thought that explained it.'

I gave him a few coins and thanked him and we left.

'It's the same woman,' McCloud said. 'Who is she?'

'A whore who got transported and came back.' He gulped
but I was too tired and too worried to be concerned about
proprieties. 'She thinks George is the key to a lot of money.
She's wrong but that's not what matters now.'

'Where will we find them?' A hopeless question so I didn't
answer it. After a few steps he asked where we were going and

I said back to Abel Yard. It was just possible that Tabby would be back with some rag of information, though I doubted it. I was thinking about George stumbling, repeating *I didn't mean to*. The scene was becoming all too clear in my mind. Emilia delivers George to Astley, waiting for them in his room. Astley starts questioning him, probably with threats, about the location of Byron's mythical treasure and George panics and kills him. Did Emilia try to prevent him? At any rate, she wasn't going to let a small thing like murder distract her from money. She'd probably seen a lot worse in her career. George goes away with her more or less willingly, in a state of shock. I knew that even with Astley dead she was not acting alone. There'd been the unidentified man at the public house near Northlands, the same man or another one with her when she took George from his lodgings in London. McCloud's disastrous decision to bring George to London had delivered him to them. My heart bled for the boy taken from his island for this.

Back at Abel Yard, Tabby was waiting for us, downcast. 'Nobody around the Garden's seen her for two or three days. Some reckon she's found somebody with money and is sticking to him, some say she's taken herself off abroad again. She shares a room for trade with another woman but she's not seen her either.'

'We're going to Mr Vickery's house,' I said. 'Food first.'

We snatched a hasty tea of bread and cold meat in the parlour, with Mrs Martley keeping an eye on Tabby all the time, presumably to make sure she didn't steal the spoons. I couldn't convince her that Tabby would never steal from us, and that if she did take an unaccountable fancy to our worn cutlery no power on earth would protect it. I left McCloud in Mrs Martley's care, claiming that somebody had to wait at home in case there were any messages. As we crossed the park towards Knightsbridge, I explained to Tabby that it was in my mind that Jolly might know more about Emilia than he'd admitted. For one thing, we needed to know whether he'd been away from the house a lot. I'd speak to him directly and she could get into conversation with some of the other servants there to check if he were speaking the truth. When we came to the house she went round to the back while I knocked on the front door. A hoarse voice from inside asked who was there. I had to shout my name twice before the door was opened by Jolly himself. He looked sick, his round cheeks sunken and dark bags under his eyes. The hall and stairs hadn't been swept for days.

'I'm sorry about the wait, Mrs Carmichael. There's tradespeople trying to send in the duns. Word's got round he's in prison.' I walked in and he shut the door quickly behind me. 'Any news?'

'Can we talk?'

He led the way into a downstairs room and hardly waited until I was sitting down before collapsing into a chair himself. In other circumstances the action of a servant making himself at home in one of the family rooms might have seemed defiant, but this time it looked more like simple weariness.

'They've all gone, apart from the cook and the boot boy. There's no money left to pay them. I've already pawned some of the silver.'

It struck me how quickly Vickery's establishments collapsed when he wasn't there to fill them with his energy. It was all part of his rootlessness. He listened, not taking his eyes off my face, while I told him about finding McCloud and so nearly finding George. If he didn't know, there seemed no harm in telling him. He gave no sign that he did. I said nothing about Astley's death.

He sighed. 'So they've got the boy.'

'They?'

'The same ones who were trying to take him back at Northlands.'

'And you don't know who, apart from Emilia?'

'I'd be wondering about McCloud.'

'He seems desperate that George has gone.'

'Easy to seem.'

Three different clocks in the room had stopped at three different times, with nobody to bother winding them. It seemed that whatever force had been driving Jolly had run down too. When I asked him where he'd been over the last few days he showed no annoyance and not much interest.

'Here all the time. We can't stir out because of the duns. Some of the time I've been playing cards for pennies with the cook and the footman and maid from next door. Apart from that, just waiting. I sleep in a chair by the front door.' He looked at me from under his eyelids. 'Are you thinking I had something to do with taking the boy? I would be, in your place.'

'Did you?'

He shook his head. 'I'm Mr Vickery's man through and through. I like the boy. If I could do anything to find him, I'd do it.'

'McCloud told me George had nightmares,' I said.

He revived a little, frowning. 'You didn't need him to tell you that. I was helping Mr Vickery deal with George's nightmares before he came on the scene. Night after night, he'd wake up terrified, screaming at somebody not to get him. Once he even picked up the little knife we kept for trimming candlewicks and stabbed me with it, got me in the throat too, thinking I was whoever he was scared of. Pretty good for a blind lad. I've still got the scar.'

He pulled down his cravat. It looked as if he hadn't taken it off for days. I went over to him and saw a pink scar about two inches long just to one side of his Adam's apple.

'When did this happen?'

'Months ago, at an inn in Italy when we were on our way back from Cephalonia. We told George I'd cut myself when my razor slipped. Mr Vickery didn't want him to know. In the morning, he was the same polite young gentleman he usually was, not remembering anything.'

'Who was it had scared him so much?'

'From the look on his face, you'd say it was the Devil.'

I thought of George in Astley's room, blind and imprisoned. Another nightmare and a more effective knife. Jolly was leaning back with his eyes closed. I asked him if he'd talked much to Emilia Panter when they were on Cephalonia.

'Not a lot, no. She was Mr Vickery's guest, worse luck. He knew what she was but Panter had brought her along and that was that. I knew about her and George, but I thought at his age it would either be her or somebody worse and at least it kept him on the premises.'

'You didn't like Emilia?'

'Not much before Panter died and not at all after that. I reckon she had something to do with him drowning.'

'Did she ever talk to you about places in England she knew?'

He shook his head. 'No call for it. I'm seeing Mr Vickery today, taking him clean linen. That's where one of the silver spoons went – the laundry bill. The trial comes off next month. When you came, I thought you might have some good news for him about finding George.'

I shook my head. 'Tell him what I've told you, if you like.'

'I'll do that.'

Something was beginning to stir in my mind. 'Mr Vickery can write and receive letters?'

'He can get them because they haven't found him guilty yet. I don't know if he can write letters out.'

'If I wrote a note for you to take in, he could tell you the answer?'

'Suppose so.'

A writing desk in the corner turned out to have paper inside and a residue of ink in the inkwell that was just usable with much stirring. Jolly showed no curiosity as I wrote a couple of blurry lines, blotted them and folded the paper over. I didn't bother to seal it because he could read it if he wanted. He took it without much interest and put it away in his jacket. Since he showed no sign of moving I let myself out and went to find Tabby. She was in the backyard of the house next door, talking to a plump girl with a great swirl of dark hair under her maid's cap. I waited by the gate till she finished and came to join me.

'She says he hasn't left the house for three or four days. Her and the footman were playing cards with him on Wednesday night. She left about midnight, she thinks. She'd won sevenpence off them by then and wanted to keep it. The footman stayed with Jolly, though. She says he staggered back at just about daylight the next morning, still half drunk and smelling of tobacco, and got a shilling stopped from his wages because he'd burned a hole in his uniform.'

As we were walking along the pavement, Tabby asked me what we did next. I said I had no notion.

'What's in my mind is Covent Garden,' she said. 'So far, most of what we know about the people who wanted George comes from near there.' She was right, I thought, the lodgings in Chandos Street, Perkins' Yard. Even where Helena Shilling had lodged wasn't so far away. Emilia, before her transportation, had worked her beat there.

'It's still a big place.'

'Not so big. And people stick near what they know.'

It seemed a wide trawl to me, but Tabby knew the area completely from the time she could stagger a few steps and hold out a hand for coins. If even a cabbage leaf got moved from its place in the gutter she'd have known about it as a child and a few years in Abel Yard wouldn't have taken away the knowledge.

'I'd be no use to you there, would I?' I said.

'Nah. See you when there's anything to say then.'

And she was gone, disappearing into the crowds by the carriage drive in a few steps. I walked back slowly across the park, playing over my conversation with Jolly, wondering whether I should have told Tabby that finding George might just be the start of new troubles.

TWENTY

On Saturday morning, McCloud and I discussed again whether to do anything about Vickery and decided, for the present, against it. I thought I could persuade Sergeant Bevan to listen to McCloud's story about what he'd seen on the night Helena Shilling died and if he believed it Vickery might be released. But it was a big if, and in any case Vickery was still guilty on the charge of burying her body. Best to leave him where he was for the present. I hoped he'd reply to my note. It might not help but I couldn't think of anything else that would. Amos was busy at the stables most of the day but managed to get to Abel Yard and report.

'I've ridden over to Perkins' Yard a couple of times. It's empty as a blown egg with a *To Let* notice on the gate. Nobody knows where Simmonds has gone and even the jockey's disappeared now there are no horses to look after. I had a proper look round it because it struck me it was as good a place as any to hide the boy, upstairs and down – all the boxes, the feed bins, the hay store. A few grains of barley, a couple of armfuls of bad hay and that was it. Apart from this, what he'd left in the tack room: an engagements diary. I don't suppose it's any use but I thought I might as well bring it.'

He put a battered accounts book with stained covers and buffed corners down on the mounting block, vaulted on his horse and went, promising to look in again the next day. I had the house to myself because McCloud had taken himself off again on one of his useless walks, Tabby was presumably in Covent Garden and Mrs Martley out shopping. For want of anything better to do, I took the book up to my office and went through it. It was a combination of engagements diary and accounts book, with various times and dates listed and sums of money beside them, usually for a few pounds, sometimes as much as ten pounds. If the ladies and gentlemen who'd hired coaches from Perkins' Yard wanted anonymity they'd been

pretty well served because most of them were simply represented
by initials, Mr C.D., Mrs Y, Sir T.S. Sometimes, but not always,
the distances travelled and the time waited were recorded, but
not always. I turned up the dates when Helena Shilling had
written that she'd be waiting in a carriage in Whitehall and
there they both were, to Mrs H.S., but no record of payment.
The second of them was almost the last entry on the list, followed
by one trip for Mr C.D. to Greenwich. After that the list stopped
halfway down the page, with no entry for Helena Shilling's trip
to Muswell Hill. I wondered if she'd travelled there alone or if
Emilia had been with her and possibly the unknown man who'd
quarrelled with her in the public house near Muswell Hill. The
same man, equally possibly, who'd shot Helena in the carriage.
The same man, also possibly, who'd collected George from his
lodgings to deliver him to Astley. Emilia certainly had one male
accomplice besides Astley but there was no sign of either of
them in the book. I tried to work out when Emilia would have
arrived back in England. Panter had drowned in May and
Vickery's party had come back soon afterwards. Two months,
say, so she might be back in England by August. It was a fallow
time in the engagements book, probably with most of their
regular or irregular clients out of town and only five bookings
in the entire month. Four of them had, as usual, initials, desti-
nations and the amount paid beside them. The fifth had
no destination and no price, simply the initials A.F. I leafed
back through the book and found nothing like it. No reason to
think that it had anything to do with the bereaved Emilia's
arrival back in England. Still, it nagged at me as I closed the
book and pigeonholed it.

Later in the day, with McCloud back and Mrs Martley making
a pie, a letter arrived from Jolly, brought by the boot boy.
Naturally Jolly himself would be reluctant to leave the house
undefended, apart from visiting Vickery. His writing was small
and neat, the letter longer than I expected.

Dear Mrs Carmichael,
I saw Mr Vickery. He is so downcast about George that I
didn't tell him all you told me, only that you are still
looking and there is no trace of him. He begs – that was

*his word – you to continue and to get word to him if there
are any developments. He showed me the note you sent
him and said I was to tell you this. He saw no harm in
Emilia, not at first. He was pretty sure she wasn't married
to Panter, otherwise Peters, but didn't say anything about
it. He's never been a man for church services and suchlike.
He says quite soon after she arrived she made an approach
to him – you'll understand what he meant by that, I'm
sure – which he resisted in case it should create bad blood
with Panter, all of them living in the same house. He never
knew for sure until now about her and George. Today he
asked me outright for the first time – were they? I said
yes they were, but only a few times, I thought. He was
angry about that now and says she's a w—, which of
course is the case, but not really surprised on account
of George is young and his father's son. At first, before
he knew what she was, he did talk to her quite a bit and
remembers she said she grew up on a farm somewhere
not far north of London but doesn't think she mentioned
exactly where, or he might have forgotten. The last thing
he said to me that I was to tell you to keep looking,
whatever happens. Yours respectfully, Hector Jolly.*

The idea of Emilia as a girl from the farm was diverting. If
it were true, she'd obviously left the place as soon as possible
and gone a long way – even if the far side of the world had
not been in her original plans. Still, the letter was no help at
all in finding her. It was now three days since George had
disappeared and we were no nearer finding him. Amos joined
us soon after it got dark, equally baffled. He, McCloud and I
sat drinking tea, not even talking because there seemed to be
nothing left to say. When Tabby's whistle sounded from the
yard I went down and brought her up to join us, not hoping for
anything. It seemed as if I was right because she had no progress
to report on finding Emilia or anybody who'd seen a blind boy,
apart from a blind beggar in the market who was a good twenty
years too old. In spite of that, she seemed less depressed than
the three of us and, after gulping down two cups of tea, well
sugared, she started telling us the gossip of the market.

'There's one of the porters got his foot hurt, quite bad. A wagon ran over it, cut his boot open, took off two of his toes and he'll maybe have to lose another one. The other porters had a collection for him because he won't be able to work for a while and raised over two pounds, even though it was partly his fault.'

'I suppose he slipped and went under a wheel,' I said, not very much interested.

'Nah, he was asleep when it happened. He'd had too much to drink after work so he rolled up in some sacks under one of the carts. He must have left his leg sticking out but nobody thought that mattered because it was quite late at night and this was where they left the empty carts that wouldn't move off till morning and he'd be awake then. But somebody drove one of the other carts out in the night and went over his foot. Of course, he yelled blue murder but the driver of the cart either didn't hear him or didn't care because he just drove off.'

'What would anybody be driving an empty farm cart at night for?' Amos said, sounding more interested than I was. 'Either the farmers turn them straight round and go back in a day, or if it's a longer journey they wait for daylight.'

The heavy carts that farmers used for bringing vegetables to market, pulled by draught horses taking time off from the plough, were below Amos's usual sphere of equine activity, but anything with hooves or wheels interested him.

'That's what everybody's asking,' Tabby said. Something in her voice caught my attention.

'When did you say this happened?'

'Last night, after midnight. People have been asking around all day who the cart belonged to but nobody seems to know and there's not a horse missing from anywhere in the market.'

'I'll have a word around,' Amos said. 'A farm cart out that late, somebody will have noticed which way it went.'

McCloud, Tabby and I went to our beds and Saturday passed with no news at all. McCloud went out early walking and came back late, again with nothing to report except one possible sighting that had turned out to be a blind girl and her mother, very respectable and suspicious of his interest. I stayed in and

tried without much success to think. It was terrible to imagine
what Emilia and her confederate, or confederates, might be
doing to George to make him reveal a secret that he'd never
had. But I couldn't get it out of my mind that even if we found
him, there was still Astley's murder to answer. On Sunday
morning – a day when we didn't normally ride – Amos arrived
on a cob with Rancie and, although I had no heart for it, I
couldn't refuse. He turned north and we walked our horses side
by side, elm leaves flying past us on a west wind.

'I've been spending a lot of time around the market,' he said.
'Tabby's been a big help. We started at the centre and worked
outwards. I haven't done so much walking since we were
rounding up the sheep back home.' I felt guilty that they'd been
doing what I should have been doing. We cantered for a while
then he picked up his story. 'It turned out I was right. A farm
cart out so late did get noticed by a few people. Somebody saw
one going up St John's Street at about one in the morning,
empty and at a trot, though not a very fast one. Now, if you're
making for the country from there, it takes you to the Islington
Road, and on the Islington Road, near the reservoir and just as
you come out in the country, there's a toll gate. I know that
toll gate a bit. The keeper'll get out of his bed and open up for
any of the big coaches but he's not going to bother with a cart
that only pays a few pence anyway, arriving there around two
in the morning. He'll take his time, let it wait. So I went back
to the stables, got a horse and rode out for a talk with him, and
it turns out I was right. A farm cart did arrive there in the early
hours of Friday, while the gate was closed, and instead of
waiting quiet and peaceful, the driver of it made a fuss.
According to the toll keeper, he was hammering on the door,
shouting "open up" as if he was a duke with a carriage and
four instead of a cart with a spavined old nag. In the end he's
making such a row that the keeper gets up and has an argument
with him, and it ends with the driver throwing a sovereign to
the keeper to open the gates, which he does, though not with
very good grace.'

'A farmer, throwing sovereigns around!'

'Yes, not very likely, is it? And according to the toll keeper
he sounded more like a gentleman than a farmer. In the end he

decided it was probably some daft form of a race, went back
to bed and that was it.'

'Did you get a description of the driver?'

'It was dark and he had the hood of his cloak up.
Ordinary-looking sort of man, the keeper thought. I asked him
if there was anybody else with the cart and he said no, it was
empty apart from some old sacks and baskets in the back.'

'Anyone can be hidden under sacks. Did the driver say where
he was going?'

'No, and the toll keeper couldn't be bothered to ask.'

Jolly's letter was in my mind, and Emilia telling Vickery that
she'd grown up on a farm to the north of London. The toll gate,
on the Islington Road, was to the north.

'I've got ladies to take out this morning,' Amos said. 'After
that, there's a carriage with a couple I'm settling to pull together
could do with a trip out in the country.'

'Carriage?' I felt ready now to put my heel to Rancie's side
and speed straight to the Islington Road.

'That way, Tabby can come with us and the Scottish fellow
too, if he wants,' Amos said.

I had doubts about taking McCloud anywhere in his mental
state but goodness knows what he'd do if left on his own. We
cut short our ride and Amos said he'd collect us in the carriage
as soon as he could get away in the afternoon. I found Tabby
and McCloud and told them we might at last have a line to
follow.

TWENTY-ONE

I t was mid-afternoon before we left because one of Amos's
ladies had suffered a fall in the park, not serious but the
cause of much weeping and wailing. By the time we were
out on the Islington Road with Amos and Tabby up on the box
and two young bays in front of us it was five o'clock, with not
enough daylight left for much in the way of serious investiga-
tion that day, but Amos knew of an inn some ten miles out
where we could put up for the night and ask questions. For all
of us, moving somewhere was a necessity after three days of
getting nowhere. We stopped briefly at the toll gate to pay our
dues and I talked to the keeper in the unlikely hope that I'd get
more out of him, but his story was exactly as told to Amos.
After the toll gate we were well out in the country with few
people to be seen because the labourers were mostly shut up
in their cottages. McCloud stared out of the windows as if the
simple intensity of looking could produce George from the
stubble fields and the hedges loaded with sloes and blackberries.
We passed several dozen lanes or farm paths where a cart might
have turned off and some of them had quite fresh tracks in the
mud, but since the countryside was full of innocent carters we
decided to press on to the inn in the hope that somebody there
might have noticed our cart going past in the early hours of
Saturday morning. If not, we'd work back over the various
tracks in the morning. Amos reckoned that, even with an empty
cart, a draught horse wouldn't have pulled much more than ten
miles out of the city. The inn when we came to it was rough
but welcoming, with a big room upstairs for Tabby and myself,
a smaller one for Amos and McCloud and stabling for the bays.
We had supper with the four of us together round a big, battered
table – good ham and eggs – and asked questions of the
landlord. He was a large man with a small head, red face and
protuberant stomach, making him look like a cheerful fairground
toy, and he was ready to talk. He assumed that we were following

the farm cart because it had been stolen and, although obviously puzzled that such an unlikely quartet as ourselves should be concerned with it, was as helpful as he could be. Unfortunately, that didn't amount to much. One thing he was certain of was that it had not passed his inn in the early hours of Saturday. His wife suffered from toothache, he said, and she'd kept him awake groaning all night. They'd hardly closed their eyes. Their bedroom looked out on the road and he was quite sure he'd have heard anything going past, especially a heavy farm cart. So somewhere between the turnpike gate and the inn it must have turned off, eight miles or so and a lot of farms and small-holdings. Luckily, he knew every farm and their owners for miles around, as they were mostly his customers. He stood there as we ate, counting them off on his fingers.

'There's the Dews at High Farm and his daughter and son-in-law at Little High – that's on your left as you go out from town. Then Meredith at Burnt Oak on the other side, the Joneses at Far Farm, though they're nearer in than the Pollards at Eastley and the Dicksons at Ashfield, then old Dexter at White Posts . . .'

'Just a minute,' I said, hastily swallowing a forkful of egg. 'What was the one before last?'

'Dicksons at Ashfield Farm.'

The appointments book with its initials came into my mind. A.F. 'What are they like, the Dicksons?'

'Quiet enough, middling well-off, farms over a hundred acres, mostly cattle, a few sheep, some acres of oats and barley. His wife brews the next best beer in the district after us so we don't see him in here much. Besides, he's getting on, in his seventies, we reckon.'

'Has he a son?' McCloud said.

The urgency of the question and McCloud's Edinburgh accent made the landlord blink. 'They've never been able to have children. There's a nephew but he's in London.'

I sensed a closing up about him. We were strangers after all and there was something here he didn't want to talk about. 'If you're wondering, Dickson's not the man to go stealing farm carts. He's a churchwarden – has been for years.'

He cleared the plates and left. Tabby went out and Amos

asked us to excuse him and went too. I knew he'd gone to
smoke his pipe in the stable yard and, after giving him some
time on his own, went out to join him. I followed the scent and
gleam of the pipe to the corner where the bays were stabled.

'The nephew in London,' Amos said.

'Simmonds, from Perkins' Yard?'

'That's what I wondered. It's far enough out for him to come
and hide.'

'And Emilia's his niece. But can you imagine a churchwarden
sheltering a pair like that?'

'Families are funny things,' Amos said. 'I'll find out first
thing tomorrow where Ashfield Farm is.'

'About a mile and a half back down the road, left-hand side
as you're going towards London. I asked the kitchen maid.'
Tabby's voice came out of the darkness inside the loose box.
'We going for a look now?'

I should have said that we'd wait till morning. It was quite
dark, no moon, and we were in unknown country. But the
restlessness that came from days without success had me in its
grip and when Amos said, 'I might, at any rate', I told him that
there was no question of going alone. Tabby and I went up to
get our cloaks and change into outdoor shoes. I was wearing
my plainest and most durable clothes and had thought to bring
my burglar's lantern with the sliding shutter. We talked and
moved quietly so as not to alert McCloud, who presumably had
gone to his room upstairs. Without discussing it we'd decided
that he'd be more of a liability than a help, but when we came
on to the landing there he was, fully dressed, so we had to
explain what was happening.

'You two stay here. I'll go with Mr Legge.'

The look Tabby gave him was answer enough so the three
of us went together downstairs. The landlord was surprised that
we were going out after supper but I told him we wanted to
take the air. From the look on his face he was beginning to
have doubts about us. The air outside was cold and moist but
not actually raining. Amos came from the stable yard to meet
us and we set out on the road back towards London. We left
my lamp unlit to save the candle for later and the darkness was
so nearly total that even Tabby had difficulty recognizing the

landmarks she'd been given – a pair of cottages standing back from the road, a milestone and finally a group of trees and a gate opposite the turning to Ashfield Farm.

'Are those things oaks?' I went close up and confirmed that they were. 'It's the opening just opposite then.'

I struck a flint, got the lantern going with some trouble and adjusted it so that only a narrow beam of light showed. It was enough to pick out the opening of a track between tall hedges, muddy underfoot.

'Cart tracks,' Amos said. 'But then there would be.'

The farmhouse wasn't visible from the road. Amos and I went first, with McCloud and Tabby following. The mud was deep and at some points came over the top of my shoes, so my stockings were cold and clammy. Our pace was slow and the path seemed never-ending, turning round a couple of bends with nothing in front of us but blackness. Then, at last, round another bend, a bar of light was below us that was probably faint enough but looked bright against the darkness. The farmhouse was down in a dip. We stopped and it gradually took shape as a more substantial block of darkness, quite large with smoke coming up from one chimney and more dark shapes around it that were probably barns. The light we could see was probably from a lamp-lit room, partly cut off by a curtain. We stared down at the residence of Mr Dickson, farmer and churchwarden. A dog barked, just two sharp barks and probably nothing to do with us yet, but it was a reminder that once we followed the path down towards the house there'd probably be a whole chorus of barking from several farm dogs. People don't pay calls after dark in the country, especially not strangers. To go on down the path would be a declaration that we were suspicious, even hostile, and we had no reason to think Mr Dickson deserved it.

'I could say I'd had an accident up on the road and wanted to borrow a spade to dig my wheel out of a bank,' Amos said. 'That way, I should get a look to see if Simmonds is there.'

'And what if he is? He'll recognize you from the park and if they've brought George here they'll get him away again. The same goes for me.'

'He's never seen me,' McCloud said.

Amos and I looked at him and I knew we were both thinking the same thing. We still weren't completely sure about McCloud and even at best his temperament seemed too excitable for such work. On the other hand, he'd be very convincing as an innocent in trouble in the country. After our muddy tramp along the path almost anything seemed better than returning with no questions answered.

'Don't take any risks,' I said. 'If there's any hostility at all, or even if they don't answer the door, come straight back. The man we're looking for is of middle years with a badly pock-marked face.'

'Just in case they offer to help dig you out, accept it,' Amos said. 'I'll meet you on the way and tell you I've managed to get the carriage out and not to worry, thank you.'

Tabby offered to go down with him and wait near the house but I decided the three of us should stay together. I gave McCloud the lantern, repeated the warning about not taking risks and watched as the darkness swallowed him and the lantern beam. About ten minutes after he'd left us, several dogs started barking.

'For it now, any road,' Amos said.

He sounded worried and so was I, more than half regretting we'd let McCloud go. We watched the light from the house's window and waited. The dogs were still tearing their throats out with barking, so we probably wouldn't hear when McCloud knocked on the door. It was strange, when I thought about it, that nobody had come out to see to the dogs. I thought it must be about twenty minutes since McCloud had left us, though I hadn't bothered to burrow through layers of clothing to the watch in my skirt pocket. Surely he'd be at the door by now. After half an hour or so, Amos said, 'He should be on his way back.'

'They didn't open the door to him. We'd have seen the light from it.'

'The door might be round at the side. Maybe they're giving him tea and a warm seat by the fire.'

It was a possibility, but I didn't think Amos believed it. Tabby said nothing, just waited. Some time afterwards I voiced what had been going round in my head almost since McCloud went.

'Suppose we were wrong about him. Suppose he's with the kidnappers.'

Amos took a long breath. 'If he is, he'll have told them that we're here. But he couldn't have depended on us sending him down there first. He'd have to be out of the common cool and clever.'

'Somebody is,' I said.

From far away, a church clock was striking. I didn't catch all the strokes but there were a lot of them – it was probably eleven or midnight. When I glanced down at the house, the one light from a window had gone out and it was in total darkness.

'I'm going down there.'

Amos was moving as he spoke but I went with him, down the path towards the house, sliding on mud. I heard Tabby following us. The barking had decreased over the past half hour or so, probably because the dogs were tired, but now it started up again. They must surely be tied up or they'd have been on us. Somebody inside must have heard them because as we came closer to the house a faint glow came from one of the upper windows. The somebody had lit a candle. Amos rapped on the door and waited, then rapped again.

'Who's there? What is it?'

The voice from above was male and angry but elderly. He'd opened the window with the candle glow just over our heads but all we could see was the dark shape of him.

'A friend of ours is lost,' I said. 'We're looking for him. We're sorry to wake you.'

'Who are you? Where are you from?'

From habit, I said I was a Miss Lane, from London, and we were staying at the inn. In a place so remote, and so late at night, we might have landed from another planet. He called a sharp command and the dogs went quiet. A female voice was saying something to him inside the room but I couldn't make out the words. He disappeared from the window and there was some sort of consultation inside, then he came back, sounding more conciliatory.

'Your friend might have gone back to the inn. If he's still missing when it's daylight, I'll help you look for him.'

'We want to find him now,' I said. 'Is there anybody in there with you?'

'Why should there be? Only the two of us.' He sounded genuinely puzzled.

'Do you have a nephew from London staying with you?' I said. It wasn't the way I'd wanted to ask the question but I could see no alternative. The front door looked stout and although Amos could probably have broken in, we could hardly think of doing that in what seemed to be an ordinary, peaceful farmhouse.

'Nephew? What's my nephew got to do with it?'

'I met him once. He kept a stable at Perkins' Yard.'

A silence, then another withdrawal into the room for consultation. I could hardly blame him for being alarmed and suspicious. His shape came to the window again.

'I know he had a stables near the market. He stays with us now and then but he's not here now. Has something happened to him?'

'Nothing that I know of, only we're looking for him.'

'I thought it was your friend you were looking for. Anyway, there's nobody here but us. If you want to come back in the morning I'll do what I can to help you find your friend. Until then, goodnight.'

The window shut and soon afterwards the candle went out. We went back up the path a little way for consultation. We'd confirmed one thing, at least, and it wasn't cheering. The driver from Perkins' Yard was Mr Dickson's nephew, so Emilia was related to them as well. But it didn't prove that Mr Dickson and his wife knew anything about what the two of them had been doing and wasn't enough to justify breaking into the house.

'Somebody could have met McCloud before he got to the house,' I said. 'It was so dark we couldn't have seen.'

'Wouldn't he have shouted out?' Amos said.

'You'd think so, yes. Unless it was somebody he knew.' The thought that McCloud might be on the other side seemed more real now. 'Anyway, willingly or unwillingly, he's here somewhere and if he's really not in the house he might be in one of the barns.'

'So I'll go down and look,' Amos said. 'You two stay here just in case he comes back.'

'I'll come with you. Tabby can . . .' I stopped because the one thing you couldn't ask Tabby to do was wait on her own in dark countryside. In London almost nothing scared her but out here almost everything did.

'I'll go with him,' she said. Her voice was husky and the fact that she'd said little so far was a sign of her overstretched nerves. Even the prospect of searching the dark humps of barns and ricks around the house seemed preferable to standing in the mud by the hedge. But one of us had to wait in case McCloud was honest and got away. So, not liking it, I said yes they should go and I'd wait here. As we'd given our one lamp to McCloud the darkness hid them after they'd taken no more than a few steps and closed round me like a candle snuffer. I wasn't worried for Tabby because I knew Amos would protect her and her cat-like acuteness of hearing might help his search. The dogs were making no sound now, which surely meant Amos was making a wide circle of the house to come to the barns. There were several of them, I thought, though it was hard to tell in the dark. A smell of cows was coming up faintly on the cold air, so one cattle byre, at least. I imagined Amos and Tabby taking a few steps, listening, then a few steps more. It would be a long business but daylight was still way off. The church clock gave one stroke, either a half hour or one o'clock, no telling. My hands, even in gloves, were cold, so I stuck them inside my cloak and under my armpits, and shifted my feet for fear they'd solidify into the mud. Something small, a vole possibly, stirred the weeds at the base of the hedge, making a sound so faint it would surely be inaudible normally. All the time I was listening for footsteps coming up the path and McCloud returning, though I didn't think he would. A cow mooed, just one, then silence again. I had too much time for thinking and it came to me that George might be down there dead and if so it was my fault. The kidnappers had wanted information from him – information which he almost certainly did not have. If McCloud were on their side after all, they now knew we were close. In the circumstances, wouldn't it be safer for them to give up their attempt, which was going nowhere in any case, to kill George and bury him on the farm or stuff him down a drain and get away? I thought of the first time I'd seen him, standing on the rock above the bright sea, surrounded by light, and wished that all of us who'd had anything to do with him had left him on his island and not brought him to this dark and cold country. Two o'clock struck, then another half. Nothing. If Amos and Tabby had found anybody, surely there'd have been conversation or a few words, at least. Even a whisper would carry a long way in such conditions. I walked a few yards up the track by the feel of it under my feet rather than sight then down again, the rustle of my petticoats sounding as loud as branches cracking. Most of the mud had got into my right shoe, clotting my toes. I was wriggling them, trying to find a drier part of my stocking foot, when I heard the scream. It came from somewhere on my left, as shrill as a fox's cry but definitely human, just the one scream but the darkness seemed to vibrate with it. Amos wouldn't sound like that, but Tabby or George might. I called out, 'Who's there?' though the scream seemed to have come from some distance. No answer. It hadn't come from the farmhouse or barns below me, more on a level where as far as I knew there were only fields. Amos must have heard it, but if he were still down at the barns he'd be further away than I was. It might even be a trap for us, but it had sounded so horribly real that I doubted it. Standing and waiting weren't possible any more. I had to try to get to whoever had screamed by the shortest way. I couldn't remember passing a gate in the hedge on the left and certainly wasn't going back up the track to look for one. The hedge seemed from its springiness to be mostly hazel, not very well kept, with gaps in it that were patched by brambles. I pulled my cloak up round my face to protect it and pushed my way through, catching a foot in a bramble and falling on my hands and knees in the next field. Not hurt, at any rate. The clean smell of turnips rose round me. I stood up, listening. Still quiet. Going across the turnip field seemed to take forever, my feet sliding on the rounded tops of the roots then sinking deep in the dips between rows. I hoped I was making for where the scream had come from but couldn't be sure. The hedge on the far side was more solid than the last one and thorny. I walked up some distance and found a gap by a slight change in the density of the darkness. It was closed in by a hurdle, quite easily moved once my fingers had found the fastening, and led to a pasture field. I'd taken a few steps when, almost beside me, a harsh cough sounded like the discharge of a shot. Then another cough and a shape blundering away from me. A sheep. More shapes moved and I knew I was in the middle of a herd of them. I staggered back, woolly sides jostling me, to make sure that I'd replaced the hurdle, even in these circumstances knowing it was unthinkable to let them get at the turnips, and walked on. At least they gave no more than a bleat or two. I thought it might be as much as half an hour since I'd heard the scream but my sense of time was going. Some of the sheep were following me as I walked across the field, no longer sure of my direction, and the smell of damp fleece took over from turnip. I came up against another hedge and stopped. Then I heard it. I thought at first it might be a hedgehog snoring but it was too high for that and too quick in rhythm – a series of shallow snorts like a person trying hard to keep breathing. I said 'Where are you?' and there was a moment of silence, then a sound between a gasp and a groan from not far away to my right. I followed the hedge along, hearing the breathing again, close now, and came to a closed gate. It was looped round with string and I dropped my gloves and tore my nails unfastening it blindly. As I squeezed through it my foot struck against something and the breathing changed to a gasp of pain. I went down on my knees and felt fabric under my hand, a lot of fabric like a skirt and, inside it, the curve of a limb. I looked along it to a pale disc of face, flat against the grass, smeared with black that in daylight would probably have been red, surrounded by a tangle of greyish-looking hair. I think I'd hardly have recognized her even if it had been daylight when the hair would have showed as yellow, but it had to be her.

'Emilia?'

She gave a groan that might have been 'yes', then something else I couldn't understand. No point in asking her what had happened. I couldn't carry her to the farmhouse so I'd have to get some help for her. Just as I was trying to decide which way to go I saw the faint glow of a lantern some distance away, probably at the far end of the field we were in. I'd been holding my breath, trying to hear what Emilia was saying, but now I let it out in a sigh of relief. Amos and Tabby had found McCloud and were coming back. Then I thought that it might be whoever had done this to Emilia, but the risk had to be taken. I told her I'd come back, not knowing if she understood me or not, and walked towards the light.

TWENTY-TWO

It took me some time to realize that the light wasn't moving. When I started, it had seemed a few hundred yards away and a little below me as the field sloped down and that's where it stayed. If it was with Amos and Tabby, they'd have been puzzled not to find me at the place we agreed and might be shining it as a signal, but I couldn't risk calling out to them. As I came closer I saw it was coming from some kind of structure, a small barn or shed, not a hand-held lantern at all. I knew I'd come quite a long way from the farmhouse, so it couldn't be one of its outbuildings. Almost certainly not Amos and Tabby then. I stopped, wondering what to do, and at that moment the lamp went out and the darkness seemed even deeper. The sheer lack of an alternative made me decide to go on. I had to find help for Emilia and if I kept on walking downhill and to the right at least I'd be going in the direction of the farmhouse. The Dicksons wouldn't react well to being woken up again at an even later hour but there was no help for it. Presumably whoever had been in the shed or barn would be well ahead of me in the darkness. Since it was quite probably the same person who'd attacked Emilia, I hoped it would stay that way. The thing where the lamp had been shining began to take shape in the darkness. It was small, a shed rather than a barn. I went right up to it, almost within touching distance. A shed on wheels, a lambing shed probably for a shepherd, left out in the pasture. But this was nowhere near lambing time. Then the whispering started out of the dark, as if the shed itself were speaking. A man's voice, low but very clear, repeating the same thing over and over again, like somebody chanting a spell.

'. . . killed me. I'll follow you always because you killed me. I'll follow you always because . . .'

There was no emotion in it, just the level coldness of something that could go on forever. 'Because you killed . . .'

In spite of the strangeness of it, I thought I'd heard the voice before but couldn't place where. Not McCloud's certainly, nor Simmonds'. Was he talking to himself? In any case, it was madness, because how could he be killed and talking? Then a memory flashed into my mind that was about as far away as it could be from this damp, dark field. All of us round the table on that summer night, most of us talking happily but one man who said little, who seemed entirely unremarkable. Then his death a few hours later had made him remarkable after all, but only in the sense that you looked back in your memory trying to find reasons to account for it. I'd thought, until that moment, that I couldn't even remember his voice, but now it came back to me so vividly that I was sure of it. The man talking in the shepherd's hut was the one I'd thought drowned in a bay in Cephalonia four months ago, Geoffrey Panter, and the person he was talking to could only be George. I wanted to go in there and prove I was right, had even taken a step towards the shorter side where the door might be, when the chanting stopped. I froze, thinking that what had happened to Emilia could also happen to me, waiting for the sound of a door opening. Nothing happened. My step must have been quieter than I thought, though it seemed to me that even my breathing would be audible inside the wooden walls of the shed. Then, after a minute or so, the voice began again.

'*Not asleep, are you? I don't think so. In any case, I shall be there even in your sleep. You've seen me, haven't you, in your dreams? Night after night, you've seen yourself drowning me. You always will. You always will.*'

Then the first sound from somebody else, a quick 'yes' and a trembling, indrawn breath. George's voice. Then Panter again.

'*Yes, was it? You see it. You admit you drowned me. You had her, didn't you? Had Emilia? That's why you drowned me. Yes?*'

And again that trembling 'yes' from George. He'd always lived in darkness. This night would be nightmare to him, like so many other nightmares. He couldn't distinguish between the voice he was hearing now in reality and the one he'd heard so often in his imagination. I thought Panter had brought him there to kill him and took another step towards where I thought the door might be, wishing that Amos were there but knowing he had no way of finding me in the dark. Panter spoke again. This time his voice was different, conciliatory.

'*You'd like to make me go away, wouldn't you? You'd like me to go away and never trouble you again. You can do it if you want to. All you have to do is tell me and you'll never hear from me again. Just tell me where.*'

I knew then that Panter was mad. He'd gone on believing in Lord Byron's mythical treasure in his seven-year exile in Van Diemen's Land and he still believed.

'*Just tell me where. Tell me where. Tell me where.*'

Then a yell of despair from George, loud enough to set the walls of the hut ringing like a violin playing a high note. '*I . . . don't . . . know.*'

For a heartbeat, everything went quiet. I gave up trying to be cautious and blundered round the hut, falling against the wall as my feet tangled in a bramble and my skirt and petti-coats bunched round my knees. I went flat on my face and pushed myself up just enough to shout, 'George, I'm here, Liberty.' For all I knew, Panter might be killing him in there. Then, from what sounded like a field away, came Amos's voice.

'Where are you? Keep shouting!'

So I shouted Amos's name, several times over as I tried to stand up. I noticed that my arm as it pressed against the hut wall was striped with diagonal yellow bars where light was coming through from the inside. Panter must have lit the lamp again. When I got upright I managed to get round the corner of the hut but there was no door on that side. Movement from inside, somebody breathing harshly. I spoke through the wall to Panter. 'Let him go. We're all around you.'

Then there was somebody else, a light body cannoning into me and Tabby's voice asking what was going on.

'Where's Amos?'

Before she could answer some violent movement happened inside the hut, everything went dark again and the smell of spilt lamp oil spread. I grabbed for Tabby's hand and we went round the hut to find the door at last, visible from the shape of a porch sticking out above it. A large dark shape was by the door, wrenching at it. It didn't matter if the door was latched or not. It came open like a page tearing from an album and a red burst of fire came out.

'Amos.'

He stood there, silhouetted against the fire, then disappeared inside before I could say anything else. Tabby's hand gripped mine as firmly as if they'd never come apart. Then he was out again, with a body draped across his arms, sparks flying behind him. He walked some way out of the firelight, with the two of us following, and laid it down on the grass.

'He's still breathing, any road.'

George, unconscious. The smell of burning was all round us: burning hair, wood, the wool of clothes. Amos knelt and beat out with his hand fragments of fire on George's jacket and the boy didn't stir. His face was so pale it practically shone out of the darkness, sightless eyes wide open. A whooshing sound like an explosion came from the shed behind us. The fire that had been burning fiercely was now something else, a red whirlwind of smoke and flame. The lamp oil, I thought, the way your mind seizes on things that don't matter when you can't help the things that do.

'The other one was on the floor in there,' Amos said. 'Wasn't time to take the two of them.'

He raised his hand to his mouth.

'You're burned?'

'Nothing to show. So who was it?'

'Panter.'

'Not dead then? Or wasn't, at any rate.'

We both looked back at the burning hut. The dark outline was still visible, etched against the flames, but as we watched it crumbled and fell. Nothing could last alive in there.

'He nearly killed Emilia too,' I said. 'She's up the field. We must go to her.'

George groaned and moved an arm.

'I reckon he layed your man out,' Amos said. 'He wasn't moving.'

George moved his head and tried to say something.

'Don't tell him,' I said. 'Don't ever tell him. It was the fire that killed Panter.'

Amos nodded. George spoke in something surprisingly like his normal voice.

'I'm awake, aren't I?'

'Awake, yes.'

Amos took off his jacket to make a pillow for him then left him there with me while he and Tabby followed my directions up the paddock to find Emilia. All the time they were gone George didn't speak another word. As the flames from the shed died down the darkness came back, so all I could see of him was his white face against the darkness.

TWENTY-THREE

L ight came slowly the next morning. At six o'clock it was still more dark than light and when Amos and I found McCloud on the floor of a shed at the back of the house my first thought was that he was dead too, until he opened his eyes and blamed us for taking so long to find him. He was cold, stiff-limbed and had a terrible headache from a lump the size of a golf ball behind his left ear. The hair round the lump was singed, which puzzled me for a while. All he could remember was being near the house then suddenly somebody coming out of the dark and a hot and explosive pain in his head. After that, nothing until he'd come to and found himself locked in with nobody responding to his shouts. Then he must have gone unconscious again. When he asked who'd hit him, I said, 'George's mother.'

'What!'

He winced from the force of his word and put a hand to the lump behind his ear.

'The woman who introduced herself to you at Northlands as George's mother. She's really a woman of the streets, named Emilia.'

'But why?'

'Because she was working with Geoffrey Panter.'

'Who's . . .?' Another wince.

'It's too long a story for now. Let's get you into the house.'

The Dicksons' farmhouse, a large and rather ramshackle building in the grey morning light, had become something of a casualty station. Emilia was stretched out on a couch covered in cracked leather in a room that was probably kept for visitors so not much used, a faded patchwork quilt spread over her, her battered face yellow-smeared from the arnica ointment that Mrs Dickson had handed in from the door, standing there with her arm stretched out like somebody not wanting to go into an animal's den. I couldn't work out then, or even now, how much the Dicksons had known. They protested total ignorance of what had gone on, shock at the probable involvement of their nephew, Simmonds, the coachman who, as far as I knew, was never seen again. They'd considered Emilia lost to the family long since and couldn't wait to get rid of her again. On that, at any rate, I was sure they weren't lying. I'd spent an hour or more with Emilia after she was carried in, sitting on the floor by the couch with an old lamp hissing on the table. She was in pain and I thought that probably her cheekbone was broken. Her nose was certainly split and she couldn't talk much. So, as I smoothed on the ointment, reasonably gently in the circumstances, I talked to her.

'I think you knew, back in Cephalonia, that Panter wasn't really drowned. He was obsessed about the treasure but he knew Mr Vickery wouldn't let him question George. So he hit on this idea of disappearing and coming back as his own ghost. He knew how superstitious George was. I think he was always a man for elaborate schemes.' His whole past pointed that way, his attempt to defraud his employers and then the confidence trick. She said nothing, just shifted her head on the pillow. 'Back in London, he decided to work with you. He wanted to get his hands on George but Mr Vickery was very protective of him. So you planned the mother trick. You couldn't approach Mr Vickery yourself because of course he'd recognize you, so you recruited Helena Shilling. I daresay you knew about her from your friends in Covent Garden. When Mr Vickery went to Northlands, she didn't want to go, but you and Panter persuaded her.'

'Paid her more than enough.' Her voice was cracked and contemptuous. I waited for her to go on but she didn't. Her eyes were on me, bright and apparently unblinking.

'Panter had an argument with her that afternoon, in a public house near Northlands. I don't know why she'd started resisting then. Perhaps she realized she'd got herself into something deeper than she thought, but you and Panter still wanted her help in getting George away from McCloud. You'd never intended to attack the house, as Mr Vickery feared. That helped you, all the attention diverted from what was happening in the lane. But Helena must have started protesting again, so Panter just shot her.'

'He said it was an accident.' She didn't sound as if she believed it.

'You and Panter went back to London. When you heard Mr Vickery had been charged with killing her, you couldn't believe your luck, but you still needed to get your hands on George. You had an ally at Northlands – Astley. Or at least you thought he was an ally. He'd been spying on George and McCloud, knew they were going to London and had them trailed. What he didn't expect was that you'd take George to his lodgings. He panicked and you stabbed him.'

'Panter. He was there in the room when I took the boy in.' Still, she didn't blink.

'I wonder. You brought George down here in the market cart. You knew the place – they're kin of yours though they'd disowned you long ago. And you and Panter quarrelled. I'm not sure what about. Perhaps you'd admitted to yourself by then that this business of the Byron treasure had driven him mad, that he was chasing a will-o'-the-wisp. You told him you were leaving.'

'I told him I was going because people were on to us.'

'People? You mean the man you hit?'

'He just came at me out of the dark. I grabbed his lantern and hit him with it. Just a tap, it was. Then I dragged him into the shed – it was all I could do. But I'd had enough. I told Panter somebody was on to us and he should let the boy go and leave it. If there ever was treasure, it wasn't worth all this.'

'And that's when he hit you?'

An attempt at a nod, cut short.

'You know Panter's dead?' I said.

'Definitely, this time?'

'Yes.'

'It wasn't me. He'd laid me out. You're a witness to that.' No expression of regret for a man who'd been her companion on the other side of the world. I was impressed by the quickness of her mind, even in these circumstances. Her face was a wreck but her eyes were still fixed on me, bright and calculating. 'None of it was my fault. It was him all along, making me.'

'You just might get the police to believe that.'

'I'm not having anything to do with them.'

'You've no choice. Helena Shilling's dead and Astley's dead and you know about both.'

'They can't pin those on me.'

'If you tell your story right, they'll blame Panter. You might get off.'

She muttered again that she wouldn't have anything to do with the police but I could tell her mind was working, preparing her account. I left her to it and went into the farm living room. McCloud and George were sitting on either side of the fire, Tabby on a stool, with Mrs Dickson hovering in the background. George smelled of the fire and one cheek had a long graze down it. He looked miserable and washed out, but conscious, at any rate.

'Amos has gone to the inn to get the carriage,' I said. 'We'll have you back in London this afternoon.'

He nodded. I sat on the mat beside him and took his hand, and his head turned slowly towards me.

'George, you do understand now that you didn't drown him?' I said. 'It was a terrible trick of Panter's. That was him alive with you in the hut, not his ghost. He killed the lawyer too. It was him, not you. You've never killed anybody.'

I tried to keep out of my voice the thought that, after all, he probably had killed Panter. That scuffle I'd heard inside the hut was what laid Panter out on the floor and left him a victim to the fire. George, being used to the dark, was probably a better scrapper than Panter. Fire, not water. I crushed that thought down in my mind, wanting more than anything to convince George. The rest of his face was still as blank as his eyes.

'You're not carrying a curse,' I said. 'There's no curse. You're just like anybody else.'

I wished with all my heart that were true. His past and the whiff of devilry that even now hung round Lord Byron's name would always single him out, but I could only hope not so disastrously.

'So you're nothing special,' Tabby said.

I'd been aware of her eyes on me and how intently she was following what I said. It was the tone of her words that did the trick, exactly as she might say them to one of her urchin friends, joshing. George turned towards her and a smile spread over his face, tentative but real. I remembered that she'd pushed the hero's son into a manure heap, and that Tabby had never known her father either. We said nothing more until the wheels of a carriage sounded in the yard and it was time to go into a world of questions and explanations.

Over the next few days it seemed that I spent more time with Sergeant Bevan in his bare interview room than at home. When he wasn't talking to me he was probably talking to Emilia. The Metropolitan Police had arrested her at the inn and brought her back to captivity in an ambulance. In one of the interviews, he told me some of the possible charges against her.

'Conspiracy to extort money, impersonation, probable conspiracy in two murders, kidnapping and a whole list more we haven't got round to yet. That woman's booked herself a one-way ticket back to Australia, at the very least.'

'But . . .?' I said, and waited.

'Would you go into the witness box against her?'

'Most of it would be hearsay, not proof.'

'All the same?'

'Not voluntarily, no.'

I wasn't even sure why. It wasn't that I liked Emilia and she'd certainly land herself in prison again sooner or later, but I didn't want to be the one to send her there.

'It really is the very devil of a case,' Bevan said, making no apology for his language. 'The one man we could certainly have convicted is dead. They've found most of a skull and some of the larger bones in the ashes of that shepherd's hut.'

'Dead twice over,' I said. 'Meanwhile, you still have an innocent man in prison for killing Helena Shilling.'

'Innocent!' He practically shouted it. 'Vickery caused all the trouble in the first place by bringing the boy here. And unlawful disposal of a dead body is a serious crime.'

But not one they hanged people for. Bevan went silent for a while after that, then sighed.

'The truth is there will probably be no prosecutions for the murders. Panter did them and Panter's dead. End of the case.'

'And Mr Vickery?'

'We're not letting him out yet. I suppose you want an order to go and see him.'

I said yes please, and left an hour later with it in my hand.

Mr Vickery seemed as relaxed and affable in the damp room in Newgate where he'd been brought to see me as he'd been in his Ionian villa. I'd come to realize that part of his power over people came from the way he adapted to any change in circumstances without regret for what he'd left behind. Only George made him vulnerable and by the time I saw him he'd already had word from Jolly that George was safe and back at his London home. Jolly had told me that Mr Vickery had even, from Newgate, contrived to get some of his money flowing again so the house in Knightsbridge was nearer what a gentleman should have. He even seemed to have made Newgate reasonably comfortable for himself. Since he hadn't been convicted he still wore his own clothes, including a spotlessly clean shirt probably also supplied by Jolly, and smelled mostly of a gentlemanly soap with just a whiff of prison. Newgate smelled of death and damp as usual and the place we talked in had so much plaster flaking off that it lay like a drift of dirty snow along the floor. A bored warden dozed, leaning across the entrance to the room. I talked to Mr Vickery across a small table, its top stained with nameless things, the edge uneven as if somebody had been trying to carve it with a blunt knife, and told him the story, every detail of it, with the warden showing no interest. He'd probably heard worse. When I described Astley's murder and my belief at the time that George might have been responsible, he shaded his eyes with his hand.

'You really believed that?'

'I thought it was possible, yes. Did you never have doubts about Astley?'

He shook his head. 'He'd suffered harm, partly because of me, some time ago. I was trying to make it up to him, as far as I could.' By the end of the story, and George's escape, both his hands were pressed over his eyes. 'Panter was different when he came back from Van Diemen's Land,' he said. 'I saw it on Cephalonia. If we'd returned to England together I'd have paid him off and had nothing more to do with him. He was totally obsessed by this idea of Lord Byron's treasure.'

'For something that never existed, it's done a great deal of damage,' I said.

I thought of it, from all those empty pits on the hillsides of Cephalonia to the shepherd's hut in the middle of the fire that I still saw every time I closed my eyes. Something like a smile was twisting Mr Vickery's mouth, though his eyes were still hard.

'For something that never existed,' he echoed. Then: 'Jolly asked if I wanted George brought to see me. Not here, I said. I'll be out soon enough, then we can pick up where we left off. You've seen him since he came back to London?'

'This morning, yes. McCloud and Mr Ridgeway are with him.' I didn't mention that Tabby was as well. George was insisting on keeping her close to him and she was being as patient as I'd ever seen her with anybody.

'How is he?' For the first time in the conversation, Mr Vickery sounded uncertain.

'Very well, considering. He has dreams about the fire.'

'They'll go. What shall I do about this McCloud?'

'Keep him,' I said. 'George needs his friends, especially with you in prison.'

'Oh, I shan't be in here much longer. They know now I didn't kill the Shilling woman and the rest is only a technicality.' Although I knew it was more than that, I couldn't help being affected by his confidence. Sooner or later – sooner quite probably – he'd be back at his house in Knightsbridge. He sent his compliments to Amos and a promise of something more substantial when he was out. Our time was near the end although the warden was now completely asleep on his feet, head on his chest and snoring slightly. Mr Vickery looked at me, his eyes holding mine.

'You needn't worry about George. He's all I care about. Besides, I owe him. I try to pay my debts.'

'Owe?'

He glanced at the snoring warden and smiled. 'You're wrong about one thing, you know. You said Lord Byron's treasure never existed. It did, and I was the one who found it, soon after his death. A matter of luck, mainly. It was never a chest of gold. Panter always would exaggerate. Still, ten thousand pounds in silver Maria Theresa dollars. I've increased it many times over since then, but that's the foundation of everything I've ever had. George will have it when he comes of age. I haven't told anybody else that but you and Legge have earned the right to know it.'

Was he joking? The mouth was smiling but the eyes as serious as I'd ever seen them. I stared at him, wondering. The warder woke himself up with a loud snore and said I should go, sharpish. I went out into the stink of the Newgate corridor, still wondering.